THE LOST CHILD

ANDREW CLEGG

ISBN-13: 9798650474678

Cover design by Hanson Suhendra & Andrew Clegg

Second Edition

To my Grandma

CHAPTER ONE
OLIVER

Oliver Hawthorne had always been amazed by the night sky. It was full of endless wonders, endless freedom. He looked up at the moon shining hopefully over the city of Maldenney. Every night it appeared exactly where it was supposed to, fulfilling its purpose. The moon was the unwavering light amongst darkness; never ceasing, never wandering from its home in the sky. Oliver wondered what that would be like — to know his place in the world, his purpose. He sat and stared a few moments longer before continuing to poke and rummage through the garbage dumpster he had hurdled himself into. As he searched for scraps of food that were still partially edible, a tattered book caught Oliver's eye.

"Bertie Wineman's Pocket Guide to Curious Creatures and Peculiar Pets," he muttered. He flipped through the pages quickly before shoving the book into his old backpack. Wasting little time searching for more food, Oliver climbed out of the dumpster and brushed the garbage off his clothes. Some fifty feet away, the streets of Maldenney beckoned for him to come explore. He took a step forward and realized his foot was in a puddle. Oliver groaned. That was his only pair of shoes. With one last longing glance, he turned and headed back down the alley where he belonged. The rest of the city was no place for someone like him.

As the capital of Omnios, Maldenney was a booming metropolis of more than ten thousand inhabitants, the likes of which Oliver had seen very little. It contained five districts, each designated for a specific purpose. The open fields of the Farmlands ran along the city's eastern length, supplying food to all of Maldenney. The Northern Quarters was home to Maldenney's richest and noblest citizens, while the Southern Quarters—or Blights, as it was often called—housed the rest of the population. The city's center was shared by the Market and Imperial Districts. The Market District was most notably home to Lucila Square, the hub of commerce and trade for all of Omnios, while the Imperial District's defining landmark was the Blackfort. Once a military stronghold, the Blackfort was the structure around which the entire city had been built. Presently, it served as a palace, home to the Lord Commander of the Legion, Kaliculous Kaeno.

Oliver reached the end of the alley where it met the city's towering outer wall. He came to a halt in front of an odd-looking door that nearly blended in with the façade of the stones around it. Stepping up to it, Oliver grabbed the handle, and—with some force from his shoulder—jammed open the broken door of the little shack he called home.

Leftover rain dripped on to the floor through a hole in the roof. The hole let the moon shine in though, so Oliver didn't mind it too much. At the far end of the shack, Nan was asleep in her bed, a simple cot that raised her a mere few inches off the ground. The sound of her labored breathing filled the air and simultaneously filled Oliver's heart with worry. Next to her lay Oliver's own cot, which was imprinted with the shape of his body. In one corner there was a makeshift table and chair that Oliver had made using rescued parts from discarded furniture. Pushed up against the opposite wall was a small wooden box filled with Oliver's few belongings. The shack was barely big enough for both Nan and him, but they made do.

Oliver was somewhat small for a boy of thirteen. Some nights he went hungry, which would not be surprising to anyone who saw his size or looked at where he lived. It was difficult having to live off scraps and there was no telling how much he would be able to find in the alley outside his shack. Sometimes when the harvest was plentiful, farmers would throw away the least appealing of their crops, leaving Oliver with an excellent selection of delicious, albeit misshapen produce. When there was a bad harvest however, he had to rely on the leftovers thrown out by the tenants of the Blights, which were far less bountiful and tasty.

Oliver often had to brush his untidy brown curls off his forehead, which always caused him a great deal of annoyance. Nan used to cut his hair before her vision went, and he couldn't do it very well on his own. Sometimes when the sun shone through the holes and cracks in his roof, his hair looked to be almost a sandy blonde. His eyes were mostly blue with a thin ring of bright yellow just around the pupil. He had a crooked smile that was quick to show itself, but remarkably straight teeth. Oliver thought he had a rather nice appearance, but only Nan was able to tell him that, so he would never really know for sure.

Oliver was an unusual boy for several reasons. For one, he really wanted to go to school. Nothing thrilled him more than the idea of running off with classmates every day and learning new and exciting things. He had read about school in so many books. It sounded like the most wonderful idea in the world to him. Secondly, he had never met either of his parents. It was Nan who had raised and cared for him since he was a baby. Lastly, he was thirteen and his only friend was…well, *old*. How old Nan was exactly, Oliver didn't know. She had never bothered to share her age with him, and he had never dared to ask. She was a great deal older than he; that much he was sure of. Truth be told, he didn't even know if Nan was her real name, but it's what he had called her for his entire life.

For a grudder like Oliver, the desire to have friends was always at the forefront of his mind. *Grudder* was the term that the Legion used for people who lived undocumented and illegally within the limits of its cities. Oliver had no birth papers or documentation of any kind, and so he had to make absolutely sure that no one ever saw him. Even Nan didn't see him anymore. Her illness and old age had caused her to lose the use of both eyes. Still, she was quick to remind Oliver just how very handsome he was, but he knew that she was only remembering what he had looked like at eleven.

Of course, Oliver's parents — whoever they were — had seen him as a baby, but they would hardly recognize him now if they looked right at him. He had no memories of either of them whatsoever. When he was a boy, he would sit at the edge of the alley for hours, waiting for his mother and father to return for him. Eventually, Nan caught him and told him he could never do that again, or he would risk being seen.

The sun was just rising over the green hills surrounding Maldenney as Oliver settled down to eat meal he had scrounged up. There was a half-eaten apple core, a nearly full loaf of bread with a few moldy spots on it, a small piece of some sort of meat that was admittedly mostly fat, and a canteen of milk that was beginning to go sour — not a bad selection.

Oliver frowned as he realized he had sat in the puddle of water that had formed from the dripping roof. Perhaps he should try to patch the hole after all. Using his pocketknife, he cut the moldy spots off the loaf of bread and began gnawing at it slowly.

"Nan," Oliver whispered, gently shaking the sleeping woman's shoulder. She did not stir. It was odd to think about how she had once been his caretaker, and now he was hers. It seemed only fitting to him. He would finally be able to repay her for all she had done for him.

"Nan," he said again, a little more loudly.

"Ah," Nan said at last, "Ollie, what is it?" Her voice was so soft it was hardly audible. She reached out with her hand, searching for him. He leaned over obligingly and placed his face in the palm of her hand, wrapping his own hand around her wrist.

"How are you feeling?" he asked. Her hand did not move from his face as he spoke.

"Oh, Ollie. Don't you worry about me. I'll be alright."

Silently, Oliver wished that were true. He suppressed a frown so she wouldn't feel the change in his face. She looked terribly frail, but even now she had as much ferocity and sass as ever. Oliver wondered what she had looked like at his age. Her hair was mostly gray now, but he could still see the remnants of when it had been thick and black. She had prominent cheeks, full lips, and vibrant brown eyes. Oliver guessed she must have been beautiful in her own time.

"Nan, I was thinking…maybe I could go and…well maybe I could try to find you some medicine."

"Find me some medicine?" she repeated. By the way she said it, you would think Oliver had told her he was trying to become the next Lord Commander. "How would you go about doing that?"

"Well, I could sneak out."

"You? Sneak out into the city?"

"I'd be really fast! And I'd stay away from the legionnaires!"

"Now you listen to me, Oliver, and you listen good. I don't want you risking your neck to help me. If someone asked for your identification papers… What if I lost you?"

"Nan, come on!"

"No, Oliver. Drop it."

Oliver sighed and slumped in defeat. He couldn't argue with Nan. He had never been able to. In any case, he knew she was right. If he were caught, what would happen to her? She wouldn't last long without him.

He returned to his food, which he ate with a reluctant grimace painted across his face.

"How were the pickings today?" Nan asked.

"Um, really good, actually," he said, holding up a piece of bread to examine a mold spot. "Feast for a king. You want some?"

"No. I'll wait a while."

"Nan, you have to eat something."

"I've been grown for some time, Ollie. I don't *have* to do anything."

Oliver felt her forehead with the back of his hand. "You have a fever."

"I feel fine."

"I can't just sit here and do nothing," Oliver pleaded with her.

"There's nothing you *can* do, sweet boy. Besides, I'm an old woman," she said feebly. "I'm not worth the trouble."

"You are to me," he said, tears welling up in his eyes. "You're all I've got."

"Promise me you won't do anything stupid, Ollie." Oliver did not respond. "Oliver," Nan said sternly, grabbing his wrist.

"Okay, Nan...I promise."

Nan released her grip on him and allowed her head to slump down into her pillow. In seemingly no time, she had drifted off to sleep.

Oliver went outside in an attempt to take his mind off Nan's failing health. It was a warm autumn day, probably one of the last they would have for a while. Just outside the shack, there was a space where the alley opened up into a sort of courtyard. The alley wrapped around the back of an old hospital ward that had been abandoned before Oliver was born. It provided good cover for his hidden home, and Nan had often told him that the hospital was what kept people away. Rumor had it the hospital was haunted, and Oliver shuddered to think what sort of spectral things came out of hiding there at night.

From the courtyard behind the hospital, Oliver could faintly hear the sounds of city life. Behind the shack, he heard songbirds chirping melodies, forest critters rustling, and the *whoosh* of the warm breeze that pranced through the trees. How nice it would be to step outside the confines of his hidden, little world, Oliver thought—to take off at a run; to splash through the river that flowed through the middle of the city; to jump, yell, and play with the other kids. He heaved a great sigh.

Stepping back inside, Oliver did what he always did when he was reminded of how miserable a grudder's life was; he read. Nan had taught him to read when he was just four years old. They had an assortment of tattered old books, from *Histories of the Lucila Dynasty, Volume Three* to *Travels and Tall-Tales of Sygmus Baylore*. He read stories of fate and destiny, dreaming of what it felt like to experience such things. Often, he would open up a book and get lost in its pages. He would become transported to another place and time. No longer would he be Oliver Hawthorne, the grudder of Maldenney, but Raytheon Lucila, the boy-king of Omnios.

He started to pick up one of his favorites when he remembered the book he had found in the dumpster. Oliver reached into his bag and pulled out *Bertie Wineman's Pocket Guide to Curious Creatures and Peculiar Plants.* He flipped it open to a random page of the *A* section and began to read.

AL-MIRAJ

While the AL-MIRAJ may present a soft exterior, do not underestimate the violent nature of these beasts. Though they resemble a common hare, the AL-MIRAJ differs in both size and speed. When standing on its hind-legs, an AL-MIRAJ may be up to five feet tall. Their most dangerous aspects, however, are their razor-sharp claws and teeth, and the spear-like horn found atop their heads. If you should find yourself in an encounter with an AL-MIRAJ, do not run. As highly territorial and intelligent creatures, they will take running as a challenge to chase. Rather, make it clear that you are not intending to fight. Speak in soft, calming tones, and take special care to not make sudden movements.

For more information on the AL-MIRAJ, look for my follow-up book The Giants of the Forest, *which will detail my studies of an AL-MIRAJ pack over a period of two months. Coming next summer.*

Beneath the paragraph there was a rather terrifying drawing of a massive creature that looked like a rabbit with a horn. Drawn next to it was the outline of a human for scale. The al-miraj was barely smaller.

Oliver grinned wildly. He had never heard of an al-miraj before. What other sort of things did Bertie Wineman have to tell him about? He was just looking for the next interesting page when a sound pierced his ear.

Bang! Bang! Bang! Oliver nearly threw the book as his heart shot up into his throat. Someone was outside in the alley beating loudly on the stone walls.

"Theo, come back here *right now!*" an impatient voice called.

Bang! Bang! Bang! The sound was growing louder.

Oliver leapt up and crept silently towards the door. Beside it, there was a small hole in the wooden wall, no bigger than Oliver's little finger. He peered through it and saw the shape of a boy skipping merrily towards the shack.

"Ohhhh no…" Oliver whispered. "Nan! *Nan!*"

He looked over his shoulder to see that she was sill fast asleep. He turned back to the peephole. It was too small to get a good look at the boy, but Oliver could tell that he was small, probably a little younger than Oliver, with thin blonde hair cut in a sort of bowl shape. He was holding a large stick in his hand, which he slammed on everything he saw with glee.

"THEO!" the voice called again, still from farther down, but this time sounding very angry. The boy, presumably Theo, did not stop. He continued towards Oliver's shack, beating his stick obnoxiously as he went.

"Okay, okay. What do I do? What do I do?" Oliver said to himself. He looked around the shack helplessly for something to bar the door from opening. Suddenly a long and thin stick of wood caught his eye—the cane Nan used when she could still walk.

As quietly and quickly as he could, Oliver grabbed the cane and slid it through the door handle, then scrambled back onto his cot. He looked at Nan resting beside him. If she woke up while the people were still outside, how would he be able to tell her to stay quiet? He sat perfectly still and tried to silence his breathing.

BANG! BANG! The thunderous sound of Theo's beating stick had reached Oliver's shack, now louder and far more petrifying.

"What the…" Theo muttered to himself. He was standing just outside Oliver's door.

"Ah, there you are!" said the older voice. "What in the heavens are you doing running around *here* of all places? Do you know what sort of filth could be infesting an alley like this?"

Thud. Nan's cane hit against the wooden frame as Theo pulled on the door.

"Help me open this!"

"No! I took you along to Lucila Square because Mother asked me to, not so you could go running off into some disgusting alley. And in the Blights of all places! Sometimes I can't believe you're my brother. Now let's go, we're going to be late for lunch with the Kyworths."

"Who cares if we're late?"

"Can you imagine what Mother will say to me if I bring you home late *and* covered in filth? Punctuality is important, Theo."

"Punctuality is important, *mweh, mweh, mweh,*" Theo said in a mocking tone.

"Some of us actually have aspirations in life, believe it or not. Father thinks I might be vying for the position of Lord Commander myself one day."

Theo snorted. "Oh, come off it. You're not even a legionnaire yet."

"I will be, come tomorrow! And when I am, you might think twice about how you talk to me. Legionnaires command a great deal of respect, you know."

"No, you'll be a *recruit* come tomorrow. It's not the same thing." The shack rattled as Theo tried to force the door open again.

Recruit or not, Oliver didn't want anyone associated with the Legion coming near his shack. He put a hand over his mouth, doing his best to not make a sound. If he was discovered now, there was no question these boys would turn him in.

"Will you cut that out!" The older boy said. "Come on now, we have a tight schedule to keep to, and Father will have both of our heads if we make him look poorly by being late for dinner."

Theo let out a long groan before releasing his grip on the door handle and resuming the beating of his stick. Oliver listened intently as the banging sound traveled farther and farther away. It wasn't until the alley was completely silent that he allowed himself to breathe again. The coast was clear, as far as he could see through the peephole. Oliver's heart was still beating fast. He had experienced close calls before, but none quite that close. Now each chirp of a songbird or rustle of a leaf that had seemed so peaceful before caused him to jump with fear.

* * *

Oliver slept terribly the next few nights. He woke up early one morning with a sweat-soaked shirt, panting after dreaming about being taken away from Nan. Once, he had asked her if there were any other grudders in the city. She told him that the Blighters were notorious for catching grudders and turning them into the Legion. A grudder's head was worth enough to buy two chickens. He hadn't told Nan about the event with Theo and his brother. What was the point in making her worry about it when there was nothing she could do? In any case, they had not come back since, and Oliver doubted they ever would. They were not the first to wander down the alley, and never had anyone liked it enough to return a second time.

Unable to fall back asleep, Oliver stayed awake until dawn watching the sky for shooting stars. No one of Oliver's days differed much from any of his others. With each setting of the sun, he found his yesterdays passing by and his tomorrows approaching. Rarely ever were they truly distinct from one another. He woke up every morning as early as the sunlight would allow and went out into the alley in search of food. Too often in his young life had he seen Nan worry that there would be nothing for him to eat, so he liked to have that part of his day done before she woke up. He would go only so far as the edge of Hawthorne Alley, always careful not to wander into the Blights. The Blights were a dangerous part of Maldenney, for Oliver even more than most.

On this particular day, the moon was still visible in the early morning sky when Oliver stepped outside. It was strange how some days the moon would disappear as the sun rose but other days it wouldn't. Perhaps it liked to see what the daytime was like every once in a while. Oliver could certainly understand that feeling. He too wondered what the days were like beyond the limits of the alley.

The young grudder yawned and rubbed his eyes as he made his journey away from the shack. He liked to play a game where he would leap between cobblestones and try not to step on the cracks that separated them. He often made up little games like this; they helped him keep his mind off things that bothered him.

Oliver could just see the golden glare of the sun peaking its way over the top of the old, abandoned hospital. He jumped off one foot and landed on the other, his toes perfectly centered on one slab of cobblestone. Before he knew it, Oliver had reached the mouth of the alley. It seemed to have approached quicker than usual today. He put his foot down and looked around. The Blights were peaceful and quiet this early in the day.

A dog's bark from up ahead made Oliver nearly jump out of his skin. A boy and girl his age came running out of a house after the animal. Oliver ducked behind a pile of garbage and watched from afar as the two played in the streets. Their clothes were tattered and dirty like Oliver's. The boy threw a stick and the dog ran to get it. She brought it back to the boy immediately, wagging her tail. The boy patted the dog on her head, then took the stick and threw it again. It seemed like such a simple game to Oliver, but time and time again he watched as the dog happily took off after the stick, never seeming to bore of doing the same old thing over and over. Perhaps Oliver needed a dog, he thought. Someone who would appreciate the simplicity of his life, day after day, after day.

He wanted so badly to go and play the game with the kids. What would he say to them if he did? He had never introduced himself to anyone before.

"Hey, it's Oliver," he said quietly to himself. He stuck his hand out into the empty air and shook it. "No, we haven't met, but I've watched you before…No that's stupid, don't say that…Okay. Hi there, my name's Oliver. I live down the street and I was just wondering if I could play with your dog…"

He looked back just in time to see the kids disappearing into their house. His shoulders slouched low as he tore himself away from his fantasy and collected a few findings. Nan perked up when she heard him reenter the shack. She sat in her cot with her glassy eyes staring blankly at the wall.

"Ollie," she said with a smile.

"Morning, Nan. How are you feeling today?"

"I'm feeling perfectly well. Why wouldn't I be?" Silently, Oliver wished Nan wouldn't try to be so tough. It was one of the things he admired most about the woman, but one of her most frustrating qualities as well. He put a hand to her forehead.

"Your fever has gotten worse," he said sourly.

"Has it? I couldn't tell."

"Nan we've got to do something about this infection or it's just going to keep getting worse."

"Ollie, I'm alright. How many times do I have to tell you that?"

"Enough times for it to become true, maybe. Want something to eat today?"

"No, no, you eat. I just need to sleep it off…" she said drearily.

"You just woke up," Oliver said, but she had already started to lie back down, her eyelids fluttering as she drifted off. She slept soundly through the next hour, while Oliver read about more curious creatures and peculiar pets. Shortly after the hour was up, however, Nan began to mumble softly. He thought she was waking up at first, but then he realized she was only talking in her sleep. He leaned in close so he could make out the words.

"Fort…clips…" she said. Oliver rested his hand on hers.

"Shhh, it's okay, Nan. I'm right here. Everything's alright."

"Fort…miss…"

"What are you saying?" he mused.

"Fort...miss...taken! Fort!" Suddenly Nan's arms began to shake and thrash.

Oliver stumbled backwards. What was going on?

"Clips..." she said one last time, and then as quickly as it began, the fit had ended.

Oliver stared, unsure of what to think. He had never seen Nan do anything like that. He didn't know whether it was caused by the fever or something else, but he did know that he had to do something soon, or Nan was going to die.

CHAPTER TWO
LIVIAH

Liviah Cain woke, as always, to find her younger sister's bed empty. She got up, dressed, and walked out to the veranda of the Cain family's cottage. Juliana and her parents were already outside, enjoying their breakfast.

"Good morning, honey," Liviah's mother said. She pushed her blonde hair back behind her ear and smiled at her daughter. She looked far too young and vibrant to be the mother of a twelve and thirteen-year-old.

The Cains were an unusual family for multiple reasons. For one, Sydarah and Jonathon Cain had gotten married at only seventeen, and they had Liviah less than a year later. Shortly after, they moved from a lovely home in Maldenney, the capital of Omnios, to a small village in the west called Glassfall. Jonathon had given up what would have been a prosperous career as a Legion official to become a fisherman, while his wife Sydarah taught at Glassfall's school. The most peculiar thing about them, however, was the magical powers that each of their daughters had developed at the age of twelve.

"Morning Livvy," Juliana said.

"Hey Jules," Liviah replied to her sister. "How'd you sleep?"

Juliana shrugged. "Bad again."

Liviah frowned. Juliana had just started having nightmares not long ago. They began around the same time her magic appeared. Juliana, who was always positive and cheery, seemed utterly unperturbed by them. Liviah guessed that the nightmares must have seemed normal to her sister by now.

Juliana's hair was a shimmering white-blonde, except for the dark brown color that existed only at her roots. She wore it pulled back into a bun at present, with a few low hanging strands around her ears. Her lips were small and she had a similarly proportioned nose that curled up just slightly at the tip. Both Cain girls were darker skinned, but Liviah's was a shade darker, like their mother's. Liviah also had fuller lips and a perfectly rounded nose. Her dark brown hair hung in large, loose curls. It matched the color of her eyes, while Juliana's eyes were the color of a cloudless sky. The girls were by no means identical, but one could tell that they were sisters well enough.

"I know what'll cheer you up," their father said to Juliana with a smile. His thin face and dark skin were youthful; his eyes held childlike excitement behind his glasses. "Today is the start of preparations for the Harvest Festival."

The Harvest Festival was the biggest event of the year for the small village of Glassfall, and it just so happened that this year the first day of the week-long celebration fell on Liviah's fourteenth birthday. The Cain girls jumped up in excitement. Liviah bumped a table with her hip, and her mother's morning coffee went tumbling off it. Moments before it hit the ground, the mug froze suspended in mid-air. The steaming liquid collected itself together and flew neatly back into the cup, which floated up to the table and set itself down softly.

"Liviah!" her mother said, looking around to make sure no one had seen. "You know the rule! Not outside the house!"

"But we're *at* the house," Liviah said snarkily.

"Liviah Cain, do not take that tone with me. Now if you can't be trusted to use magic according to the rules your father and I set for you then we simply won't allow it at all."

"Fine," Liviah said with an eye roll. "Not like you could stop me though..."

"What did you say?" her mother said. There was a certain severity in her tone that told Liviah she had gone too far.

"Nothing..."

"You need to learn to watch your mouth, young lady."

"Uh, oh. I hope I'm not interrupting something," a voice said from behind Liviah.

"Ramsey!" both girls yelled as they ran off the porch towards the man. He wore all black pants and shirt, and a vest of black leather tied with a belt that hung down from his waist. On his chest was a golden pin in the shape of a crescent moon with a spear through the center, identifying him as a Legion official.

"How are my favorite girls this morning?" Ramsey said, grinning as he knelt to hug Juliana and Liviah.

"Girls, please. Address Lord Ambersen with his proper title," their mother said, but her smile showed her lack of concern.

"Oh nonsense, Darah," Ramsey said with a grin. "They can call me whatever they like!"

The title was no more than a formality anyway. The Legion had no Lords, only officers and commanders. *Lord* and *Madame* were honorary now, titles of the old world whose use never died out. Still, they were well respected, and most Lords were men in positions of great esteem.

Ramsey was nearly half a decade older than Liviah's mother and father, but his expressive brown eyes gave him a certain youth. He had black hair that was just beginning to gray, a cleft chin, and full lips. The cloaks he wore were mostly dark colors—black, navy, dark emerald, or gray. It was a habit that he had picked up in his younger days as a legionnaire.

"Why didn't you write to us and tell us you were coming?" Liviah asked.

"I like to give you a surprise! And in any case, the trip was made on rather short notice. I doubt a messenger falcon would have arrived much before myself." Ramsey stepped up to the porch to greet his old friends. "Sydarah," he said with a kiss of her hand, "looking beautiful as ever. Jonathon, how have you been, old friend?" They shook hands before clapping each other on the back in a hug.

"It's great to see you, Ramsey," Liviah's father said. Seldom did Liviah see her father as cheery as when Ramsey came to visit. They had been close during Jonathon's days in the Legion, and he always spoke fondly of his friends from that time. "How is your family?"

"Healthy and prosperous. My wife sends her regards."

"You'll have to bring her along with you sometime," Liviah's mother said.

"Oh, I couldn't do that to you," Ramsey said, then lowering his voice, "she wouldn't be a pleasant woman after a few days journey in a carriage." The three adults laughed together.

"Say, how's old Etzra doing?" Liviah's father asked.

"He seems to be getting grouchier by the minute," Ramsey replied, "but he still makes his way over for supper now and again. Rambles on about politics for hours on end."

"So, the same as twelve years ago, then?" The pair roared in laughter again.

"Exactly."

"What brings you to our neck of the woods this time?" Liviah's father asked once both men had collected themselves.

"Lord Commander Kaeno has had me running all over the realm for him," Ramsey said tiredly. "I thought I'd better make all the travel worth it with a trip to Glassfall on my way back from the Bastion."

"What's the Bastion?" Juliana asked.

"It's a fort being built just two days north of the capital. Lord Commander Kaeno sent me there to check on its progress."

"Well, we're happy you could stop by," Sydarah said. "You're welcome to stay with us as long as you like."

"Oh, I couldn't intrude. There's a house at the edge of town for Legion officials to stay in on occasions such as this. In any case, I won't be able to stay long."

"You won't leave before the Harvest Festival though, right?" said Juliana. "You'll stay until it's over?"

Ramsey ruffled her hair slightly. "We'll see," he offered. "I'd like to see the festival again, but I suspect the Lord Commander will want me back in the capital sooner than that."

"What for?" Liviah asked. Ramsey looked hesitantly from Liviah to her parents.

"Best not heard by children's ears," he said with a smile.

"Girls why don't you go on and play," their mother said. "Didn't you say you had plans with Addi? Ramsey, if you'd like to come inside for some tea, Jonathon can go and fetch Philius, I know he'd like to see you."

"What? Oh uh, yes!"

Juliana and Liviah giggled as their father hurried off in a fluster.

"Thank you, Darah. That would be lovely," Ramsey said.

"We'll see you later, Ramsey!" Liviah said. Both she and her sister gave Ramsey a great big hug before running off towards the woods.

"Liviah, remember my rule!" her mother called after her.

"Yes mum!" Liviah replied. She and Juliana reached the line of trees, covered the crest of a hill, and made their way down to the river where Addi was already waiting. Addisarah Crey was the daughter of one of the farmers, an olive-skinned girl with straight, jet-black hair. She was in Liviah's year at Glassfall's school but was only Juliana's age. Most importantly, she was both girls' very best friend. Addi pranced around the water's edge gracefully as she tossed stones at the surface. She had been skipping stones since she was eight, she boasted, while Juliana and Liviah's father had taught them only last week.

"Hey Addi!" Juliana and Liviah said in turn as they approached the river's bank.

"Hey Jules! Hey Liviah!" Addi said as she flicked another stone. It skipped four times before sinking below the surface.

"Guess what! Our parents' friend Ramsey is in town!" Julianna said.

"The one who works for the Legion?"

"Yeah!"

"Why aren't you with him?"

"They're talking about some boring Legion stuff," Liviah said dismissively.

"Watch this Livvy," Juliana said. She cocked back her arm and flung it forward, releasing a thin, smooth stone down the stream. The stone skipped once, twice, and then sank into the water. Juliana smiled at her sister proudly, waiting for her response.

Liviah bent down, chose a suitable rock, and flicked it at the water. It leapt downstream for as far as the girls could see, bouncing off the surface at least ten times before they heard the far-off *plop*. Liviah smirked at her sister with folded arms. Juliana wrinkled her nose.

"It's not *fair* if you use magic..." she muttered. "Why do you always take away the fun?"

"I don't!" Liviah said, "It's not my fault that you can't do it."

"I can too!"

"No, you can do *other* magic, and you're jealous that mine is cooler."

"I am not! And yours isn't cooler!"

Liviah smirked as a small stone floated up and hung suspended in mid-air next to her. "Admit it," she said. "You're jealous."

"Come on," Addi groaned. "Why do you two always have to fight?"

"If she wasn't such a baby!" Liviah said.

"I'm not a baby!" Juliana retorted. "You're just a jerk!"

Suddenly the riverbank erupted in voices. Juliana and Liviah hurled names at each other, while Addi reprimanded them both for their immaturity.

"Hey Cain!" a voice interjected. The stone dropped to the ground as Liviah's attention snapped to the crest of the hill behind them. She desperately hoped that none of the three boys standing there had seen her floating the stone. One of them jogged down towards the girls. It was Ambry Delphi, a common troublemaker in Glassfall, and his two henchmen following close behind him.

"What do you want, Ambry?" Liviah asked, being clear to step between the boys and her sister.

"You hear the big news?" Ambry said with a tone of mock sarcasm. "Turns out, you and your little sister here are a pair of freaks!"

The boys behind Ambry—Shaunnard and Polack—snickered.

"Leave them alone," Addi said sternly.

"This don't concern you, Crey! I'd get lost if I was you. Stop hanging out with these two before they sacrifice you to their freaky magic gods."

"Shut up!" Juliana said.

"I mean look at them. You can see it in their eyes. They're crazy."

Liviah glared at each of the boys in turn. Their faces were covered in a bit of dirt, and all of their hairs were tangled and messy. She drew her mouth into a half grin.

"You should probably be more careful around us then. You never know when we might *snap!*"

Ambry's henchmen flinched as Liviah took a quick half-step towards them. She cocked her head back in laughter and then grabbed Juliana by the shoulders as she turned and walked away.

"I seen what you are," Ambry said. "I seen what kinda dark magic you do. Both of you!"

Liviah stopped walking and glanced slightly over her shoulder. "I don't know what you're talking about."

"I reckon you do. See I'm an augur now. I see things. All things. Sometimes things people don't want me to see."

Liviah whirled around; her eyebrows narrowed at Ambry.

"Liviah, cool it," Addi instructed.

"You're lying," Liviah said.

"Swear I'm not," said Ambry. "Had my first vision a month ago. Normal stuff, nothing big. Dad did appreciate knowing the weather a few weeks in advance. But then last night, I had a dream about you and your little sister here on her last birthday doing all sorts of freaky magic. You know what they say about an augur's dream always being true?"

"That doesn't even make sense, Ambry," Addi said impatiently. "Augurs make predictions of the future, not the past."

"Your friends are monsters! Both of 'em!"

Liviah stepped towards Ambry and grabbed his tattered shirt collar faster than he could react. She was just slightly taller than him when they stood this close together.

"Tell anyone what you saw, and you'll wish you hadn't!" Liviah said.

"Get off me you freak!"

"Livvy, come on. Let's go home," Juliana said. She tugged hopelessly on her sister's sleeve. "Liviah let's leave. Please, Liviah!"

"Pol! Shaun! Get her off me!" Ambry commanded his henchmen.

The other two boys rushed to pull Liviah off him. She released her grip on Ambry's shirt just as Pol pushed her. Liviah fell backwards, toppling into Juliana. Juliana squealed as she hit the rocky ground. Blood oozed from her forearm where one of the stones had cut her.

Liviah stood up with blistering speed, her eyes wide in fury. Ambry looked quite satisfied with his companion's work, but Pol raised two surrendering palms as he backed away from Liviah.

"I—I'm sorry," he stammered. "I didn't mean—it was an accident!"

Liviah clenched her fists, and the rocks on the ground around her rushed to encase his feet. They wrapped around his ankles, then his shins, and eventually his knees. He struggled to move as Liviah continued towards him.

"Liviah, don't! He's not worth it!" said Addi.

"What's she doing to him?" Ambry yelled. The smile was eradicated from his face. "What are you doing to him? Stop it! Make her stop!"

Pol let out a scream as the rocks grew tighter and tighter around his legs. "Ahh! Please!" he yelled to Liviah, "Please, I'm sorry!"

"Stop it!" said Ambry.

"You're hurting him!" Shaun yelled.

"Livvy!" said Juliana. "Livvy, stop it, please! Liviah!"

It was Juliana's voice that broke through. Liviah turned towards her sister. The blood had already disappeared from Juliana's arm and the cut had already healed. Liviah's fists relaxed, and the boy fell to his knees as the rocks around his legs toppled down. Juliana rushed over to him, now blind to any previous fear she had for her own safety.

Juliana placed a hand over each of the boy's bloodied legs, and a faint yellow glow emanated from her palms. He winced as she touched him, but in a matter of moments the blood began to trickle back into his body. The bruising and gashes in his skin faded way. His breathing slowed to a normal pace and he sat in amazement, staring at Juliana.

"Please," Juliana said, "please don't tell anyone. We'll never bother you again. We'll leave you all alone. I promise."

"Come on guys," Ambry said, hitting each of his mates once on the shoulder. "Come on! Let's get out of here!"

The boys scrambled up the hill as fast as they could. Only Pol looked back for a moment once he had reached the top. Juliana slumped to the ground.

"You shouldn't have done that," she said to Liviah.

"*You* shouldn't have done that," Liviah replied.

"If I hadn't healed him, he could have been crippled the rest of his life, and he would have told everyone it was you who did it!"

"So? No one would have believed him. And who cares if he's crippled. He needed to learn a lesson."

"It was an accident."

"They came after us! He wouldn't have *accidentally* hurt you if they hadn't been here in the first place."

"But it doesn't matter, anyway! I can heal myself just fine. Now what are we going to do if they tell people what we did?"

"They won't tell."

"But what if they do?"

Addi shook her head without a word. Liviah already knew everything she was thinking. Her parents had one rule—never be seen using your magic—and both her and Juliana had broken it.

* * *

Now only one day before the start of the Harvest Festival and her fourteenth birthday, Liviah set the places at the dinner table with quiet anticipation. She had a whole day of excitement waiting for her tomorrow, and the rest of the week to follow as well. She was prancing around the table without a worry in the world when Juliana bumped into her.

"Look where you're going," Liviah said, but her sister's solemn face told her something was wrong.

"One of the boys told their parents!" Juliana whispered.

"What?"

"Ambry and his friends! One of them told their parents what happened, and Mum and Dad know too. I just heard Uncle Philius talking to them about it."

Liviah had been so preoccupied thinking about her birthday and the festival that she had almost forgotten about the incident by the river. She had known at the time that she had pushed her luck too far, but after a few days it had slipped clear out of her mind.

Liviah glanced uncomfortably into the kitchen where her Uncle Philius was talking in a hushed voice to her mother and father. That was the problem with having the village's chief augur as your uncle—you could never get away with anything being kept secret from your parents.

"Liviah!" her mother called from the kitchen. "Get in here, now!" Liviah dropped her silverware on the table and stepped into the kitchen, unsure of what to expect. "Uncle Philius seemed to have some interesting information to share with us about you," her mother said.

"I can explain," Liviah said timidly as all three adults glared down at her.

"Oh! Please do!" her father said, throwing his hands up in the air.

"Ambry was saying that he's an augur, and he knew about what Juliana and I could do! And I told him not to say anything to anyone, but he was going to anyway. And then they shoved Juliana and she hurt her arm!"

Juliana, who had been standing in the doorway behind her sister, shrank back into the dining room at the mention of her name.

"LIVIAH CAIN! We have one rule in this household. Do you know what that is?" said her mother.

"I know the rule! Never use magic in front of other people, but—"

"But nothing! Never use magic in front of other people, and I would certainly think if you were going to break that rule you would know better than to use it to harm someone! Do you even know what kind of damage you could have done to that poor boy if your sister hadn't been there to heal his legs? Juliana is twelve years old for heaven's sake! I would expect you to be the more mature one of the pair of you!"

"What was I supposed to do? Just let them hurt her? They called us freaks, Mum! They said they would tell everyone what we were and what we could do! They hate us because we're better than them, and they would have made everyone else hate us too! Would you rather I just let them treat us like monsters?"

"Liviah, haven't I always protected you?" Uncle Philius interjected. "This isn't the first time that a young augur has had visions pertaining to this family, and haven't I always convinced them not to expose you? Haven't I always kept you safe?"

Liviah scowled at the floor. "Go to your room, girls," her father said with a hand pressed to his forehead. "Your mother and I have a lot to discuss."

Liviah filled with fury. Did her parents really expect her to do nothing to the boys who hurt Juliana? She couldn't understand it.

Juliana followed quietly behind as Liviah marched towards their bedroom door, which she swung open without a touch. Just as the girls were entering the room, a banging at the front door of the cottage stopped them in their tracks.

The Cains looked to the door and then to each other, not moving a muscle. They were all still on edge from the conversation that had just taken place. The person at the door knocked again. Liviah knew it was foolish to be scared of a simple knock on the door, but she couldn't help it. From what she could tell, the rest of her family felt the same way.

"Open up!" a voice called from outside. Liviah nearly jumped out of her skin. Juliana reached over and grabbed her by the arm.

"Everyone relax," Philius said. "I'll just go and see who it is."

"Wait!" Liviah whispered. "Juliana, get the lights."

Jonathon nodded his agreement. Juliana blinked hard once and the light of every lantern in the house disappeared to darkness, with only the candle in their father's hand remaining lit.

Liviah and Juliana stepped fully into their room and rushed to the window, ever so slightly pulling the curtains so they could peek out of them without being seen.

"Philius!" the man at the door said. "I wasn't expecting to see you here."

"That's Ambry's father," Juliana whispered in Liviah's ear. Liviah swatted her sister back.

"*Shh!*"

"Yes, hello Rolan," Philius replied politely. "Jonathon has taken Sydarah and the girls on a trip to the city. I'm watching over the cottage while they're away. Actually, I was just heading to bed so, if you don't mind."

"Just a minute," Rolan said, stopping the door with his foot as Uncle Philius tried to shut it. "I think you know why we're here, Philius."

It wasn't until now that Liviah realized there was a crowd of others with Rolan, standing at the base of the stairs that led up to the veranda.

"Ambry is telling me that one of your nieces smashed in his mate's legs with some rocks," Rolan said.

"Oh dear, the boy's legs are hurt?" Philius did a poor job concealing his sarcasm.

"Let's not make this harder than it needs to be, Philius. We've all heard the rumors about your brother's family."

"I'm afraid I haven't."

"The black magic, the blood curse, whatever you want to call it. This isn't the first time there have been whispers of their...*abnormalities*."

"Forgive me Rolan, but I don't have the patience to sit here all night entertaining crude gossip. Is there something that you want?"

"What I want...what we all want," Rolan raised his hands in a gesture to the crowd behind him, "is for our children and our families to be safe. Unfortunately, that means your brother and his family have got to go."

"These are very serious accusations, Rolan. I assume you have proof?"

"You know Ambry's an augur. You're the one who told him for gods' sake. He's seen—"

"I know that Ambry is a young augur whose first vision was no more than a month ago. His word can hardly be taken as law."

Rolan glared and took a step towards Uncle Philius. Liviah knew if anyone else had opened the door Rolan would have probably hit them by now, but the village augur did command some level of respect.

"What is going on here?" a new voice said outside. Liviah's heart leapt with relief.

"That's Ramsey," she whispered to Juliana. She could see him coming around the side of the house. His face, usually warm and kind, was harsh and commanding.

"We won't live with blood magicians in our midst!" a woman in the crowd behind Rolan shouted.

"Get the freaks out of here!" a man seconded.

"What?" Ramsey said with an almost lighthearted chuckle. "I've known the Cain family my whole life, and I can assure you they are not blood magicians. They have as much right to be here as any of you have. How many of you have bought fish from Jonathon Cain to feed your families? Or sent your children to be educated by Sydarah at the school?" His tone was relaxed, though his grip was firm on the hilt of his sword.

"What do you know?" Rolan said. "You come here once or twice a year and think you know us. You think that golden Legion pin on your chest gives you some sort of special power here? Look around, there are no legionnaires patrolling our streets or protecting our people. The Legion has no claim on my home! Glassfall has always been run by the people, and the people have spoken!"

There was a roar of approval from the mob of villagers. Liviah felt her little sister's hand squeeze her own. Ramsey worked his way through the villagers until he was face to face with Rolan on the veranda.

"And what will the Lord Commander say when I send word to him that Glassfall has declared itself an independent state? Do you think you will be able to hold your own against the force of legionnaires he sends to retake your land? How many innocents will be expended?"

Rolan bared his teeth but said nothing.

"Down with the Legion!" one of the villagers yelled, as a flying rock struck Ramsey above the eyebrow.

Liviah gasped as Ramsey stumbled to his knees. Blood began pouring from his forehead. Her mother and father abandoned all caution, flying past Philius and out of the house.

Ramsey rose wearily and drew his sword. Without a moment's hesitation, Rolan bolted. The crowd of unarmed villagers scattered after him. Once they had gone, Ramsey dropped his sword and stumbled towards the banister of the Cain's veranda for support.

"Ramsey!" Jonathon said.

"I'm alright," Ramsey said, but blood continued to trickle down his face and onto his robes.

"Jonathon, let's get him inside!" Sydarah said.

Liviah's parents each slung one of Ramsey's arms over their shoulders and carried him into the house, while Philius picked up the fallen sword. Juliana and Liviah sprinted out of their room.

"Here, on the table," Jonathon said, pushing aside the dishes that remained on the dinner table. They hoisted Ramsey up and lay him flat on his back. Sydarah grabbed a cloth which she held to Ramsey's bleeding forehead.

"He looks bad, Jonathon," she said. "I don't know if I can do anything for him."

Jonathon took off his glasses and rubbed his forehead. Was he about to do what Liviah thought he was? Her father had always said there were no exceptions to the rule, but it looked as though he was about to make one.

"Juliana, heal him," he said.

"But...you told me—"

"I know what I've told you. Now I'm telling you to heal him."

Ramsey looked confused, but Liviah couldn't be sure if that was genuine or simply because he had taken a blow to the head. It was probably a bit of both, she assumed.

Tentatively, Juliana placed her hand over the cloth on Ramsey's head and closed her eyes. The blood on his face began to flow back towards the wound until there was none left.

Ramsey raised a hand to his forehead to feel that the wound was completely gone. He sat up, his eyes never moving from Juliana.

"Remarkable," he said. "All of this time..."

Liviah looked from Juliana to her parents, but their perplexed expressions told her that they didn't understand what Ramsey was saying any more than she did.

"All of this time...what?" her father asked.

"Juliana is an *Eclipse*," Ramsey said with an astonishment.

"A what?" Sydarah asked.

"An Eclipse! Individuals with great magical abilities! The ancient stories call them by different names—warlocks, shamans, gods even, but they're all essentially the same. In times of great peril, the Eclipse have been known to come to light! I've studied the legends for years! I just can't believe all this time...Juliana has been one."

"We...never knew it had a name," Liviah's mother said, unable to hide the worry in her eyes.

"Lord Ambersen, what do you mean, 'in times of great peril?'" Uncle Philius asked.

"In all of the legends, the Eclipse manifested themselves to usher the world through its greatest conflicts, beginning with the War of the Sun King four hundred years ago. If this means what I think it does..."

"What?" Liviah's father asked.

"Then Juliana will have a role to play in the upcoming events."

"What events?" her mother said. "Omnios is at peace."

"I believe any more specific predictions of the future would fall under your area of expertise, Philius."

The words made Liviah's stomach churn. Apprehension grew inside her, clutching tightly onto her heart, for she knew the one thing about the Eclipse that Ramsey did not; Juliana was not the only one in the family.

CHAPTER THREE
RIDLEY

Ridley Ambersen bent doubled over his toilet, throwing up his breakfast from earlier that morning. He wiped his mouth and turned to look in the mirror. His face was ghastly white.

"Ridley!" his mother called from downstairs. "Come! We're going to be late for the ceremony."

Ridley groaned. It wasn't that he didn't want to become a legionnaire; it was just the opposite in fact. He *needed* to become one, more than he had needed anything in his entire life. From the moment he was born, his father began preparing for Ridley to become the greatest soldier in history. Yet somehow even after nearly every moment of his fifteen years being spent planning, learning, practicing, and drilling, Ridley could not shake the fear that he wasn't going to amount to the success his father hoped he would.

To make his father proud was all Ridley had ever wanted. His father wasn't a cruel man, but he had always had such high expectations as far as Ridley was concerned. Every improvement Ridley made, every stride he took towards achieving the goal his father had set for him was met with a desire for him to be faster, smarter, stronger, better.

Ridley put on his most formal attire—a black shirt and pants, a black belt with a golden buckle, and a finely woven gray robe. Topping off his wear, he placed on the front of his shirt a golden pin bearing the insignia of the Legion. It was his father's first pin, one of the originals that only the founding members of the Legion had. They weren't even made out of real gold, because the Legion couldn't afford the precious metal back then.

Ridley's father had given him the pin when he turned ten years old, and it had been his most prized possession ever since. He looked at it in the mirror, twisting it to make sure it sat straight on his chest. The crescent moon was meant to represent the light amongst darkness—hope during times of despair. This idea had been crucial to the Legion during its conquest to reclaim the world from the criminals and warlords that once ruled it. Pointing up through the center of the moon was a weapon with the head of a spear on one end and a hook on the other. More specifically, it was called a *reaper*. It was a special kind of weapon that was signature to the legionnaires.

Ridley pulled his boots onto his feet and walked down the stairs. Elma, the Ambersens' maid, was furiously attempting to brush his little brother's tangled mop of hair into something presentable. Elma was older than Ridley's parents and a bit on the larger side. Ridley thought she could be a bit pompous at times, but mostly he liked her. She spent a great number of her days scolding Theo for his bad behavior and telling him he'd better straighten out, or he'd end up broke and lonely like her own no-good father.

"*Ouch!*" Theo said.

"Hush lad!" Elma said. Her voice was shrill and piercing. "It wouldn't be such a chore if you would take a bath once in a while! *Hmph!*"

"Oh, Ridley," his mother said matter-of-factly as he walked into the living room of their home. "There you are. Ready to go?"

Elma came rushing over to him and pressed the wrinkles out of his shirt. She clasped both hands over her mouth, and tears welled up in her eyes. "You look so handsome. Just like your father."

Ridley smiled uncomfortably and ran his hands through his perfectly combed, thick dark hair. His mother was never very warm to him, and at a very young age it was Elma who took up that cause. He was, as she said, the spitting image of his father. They had the same sharp jawline and cheekbones, the same daunting look in their dark brown eyes.

"Any news from Father?" Ridley asked.

"Yes actually," his mother said. "He sent a falcon with a letter last night. His business is taking longer than expected. He won't return for at least another week."

Ridley nodded his head and faked a smile.

"Oh, I know you wanted him to be here, but your father's work is very important," said Elma. "You know he would be here if he could. This day means everything to him."

Ridley knew he shouldn't have been surprised. Work always came first with his father.

"Who cares if he's there?" Theo said. "He'd probably just tell you that you're standing wrong or breathing too loudly." He snickered to himself.

"Theodor!" Elma snapped. "You will speak of Lord Ambersen with respect or you will not speak at all!"

Theo only shrugged. Ridley's little brother could not have been more different from him. Theo, who would be turning twelve in just a few days' time, had no goals or ambitions, no plans of any sort for what he was going to do with his life. Theo had never cared about their father's opinion either. Ridley couldn't blame him though. Their father was a hard man to please, while on the other hand, their mother babied Theo and gave him everything he ever wanted. How could Ridley expect Theo to turn out any differently when he had grown up never having to work for anything? Still, he drove Ridley mad on a near-daily basis. On top of their personal differences, they looked nothing alike. Theo looked like their mother, with rounder features and bright eyes. His hair was blond and thin like hers as well, but unlike her perfectly straight locks, his was always a tangled mess.

"Do I really have to go to this?" Theo groaned. "It's not like it's *my* induction ceremony."

"No, it's not," Ridley retorted, "because at the rate you're going, you'll never have one." Theo curled up his lip and made a face at Ridley.

"Yes, you have to go," Elma said. "Your brother is joining a highly prestigious and respected group and you will be there to support him."

"Honestly though, what's the point?" Ridley asked. "He'll only sit there and complain the whole time. He'll be a bother to all the people who actually care."

"Wow, Rid!" Theo said, his voice teeming with mock sarcasm. "For once that huge head of yours had a good idea."

"Shut up you dirty grudder—"

"Ridley!" his mother interjected. "You will not use that foul language in my house! Apologize to your brother!"

Ridley gritted his teeth. "Sorry," he muttered.

"Now Theodor, darling," their mother continued, "You'd like to go and see the Blackfort, right? Lovely food, important company. It would make me so happy if you would go."

Theo feigned an innocent smile. "Yes, of course, mother. I'll be happy to go."

Ridley rolled his eyes. Theo knew how to play their mother. Most times he wouldn't have let it go until he got his way, but Ridley supposed that part of Theo's craft was knowing when to suck up.

Ridley stepped out of the door without so much as another look at Theo or his mother. They followed close behind him, leaving the house to Elma who wished Ridley luck as she waved them off. The two horses in the stables outside whinnied as the three Ambersens began their walk through the Northern Quarters District of Maldenney in silence. Off in the distance, Ridley could see the golden gates surrounding the Blackfort, where two legionnaires stood guard. One of them held his reaper lazily at his side, and the other had his leaned up against the stone ledge behind him. Instead, he held a piece of parchment, upon which he marked off names of those who went inside. Ridley wondered what kind of legionnaires these two must have been, to get stuck with a job like this. Then again, they didn't look to him like they would be good for much else.

"Name?" the one with the parchment said gruffly. Neither he nor his companion looked up as Ridley and his family approached.

"*Ambersen,*" Ridley's mother said sternly. Both legionnaires perked up.

"Madame Alana! Of course," the guard said. He checked his list, "Ridley and Theodor? Right this way."

"Thank you so much," she said with a smile. "And do look a bit more alert in the future, won't you?"

"Yes, Madame. Absolutely, Madame."

Inside the gates, the Blackfort loomed like a giant. Its massive towers and ramparts rose high above the courtyard. The castle truly lived up to its name, as every stone was the color of dark granite. The glow of orange torchlight could be seen through the windows, and it gave the castle an ominous feeling. The courtyard outside was far less intimidating. It was full of hedges, shrubs, trees, and flowers. Several well-dressed people were talking and enjoying refreshments around a grand fountain in the center of the courtyard. Ridley noticed a particularly giggly group of girls gazing in his direction, but he was far too anxious to care about that right now.

"It looks like you're supposed to go inside with the other recruits," his mother said. "Go on."

Ridley swallowed and strode towards the Blackfort doors. His legs felt awkward and wonky, like they had forgotten how to walk. He glanced back at the giggling girls. Did he look as nervous as he felt?

Ridley stepped through massive iron doors and into the throne room of the Blackfort. It was much smaller than he had always imagined it. His father told him the Blackfort was the most magnificent structure ever assembled, but Ridley found it cold and hollow. He laughed silently to himself. That sounded like a building his father would call magnificent. This was not to say the castle was unspectacular, however. Nearly everything seemed to be made in tones of black and gray. The only color came from stained-glass windows, depicting scenes from battles throughout history. The insignia of the Legion was displayed proudly on the banners that hung from the walls.

The throne room was filled with at least twenty other fifteen-year-old boys. Some looked terribly uncomfortable, probably due to nerves, while others talked and laughed as if they didn't have a care in the world. Ridley had no desire to converse with anyone at the moment, so he sat on a ledge off on his own. He watched a group of boys in the middle of the room, all listening to one tell a story. The speaker had dark skin and short black hair. He was wearing a navy cloak that looked much older than Ridley's. He and the boy locked eyes for a second, and Ridley quickly looked away.

"Aye, you!" the boy said. He approached Ridley and glared down at him. Now that he was closer Ridley could see that his clothes were a bit dingy.

"Sayben," the boy said as he stuck out his hand.

"Ridley," he said, shaking the hand in response.

"You look just like that Lord Amber-something, you know?" Sayben's accent was one Ridley had never heard before.

"My father," Ridley replied coolly.

"Ah, your father," said Sayben, though it was clear to Ridley that he had known that before he asked. "I bet you live in a big house, don't you?"

Ridley said nothing. He was determined not to let this boy get a rise out of him.

"You know me and the boys here were just talking," Sayben continued. "I told them I could beat anyone in a fight, anytime, anyplace, and you know what they told me?"

Ridley looked forward uncaringly, and Sayben pointed his forefinger at him.

"They said not you. 'Not that Ambersen boy,' they said." Sayben imitated the other boys in a loud, mocking voice. "'He's got training,' they said. 'You can't beat him!'"

Ridley raised his eyebrows. "It sounds like they know what they're talking about."

"Oh so he *can* say more than three words!" Sayben proclaimed. The crowd of boys laughed around him. "Let's get one thing straight, Prodigy. I'm not highborn. I'm from the Blights, born and raised, and no amount of training can beat years of living off street smarts. You wouldn't last a day down where I'm from."

"Do you have a point to all of this?" Ridley asked. "It's getting very boring if I'm honest with you."

Sayben smiled. "A point…a point…what was the point? Oh, that's right! My point is that I'm the best recruit here, and by the time training is over, no one is going to be able to say otherwise. Not even you." As he said the last word, Sayben tapped Ridley on the nose with his pointer finger and turned to walk away. Ridley's blood began to boil. He stood up and grabbed Sayben on the shoulder, turning him back around.

"Do not do that again," Ridley said. Something about that tap, that small action that meant seemingly nothing, had been one of the most humiliating things Ridley had ever experienced.

"Why, what are you gonna do? You gonna fight me?" Sayben raised his fist and boxed at the air as he hopped back and forth between his feet.

"No," Ridley said.

"Come on, why not? You and me, toe to toe, right now. No hair pulling though!" Sayben said tauntingly, running a hand over his tightly curled hair that was no more than a centimeter long.

Ridley stepped forward so that their faces were only a few inches apart. He stared into Sayben's almost black eyes. They were unflinching. The crowd of other recruits had drawn in close, waiting in anticipation for Ridley's response. He shoved Sayben in the chest, just hard enough to make him stumble a bit. A chorus of approval erupted from the circle of boys.

"Yeah, here we go!" Sayben said. He swung at Ridley with his right arm. Ridley dodged the fist and swiftly took Sayben's legs out from under him. Unable to stop his momentum, Sayben fell flat on his stomach. The boys roared with laughter. Ridley looked around at them and grinned. Sayben jumped to his feet. "You're good," he said, still smiling. He came at Ridley with his head down and grabbed him around the torso. He punched

Ridley twice in the side, then turned him over and slammed him onto the ground. Ridley groaned in pain. "Come on, you got more in you," Sayben taunted. Ridley stood up and swung at him. Sayben blocked it with his forearm and swung back violently at Ridley. There was no pattern or technique to his action. Ridley dodged or blocked them all and waited for his opening, then he punched Sayben square in the face. Sayben yelled and stumbled back. All of the boys cheered and clapped Ridley on the back. Ridley smiled back at the other recruits, a new confidence rising in him. This had been his first trial, and he had passed it. Years of training were finally paying off.

As he was accepting his congratulations from his new comrades, Ridley felt a hand grab his shoulder. He turned around to feel Sayben land a fist deep in his stomach. Ridley gasped for air as the Blighter hit him again, one fist after the other. The crowd was eating the fight up, hollering with each new blow dealt.

"What is going on here?" a menacing, guttural voice pierced the applause and laughter in the room. Sayben wiped the blood from his nose and spat on the ground beside where Ridley had fallen to catch his breath. Every boy fell silent as they turned to look at the door behind the throne. They had all been so preoccupied with the brawl that they hadn't noticed anyone entering the room. A massive, olive-skinned man with a bald head stepped out in front of the throne so that he was in clear view. Through his trimmed beard, Ridley could see that his chin and nose came to sharp points. He held his lips pursed tight, as if he were stifling rage from bursting out. He wore black armor, separating himself from the gold of the legionnaires. Every boy in the hall recognized him as Kaliculous Kaeno, the Lord Commander of the Legion.

Kaeno's eyes darted from Sayben to Ridley. They were dark and had sunken deep into his head, but they still made Ridley feel as if they were piercing his very soul. "You two, to the front," he ordered. Ridley immediately stepped forward and looked up the four steps at the Lord Commander, holding his hands behind his back. A few moments later, he saw Sayben step up next to him. "What's your name?" Kaeno said to Sayben, who was still wiping the blood off his lip.

"Sayben, my Lord." Ridley noticed that his opponent's dialect had suddenly become much more formal than it had been before.

"Sayben...?"

"Just Sayben, my Lord. I don't use my father's name."

"And why is that?" Kaeno growled, obviously getting fed up.

"Because he's a self-serving waste of air, and I don't owe him anything...my Lord." Kaeno considered the response for a while before apparently deciding it was acceptable.

"And where is it that you're from, Sayben?"

"Maldenney, my Lord. The Blights."

"The Southern Quarters."

"The Southern Quarters, my Lord."

Kaeno nodded, apparently finding this answer acceptable. He then turned and looked at Ridley, his expression growing graver as he did so.

"Ambersen," he said, "you think you're ready to become a legionnaire, do you?"

Ridley was startled by this question. He hesitated for a moment before answering.

"Yes, my Lord."

"How many years have you been preparing for the legionnaires?"

"All my life, my Lord."

"And who is your father?"

Ridley sighed.

"Lord Ramsey Ambersen, legionnaire First Officer and Delegate of the Legion."

"Ah yes, that's correct. And given my familiarity with Lord Ambersen I feel confident in assuming that he must have spared no expense in your training, correct? Who was your fighting instructor?"

"I trained under two, my Lord. Talloway of the Isle and Duggard of the Rift."

"Talloway, as in the archer? And Duggard, the master swordsman?"

"Yes, my Lord."

"*Very* impressive."

"Thank you, Lord Commander," Ridley said with a smile and a glance at Sayben.

"No formal instruction with a reaper though?"

Ridley's face fell. "Er—no, my Lord," he said.

"How disappointing...Nevertheless, I'm sure your abilities will transition well. There's no doubt you are a well-rounded fighter." Ridley felt a jolt in his heart yet again. What was the Lord Commander trying to do? Ridley watched as the man stroked his bearded chin, seemingly deciding whether to compliment or insult him again. "Tell me Ridley, do you enjoy picking fights with those who have had far less training than you? Does it make you feel tough to beat a lad who's never been told how to properly take down his enemy?"

"I wasn't—no, my Lord."

"I would have at least expected you to be *winning* the fight." Ridley felt his face burn red hot as the boys around him snickered quietly. "The Legion is a brotherhood," Kaeno continued, "the bonds of which go far beyond whatever childish squabbles the two of you were at each other's throats about. If that's not something you two can understand..."

"No!" Ridley and Sayben said together. Their eyes locked for a moment before Sayben looked away.

"We can, my Lord," Ridley said.

"Good. I'll speak to your training instructor at the Academy. The two of you will be assigned as bunkmates while you're there. You can learn to settle your differences then." Ridley risked another glance over to Sayben, who was glaring angrily out of the corner of his eye. Kaeno turned his attention back to the rest of the boys. "Secure the Peace, Protect the People, Maintain the Order," the Lord Commander's voice boomed in the open hall. "Since its inception, the Legion has operated under these three ideals, and through them we've created a better world. The road to where we are today was not an easy one. There are many men, myself included, who have sacrificed and suffered to establish a society in which these ideals flourished.

"Initiation into the Legion is a great honor. More importantly, it is a tremendous responsibility. You've come to us from different backgrounds"—he eyed Ridley and Sayben—"but none of that matters anymore. After today, you'll all be brothers.

"Your training will push you to your limits. Your strength, your wits...even your loyalty will be tested. If you make it through the next ten weeks, you'll become full-fledged legionnaires. Saviors of the realm!" All around Ridley, the other boys erupted in cheers. "Now enough of these formalities," Kaeno said, smiling for the first time. "Induction is cause for celebration. Your families are waiting for us in the banquet hall. Let's eat!"

* * *

The banquet hall of the Blackfort was far more ornate than the throne room. Chandeliers and glass ornaments hung from the ceiling;

banners of gold and white were draped from the pillars along the edge of the room. Ridley had taken up the seat by the Lord Commander's chair at the head of the table. Across from him sat an olive-skinned boy whom he recognized as Fletcher Oswood, the son of another Legion Lord. For some unknown reason, Sayben had decided to occupy the seat beside Ridley, while Theo and his mother sat at the far end of the table with the other noble families. Ridley could see her making pampered small talk with the other Lords and Madams, but he knew it was all an act. His mother didn't really care about any of them or their lives, she just had to see to it that the Ambersens remain one of the most notable and respected families in Maldenney. It was her duty to make them think she cared, to make them crave her attention. She was quite good at it too, and it was no wonder where Theo had picked up that talent.

"I remember when I was initiated. Your father ever tell you about those days, Ambersen?" said Kaeno, pulling Ridley's attention away from his mother.

"He doesn't speak of it much, my Lord."

"You see lads, Ridley's father was with me when it all started under Lord Commander Baymore. Ah, the first legionnaires," Kaeno said reminiscently. Fletcher, Sayben, and the other boys around Ridley perked up to hear Kaeno's story. "That was before the Legion was in power of course. It was just a small group of us back then, dedicated to traveling the world and instilling order where it lacked. We were a few thousand men, but nothing compared to the numbers we have now."

"That must have been very exciting, my Lord," Ridley said, "to be a part of the group that made the Legion's dream come to fruition."

"Aye, it was. Damn, we were glorious back then! I could have killed any bandit or brigand with one hand tied behind my back! I did on more than one occasion, as a matter of fact!" Kaeno laughed violently and took a swig from his tankard of whiskey. "But don't think I've forgotten who helped me along the way, Ridley. Balfour was the one who gave the Legion its good name. Before he joined us, we were vigilantes. He made us heroes. He was always the one that the people loved."

"I'm sorry, my Lord," Ridley said. "I'm afraid I don't know who that is."

The Lord Commander erupted in laughter again but stopped abruptly at Ridley's continued look of confusion.

"Don't tell me...your father never told you about his brother?"

"My father has a brother?" Ridley said. "I have an uncle?" He could feel the other recruits' eyes turn on him.

"Aye you do! The great Balfour Ambersen! By the heavens, I forget you were just a little one when he died. Still, I can't believe no one has ever told you about him! Balfour and your father came to the Legion in a time when we were not very well admired throughout Omnios. We would travel from town to town, kill those who had done wrong, and we asked for nothing more in return than hot food to eat and warm beds to sleep. We were greatly feared, as some would have preferred it, no doubt, but most of us wanted to be seen for what we truly were—men and boys with good hearts and a talent for getting justice. Albeit our means were not always the gentlest, our intentions were always kind-hearted. Balfour saw that in us, and he always knew just what to say to make people see the good in what we were doing. He made all of this"—he gestured around himself to the grand banquet hall—"possible."

"I can't believe...my father never told me."

"Balfour and Ramsey didn't get along often. Ramsey was a bit jealous of him at times, I think. But that's no excuse for not telling a boy about his own family! Especially a man so loved and adored as Balfour was."

"If everyone loved him so much, how come you ended up Lord Commander?" Sayben asked. Ridley shot him a disgusted look. The *nerve* he had to say something like that to the Lord Commander's face. Kaeno, however, was not coherent enough to be phased by it.

"My predecessor, Lord Commander Baymore, loved me," Kaeno said. "I was willing to do what needed to be done for the good of the cause. See, as the Legion grew in power, it became the job of the legionnaires to keep that power. I knew if I slipped up, if I showed any mercy, I would be making the Legion look weak. I was able to make the hard decisions that had to be made, that's why my Lord Commander knew I would be fit for the job. Balfour never could have made the tough calls I had to make. He always wanted to forgive. Sometimes I think he cared about people a bit too much...But still, it never would have been possible if he hadn't been there to clean up my messes! I'll always give him credit for that."

"So, what happened to him?" Ridley asked. All of the other boys seemed to be leaning in now, scared to miss a word of what was said. Kaeno's face fell low.

"By the time King Talmund died there was no heir to take his place. His child sister disappeared, and for the first time in history, the realm had no King. That's when the Legion formed, to fight the chaos that came with not having a ruler. When Lord Commander Baymore died, may his soul rest peacefully, I became the new Lord Commander. But the people wanted more than a military regime. They wanted a king. They wanted Balfour. He was the face of our cause, after all, even more than Baymore himself had been. I wanted him to take reign as well, but he was never one for much power. Preferred to leave that to 'better men,' as he always said, but being liked was Balfour's curse. He couldn't bear to refuse everyone's wishes. He finally agreed to be coronated as King of Omnios, but he died soon after. Tragic accident."

"How did he die, though?" Ridley demanded. "What happened?"

"He had gone out hunting, in the forest just outside these walls, in fact. Said he wanted to clear his mind before his coronation. When he didn't turn up a few days later, a few of his closest friends went to look for him, but they never returned either. A few days later, a legionnaire patrol found a pile of bodies right in the area Balfour had set out to. They were shredded down to the bones. We couldn't tell who was who."

"They were eaten?"

"Not eaten, no. The flesh wasn't gone, just ripped apart and thrashed to pieces until they were unrecognizable. Some speculated it was an al-miraj, the vicious beasts."

"An al-mi-what?" Sayben said.

"Massive creatures that resemble hares, only they have razor sharp teeth and a horn on their heads. Not to mention they're masters of camouflage."

Sayben made no attempt to control his laughter. "Hold on, hold on. You're telling me that Ambersen's uncle was killed by a giant unicorn bunny?"

"An *al-miraj*," Ridley corrected him.

"Right, whatever."

"Lord Commander, I don't understand," Ridley said. "What kind of an animal would kill its prey and then not eat it?"

"Maybe it wasn't killing for food," Kaeno shrugged. "Maybe it was just defending itself. Balfour was hunting after all."

Ridley slumped down into his seat. He still couldn't believe his father had never told him all of this.

"You just keep getting more and more interesting, Ambersen," Sayben said smugly. "Got some big expectations to live up to, huh?"

"Aye, that he does," said Kaeno, downing another whiskey in one draft. "Probably already planning his rise to take my place as Lord Commander!" Ridley's face flushed red, but Kaeno laughed haughtily, nearly choking on the bone of a roast pork he had been eating. "You know I was Lord Commander by the age of seventeen?" he said. "Joined up at thirteen when my mother died. Never had a father, so I was used to looking after myself. Lord Commander Baymore saw that I took initiative, that I could get things done on my own, so he made me his second in command before he was killed. That's what being a legionnaire is all about, you see. Getting the hard things done, especially when no one else can. Remember that, and you'll make a fine Lord Commander someday, son."

CHAPTER FOUR
LIVIAH

"Jonathon, I would strongly encourage you to consider returning to the capital with me."

Liviah listened closely through her parents' bedroom door as they spoke in hushed voices with Ramsey. Juliana sat next to her, perched down on all fours, waiting in anticipation to know what Liviah found out.

"We aren't going to Maldenney," her father said. "We decided long ago that we didn't want the girls growing up there. Glassfall is our home."

"Glassfall is not *safe* anymore. Don't you see that? If the townspeople know about—"

"They don't know anything. Besides, we've been members of this community for twelve years. We can't just pack up and leave; we have roots here. It's the word of one twelve-year-old boy against ours. That's hardly grounds for anyone to take action against us."

"One twelve-year-old *augur*, Jonathon."

"That doesn't mean anything more. Kids are kids. They make things up all the time. And young augurs misinterpret visions all the time. We have Philius to back us up for that."

"What are they saying?" Juliana asked.

"Shush, I'm trying to hear!" Liviah whispered back.

"Ramsey," Liviah's mother said, "if we're in danger here what makes you think we won't be in the capital?"

"I can't protect you here. In the capital I can assign you legionnaires, the girls will have guards to protect them. We could even give you a safe house."

"We'd be like prisoners in our own city then," Liviah's father said. "I appreciate all of your efforts, Ramsey, but I won't do that to my family. The girls have friends here."

"And we won't teach our daughters to live in fear," her mother added. "Moving to another city every time we come across someone who doesn't like us? That's no life for kids to have."

Ramsey let out a long low breath. "I understand," he said, "but I do worry about you here."

"We'll be alright. I promise."

Footsteps approached the door.

"They're coming!" Liviah said. She and Juliana scrambled away from the door as fast as possible and into the living room. They sat down onto the sofa just as their parents and Ramsey emerged from the bedroom.

"Oh, Mum, Dad. What's going on?" Liviah said, trying to act natural. Her mother looked happy and untroubled, as always. Liviah often wondered how she always managed to keep her composure in front of her daughters. The world could be falling apart, and Liviah's mother wouldn't let it show.

"What's going on with you two?" she asked, regarding her daughters suspiciously.

"Nothing, just hanging out," Juliana said nonchalantly.

"Oh?" she said with a smile. "I guess it's just been a while since I've seen the two of you sit on the sofa in silence, facing perfectly forward with your feet on the floor and your hands in your laps."

Liviah and Juliana laughed uncomfortably.

"Well...we better get to bed!" Liviah said.

"*And* you're going to bed early?" their father asked.

"I have a big day tomorrow."

"You do? What is it? I can't remember."

"Oh, I know Jonathon," their mother said. "It's Aaron the stable master's birthday."

"Oh, that's it! We'll have to wish him a happy birthday."

"It's *my* birthday," Liviah said, "and I want to be well rested, so I'm going to bed."

"I'm going too," Juliana said, unable to suppress the guilty look on her face. "Goodnight!"

"Goodnight," Liviah seconded. They hugged their parents and Ramsey, then ran down the hall to their bedroom. Juliana jumped in her bed and Liviah shut the door behind them.

"What did they say?" Juliana asked eagerly. She was trying to sound brave, perched on the edge of her bed, but Liviah knew better. She sensed the fear that was coming through in Juliana's voice.

"They said...there was nothing to worry about. Mum and Dad asked Ramsey if he thought we were in danger. He said no. Everything is fine."

"Oh, that's a relief," Juliana said with a smile.

Liviah nodded and lay down on her bed. She didn't have the heart to tell Juliana the truth—that Ramsey was scared, but their parents wouldn't listen to him. Liviah didn't want to doubt her parents, but she couldn't help feeling that Ramsey would know better than they. He was a Legion official, after all. It was his job to protect the realm. There was nothing she could do about it though, so she pushed the thought out of her mind.

"Well, I think I am going to get some sleep," she said, lying down on her own bed. She faced the wall so that Juliana wouldn't see the look on her face. She didn't want her sister to be scared. There just wasn't a point. "Can you get the lights?"

"Yep," Juliana said. "Goodnight Liviah."

"Night Jules, sleep tight," Liviah said, knowing full well that her sister's nightmares wouldn't allow that.

"You too," Juliana said softly. In a blink of her eyes, the light emanating from the candles on their nightstands flickered out, and the room went dark.

Dreams rushed in and out of Liviah's mind that night. She dreamed about the Harvest Festival and her upcoming birthday. She dreamed that she and Juliana switched magic, and Juliana went all over Glassfall making things float around in the air. Then suddenly, everything went black, and Liviah was standing in empty darkness. Off in the distance, she could see a dim light. It grew rapidly as she walked towards it, and after a while she realized that it wasn't just a light. A wall of flames six feet high came chasing after her. Liviah turned and ran as fast as her legs would take her, but she didn't go anywhere. The wall of flames grew closer, and her face dripped with sweat. The heat of the fire licked at her skin, burning hotter, hotter, hotter. The harder she ran, the quicker the flames engulfed her.

She woke up from her dream panting and immediately choked on the smoke that filled her room. Liviah looked around to find that the Riverside cottage truly was on fire. She threw off her blanket and ran to her sister's bed.

"Juliana," she coughed. "Juliana! Get up!" Liviah pulled away her sister's sheets, but the bed was already empty. Stumbling towards the bedroom door, she pushed it open. She made her way towards the back of the house. "Mum! Dad!" she called through the thick smoke. She couldn't see a thing. The light of the fire was blindingly bright, yet at the same time, the house seemed to be filled with darkness. She was just about to reach her parents' bedroom when the ceiling began to collapse.

"Agh!" Liviah cried. A burning plank of wood fell on her back and knocked her flat. The smoke was beginning to choke her, and tears were welling in her eyes. Summoning her strength, Liviah willed the plank to rise, floating it off of her back and dropping it on the floor beside her. She staggered to her feet and strained her eyes to see through the smoke. She could just barely make out a mass of debris that had fallen in front of her parents' bedroom door.

"Mum! Dad!" Liviah raised two hands towards the blocked door and tried to force the debris to lift away. Two fallen support beams creaked and trembled, lifting slightly off the ground before falling back. Liviah let out a scream and closed her eyes. The debris shifted slightly but failed to move. Tears ran from her eyes, and blood dripped from her nose. Liviah fell to her knees.

Lying on the cottage floor, surrounded by smoke and flames, she closed her eyes. She was done for. These would be the last moments of her life. Her parents were trapped in their room. They would be dead soon if they were not already. And Juliana—where was Juliana? She hadn't been in her bed when Liviah woke. Perhaps she had made it out; perhaps she was alright. But then, why hadn't she woken Liviah when she fled the house? Maybe something was wrong. Liviah didn't know how the house had caught fire. What if it was set aflame on purpose, and whoever had done so had taken Juliana? Rolan and the others did want the Cains gone, after all. Liviah opened her eyes. She had to make it out of the house. She had to make sure her sister was safe.

Her body trembling, Liviah stood and felt her way to the front door of the house. Smoke and dust had caked her face and her lungs screamed in pain with every breath. Somehow, without seeing, Liviah reached the front room and burst out onto the veranda. She coughed and gagged, trying to inhale the outside air.

"Juliana! Juliana, where are you?" Liviah yelled. She squinted her eyes, struggling to see through the dark haze around. She could just barely make out a figure approaching her. "Juliana!" she called again.

As the figure drew closer, Liviah could see that it was much larger than her sister. It stopped about fifteen paces away — a man, staring at Liviah through a black mask. He ran forward, aiming a spear at her. Liviah dug her feet into the dirt and screwed up her face. She stuck out her hands and envisioned the man being immobilized in his tracks, but she didn't have the strength to make it happen. Her head pounded, and blood dripped from her nose. She couldn't stop him.

"Duck!" a voice said. Without knowing what she was doing, Liviah dropped to the ground. There was a *whoosh* sound overhead as a sharp blade cut through the air. Liviah heard the clash of steel as a sword deflected the reaper's blow, and suddenly there was a third body between her and the masked man. The new man's black clothes flowed in the darkness as he twisted and spun on the spot, dodging each of the masked man's attacks. He beat in the attacker's breastplate with the edge of his sword and then slammed its hilt hard into the side of his head. The masked man fell to the ground and crumpled unconsciously in the dirt.

"Liviah, you've got to get yourself out of here!" The cloaked figure grabbed her by the shoulders.

"Ramsey! I don't understand, what's going on?"

"I don't know! There was a crashing sound that woke me. When I walked outside to see what was going on I thought I must be going absolutely mad. Where are your parents and your sister?"

"I-I don't know. My p-parents' room was…b-blocked." Now that Ramsey was present, Liviah allowed herself to lower her guard. Suddenly she couldn't stop the tears that rushed from her eyes. "I don't know if they were still inside. When I w-woke up Juliana was already g-gone." Ramsey squeezed her and held her close.

"It's alright. It will be alright."

"Philius!" she gasped, remembering her uncle. Ramsey frowned.

"I don't know if he was in the Augury or not," he said solemnly. "Someone set it on fire as well. I haven't seen your uncle." Liviah buried her head into Ramsey's cloak. "Liviah, there could be more of them. You've got to get out of here! Run into the forest and don't look back."

"But, y-you're a Legion official. Can't you s-stop them?"

"I'll do all I can."

"I d-don't understand. Why is this h-happening?"

"Liviah, listen to me!" Ramsey bent down to look her in the eyes as he held her by the shoulders. "There are people here who want to hurt your family. Those villagers who came to your door last night, they know what Juliana can do—what she is—and they hate your family for it."

"But why?" Liviah wailed.

"People fear what they don't understand! And I'm afraid they'll stop at nothing to destroy you if they think you're a threat to them."

"You have to stop them, Ramsey! You can't let them get away with this!"

"I'll do everything I can, but you *must* go, Liviah!"

"I can't leave! Not without Juliana!"

"Look at me, Liviah. Look at me. Did you know that when you were born your parents chose *me* to be your guardian should anything ever happen to them? It's my responsibility to look after you and Juliana. I won't let anything happen to her, or you." He wiped the tears from Liviah's eyes. "I'll find your sister, but you must leave. Get into the forest and follow the river. Don't stop until you can't smell the smoke anymore. I'll come find you when I can. Understand?" Liviah nodded. "Good. Now go!"

Ramsey took off running back towards the flames. Within seconds he had disappeared into the smoke. Liviah started in the direction of the forest, but something held her back. She glanced back at the unconscious figure on the ground, and a hateful longing filled her heart. She wanted to look at the man who attacked her, to see the evil in his eyes and know what sort of monster he was. She walked back to where he lay on the ground and slowly pulled off the mask.

What Liviah saw shocked her more than anything she could have imagined. The person behind the mask was a mere boy, no more than fifteen or sixteen years old. His hair was draped softly over his forehead, like it had fallen there as he drifted off to sleep. Blood dripped down from his temple where Ramsey's hilt had struck. In the dim light of the fires, Liviah could see the calm expression on his unconscious face.

She leaned in close to him, noticing his slow, consistent breathing. Her gaze fell to the spear that lie on the ground next to him. Liviah curled her fingers around it, and the touch of the cool metal made her feel secure. She held the spear in both hands and loomed over her would-be killer.

Something around his neck caught her eye—a thin, silver chain with a crescent moon pendant. Liviah snatched the necklace from the boy and looked more closely at it. She could hardly believe what she was seeing. It was the symbol of the Legion.

"Ramsey!" she yelled instinctively. Ramsey would know what this meant. He would know what to do. Another voice returned her call.

"There!" a guttural voice shouted. Liviah watched in horror as the images of two men began to solidify through the smoke. She hurled the spear at them clumsily and ran as hard as she could towards the woods, clutching the pendant in her fist. By the time she reached the river she was coughing incessantly, choking on the smoke in her lungs. She ran through the pain, not daring to stop. Every so often she would look over her shoulder, but there was no sign of the men behind her.

Following Ramsey's instructions, Liviah didn't stop running until she no longer noticed the scent of her burning home. She bent down in the river to wash the ash from her hands and face. She put her lips to the flowing water and began to drink. Immediately she started to cough; so much smoke had filled her lungs. She couldn't help but wonder if Juliana's healing would be able to do anything about that. The thought of her sister made her sad, hopeless, and angry all at once.

Liviah sat in waiting for Ramsey to appear. How much time had passed? A half hour? Several hours? Her mind was too numb to tell, but she was beginning to feel the pangs of hunger in her stomach. She stood and walked up and down the river. There was no sign of Ramsey whatsoever. Liviah wondered if he hadn't made it out. Her head began to hurt as she held back tears. This was no way to spend her birthday.

Her birthday…Somehow the thought of it just slipped its way into her mind without her realizing. Before she knew it, she was sobbing. She had been fourteen years old for at least a few hours now without knowing it. What did she have to celebrate? Someone had attacked her family, and somehow it was still her birthday. How could that be? Birthdays were happy days with cakes and presents. They were days you spent playing with friends and laughing. Birthdays certainly were not this.

Liviah sat down on a fallen tree trunk by the river and waited for Ramsey just as he had instructed her. He would come along soon enough, and when he did, she would tell him about the pendant. She sat on the log for hours, waiting as the sun rose in the sky. Bugs began to fly around and bite at her skin. Liviah smacked them off her neck, growing more and more annoyed with each passing moment. Where *was* Ramsey, she wondered.

She thought about the boy who attacked her. Why had he been wearing the symbol of the Legion? She entertained the possibility that the pendant had been a coincidence, that it didn't mean anything. Something in her heart told her otherwise, however. Perhaps Rolan had bribed legionnaires to attack the Cains. The thought of rogue legionnaires was terrifying, but the idea that they hadn't been rogue was even worse.

Despite her best efforts, thoughts of her family entered Liviah's mind. The anger she felt looking at the boy in the mask came rushing back like a tidal wave. She *hated* that boy. She hated Ambry and his father. She hated everyone who had come to Riverside Cottage and called them monsters. She wanted them all to be dead.

Liviah furrowed her brow and looked east down the river. Her father had taught her that it flowed straight to the Legion's capital. She reached into her pocket and pulled out the crescent moon pendant. Her gut was telling her that it wasn't just a coincidence; this necklace meant something important. If the Legion was tied to the attack, Maldenney was where she would find answers. She looked down the river in the direction of her home, giving one last chance for Ramsey to emerge from the trees. For all she knew something had happened to him and he wasn't going to come along at all. She couldn't wait there forever.

Liviah stood and walked east along the banks, determined not to be a victim. She was going to go to Maldenney, she was going to find out what happened to her sister, and she was going to avenge her family.

CHAPTER FIVE
RIDLEY

The Legionnaire Academy was a large cluster of buildings on the east end of the Imperial District of Maldenney. It had barracks, a mess hall, an armory, a drill yard, stables, a library, agility courses, archery ranges, and the quarters of several legionnaire officers. To its east was a secondary entrance to the city, a smaller gate that was only used for Legion purposes, and to its south was the Farmlands, which gave the Academy easy access to plenty of food for its recruits.

Ridley rolled his trunk down the narrow hallway inside the recruits' barracks. Today would be the start of his new life, a life that would bring fame and glory to the Ambersen name. Some of the other recruits were also making their way up and down the hallway, finding room assignments and unpacking their things. A legionnaire in full armor, save for his helmet, was roaming amongst the recruits directing them to their rooms. He was a tall, strapping soldier who looked to be in his early twenties. He had long brown hair pulled back into a bun, and his face was covered in freckles.

"Excuse me," Ridley said as he approached him. "Could you tell me which room is mine?"

"Sure thing," the legionnaire said, straight-faced. "Name?"

"Ridley Ambersen."

The legionnaire paused, "Ambersen, huh?" He shook Ridley's hand before turning to lead him down the hallway. "I'm Orion Cormack. I'll be your Academy training instructor over the next ten weeks. I've been a legionnaire six years, people always ask. Anyway, this room right here is yours, and we're meeting at the armory in half an hour to get fitted."

"Thanks," Ridley said, and he pushed open the wooden door that was engraved with the number *301*.

"Hey roomie," Sayben said snarkily as Ridley entered the room. "I took the bottom bunk. Hope you don't mind." He was lounging on the bed with his hands clasped behind his head. Ridley groaned heavily. He hadn't been able to forget that Lord Commander assigned Sayben to be his roommate. He tried to not let it ruin this day for him, but hearing Sayben's smug comment quickly reminded him of the loathing he felt for the Blighter.

Ridley said nothing. He heaved his trunk up onto the top bunk. On the opposite wall was a pair of chests and desks. Ridley unlatched his trunk and began moving his belongings into one of the chests.

"Ah, that one's mine," Sayben said. Ridley sighed and moved to the other. This was going to be a long ten weeks.

"You know, I've been doing some soul searching," Sayben said, "and I think this whole thing could be a lot more enjoyable if we get along. Of course, I'm still going to beat you and humiliate you in front of Kaeno, your father, and everyone else...but I think if you learn to look past that we can get along just fine." Ridley continued to unpack his things without a word. "Man, you're boring!" Sayben said. "I mean, really? Nothing?"

"I've been doing some thinking too," Ridley said, "and I think this will go better if you and I don't talk."

Sayben clutched at his heart. "You hurt me," he said. "You know, me and you are a lot alike."

Ridley slammed the chest shut and turned around.

"You and I are *nothing* alike."

"Oh yes we are."

"How so?"

"We both think we're the best. Only one of us is right, but still. We're both ambitious, both good looking—again, me more than you, but I'll give you some credit."

"You're arrogant," Ridley scoffed.

"And you're not?"

"I know my own capabilities, and I've earned the right to be confident after spending my whole life refining them. You, on the other hand, pull stupid stunts like getting me to fight you. Which, in case you'd forgotten, is the reason we're stuck here together."

Sayben stood up and narrowed his eyes. "It takes two to fight," he said, and he walked out of the room.

Ridley shook his head and finished unpacking his things. He had dreamed of joining the legionnaires his whole life, and now Sayben was ruining it. If they continued on like this, Ridley didn't know how long he would be able to stand living with him.

After a quarter hour, Ridley went outside, across the courtyard, under the stone archway on the right, and into the large open room that housed the armory and forge. He had been there a few times before. Growing up with your father as a Legion official meant spending a lot of time in the Imperial District. As he was a bit early, Ridley was the first of the recruits to arrive. The blacksmith working the forge was a massive brute of a man. He wore a burnt-red shirt under a filthy, black apron. His pants and boots were covered in ash. A hardened expression was painted on his face. He had long black hair pulled back into a curly bun. His hammer rang out loudly as it connected with the anvil.

"You want something boy?" the blacksmith uttered without looking up.

"The recruits are supposed to come here for armor fitting," Ridley said. The smith looked around the armory to see only himself and Ridley.

"They didn't recruit anyone else?" he said gruffly.

"No," Ridley said awkwardly, "the others just aren't here yet." The blacksmith turned his head to reveal a grin. Ridley felt embarrassed as he realized the joke.

"Not one for sarcasm, eh?" the blacksmith said. He pounded on his anvil again, sending sparks flying through the air. "You got a name?"

"Ridley."

"Ridley..."

Ridley chewed his lip before answering. "Ambersen," he said at last. The smith looked up from his work.

"Ramsey's son?"

Ridley grimaced. He had been hoping to avoid interactions like this as much as possible. He wanted his name to be known for his own actions and his own achievements, but it seemed his father was too well known. "Yes," he answered. The smith nodded and dropped his gaze back to the anvil.

"I've only met him once personally. Had me forge a sword for him. But I've heard good things. He sounds like a good man. I'm sure he was proud to see you join up."

"I'm sure he would have been," Ridley retorted. The smith raised an eyebrow. "He didn't come to the ceremony. He's away doing work for Lord Commander Kaeno."

"Either way," the smith said, "I'm sure he's proud."

Ridley wished he could believe that as easily as everyone else could. His whole life everyone had told him, "You'll bring honor to your family's name! I bet your father is so proud of you," but never had he been given a reason to believe his father really felt that way.

By the time he had finished talking to the smith other recruits were showing up at the armory. He saw Fletcher, whom he sat across from at the initiation feast, as well as several other boys he recognized from the ceremony. There was no sign of Sayben in the crowd, and Ridley started hoping that the Blighter wouldn't show. The smith continued working as if no one else was present. Most of the boys talked among themselves until finally, Cormack showed up.

"Alright!" he called, quieting them all down. The hammering stopped as the blacksmith took temporary leave of his work. This was the first time Ridley had seen him stand straight, and he now realized that the man must have been seven feet tall.

"This is Villis Cantar," Cormack said, gesturing to the man-giant. "He's the finest blacksmith in all of Omnios, and Forgemaster to the Legion for twelve years now. He will be forging all of your armor personally, which is a truly great gift for you to receive. He has iron samples of different sized pieces. Breastplates, helms, gauntlets, greaves—the works. Try them on and give him your sizings."

The boys all looked on at the behemoth of a man who stood before them. His hammer must have been the size of a normal man's arm. Cantar did not speak, nor even smile. He seemed an entirely different beast than the person Ridley had spoken with moments before.

"Not everyone at once!" Cormack yelled, and the recruits sprang into action. Ridley walked over to the helmets and began trying them on. They were hot and sticky inside, but he didn't mind. He had grown up in helmets and breastplates, practically living his whole life in armor. He tried on several before finding the perfect fit. It felt natural as he put it on, like wearing the helmet made him whole. He could see better through the slits than he could with his own eyes. He heard better when the sound bounced off the metal. He knew the movements of those to his sides and behind him, counting on his senses rather than his eyes.

He moved over to the bench where others were trying on gauntlets and greaves, and Fletcher sat down beside him. Fletcher was a gangly boy with olive skin and spiky black hair that came to a widow's peak on his forehead. His cheeks were somewhat gaunt, and he had dark brown eyes.

"Ridley, right?" he said, holding out a hand. Ridley shook it.

"Yeah."

"Fletcher Oswood. We sat across from each other at the banquet."

"Sure, I remember," Ridley said.

"This guy's really something, huh?"

Ridley looked again at Cantar, who was pounding away furiously with his giant hammer. "He's got to be the biggest man I've ever seen. Do you think he's got giant's blood in him?"

"Oh him? Yeah, definitely. I was talking about Cormack though."

"Cormack?"

"Haven't you heard about him?"

"No. What's the big deal?"

"Guy's a legend. He's the youngest legionnaire officer since Kaeno himself."

"For now," Ridley said. Fletcher laughed.

"You're planning on taking that title from him?"

"Something like that..." Ridley's voice trailed off as he saw Sayben enter the room. "I can't believe they really let someone like him into the Academy."

"The Blighter?"

"Yeah."

"The Legion's always accepted Blighters into its ranks. Only a little over half of us northerners."

"So make him a stable boy or something he can be useful at. Don't let him into the Academy."

"I don't know...From what I hear he's pretty good."

Ridley only shrugged.

"You're late," he heard Cormack telling Sayben.

"It's not my fault," Sayben replied.

"I didn't ask whose fault it was."

"You don't even want to know why?"

"No. Now hurry up and try the armor on. We're not waiting for you."

Sayben made an annoyed face and walked over to the bench where Ridley and Fletcher were sitting. "What's that guy's problem?" he said to Ridley.

"You were late," Ridley replied.

"Yeah, but I had a good reason."

"Doesn't matter. The Legion tells you to show up, you do it. End of story."

"You got a problem with me, Prodigy?"

"What gave you that idea?"

"Man, we fought, you got hit, get over it."

"Please, you think that's what this is about?"

"No. I know what this is about."

"Oh, do you?"

Ridley stood up, and suddenly he and Sayben were in each other's faces again. Ridley could feel the eyes on him. Cormack was sure to be watching now too, but Ridley didn't care.

"You don't think I deserve to be here, do you Prodigy?"

"No, I don't. We've been here a few hours and already you've been disrespectful and lazy!"

"Nuh uh, that's not why. You know why you don't want me here. Go on, say it!"

"You're scum!" Ridley yelled. "You belong in the Blights, not the Legionnaire Academy! You don't even have a family name for heaven's sake! You're an infestation in the Legion, and it's people like you that are going to see it ruined!"

Sayben glowered at him. It was the first time Ridley had seen that obnoxiously smug smile leave his face for more than a second. "Prove it then," Sayben said.

"What?"

"Prove that you're better than me. We get scored during training, right? If I finish with a higher score than you, you drop out."

"You're insane."

"You're scared."

Of all the things Ridley could be! Angry, frustrated, annoyed, yes. But scared? Scared was certainly not one of them. He knew he would beat Sayben. How could he not? Sayben hadn't spent his whole life training for this. Sayben didn't have half the expertise Ridley had when it came to being a legionnaire.

"Alright, fine. And what happens when I win?" Ridley asked.

"Then I'm gone," Sayben said, his smile returning. "Winner stays, loser leaves. Deal?"

"Deal," Ridley said, and they shook hands.

"You just signed your life away, Prodigy." Sayben walked away and the crowd dissipated. Ridley sat back down on his bench and continued testing out different sizes of armor.

"Have you gone *mad*?" Fletcher asked.

"I'm going to beat him," Ridley said casually.

"You're risking your future as a legionnaire!"

"No, I'm not. I appreciate your concern, Fletcher, but you don't know what I can do and neither does he. If this gets Sayben out of my way, then I'm going to do it."

"I just hope you're right about this."

"I am," Ridley said, and he knew it was true.

* * *

In the coming days, Ridley managed to rise above his classmates in every category of training they faced at the Academy. He was the best rider of the group, with or without a saddle. In the fire-starting competition, he had made a torch from spare materials and lit it faster than any of the other boys. He had known the most about animal tracking and which plants to eat in the wild, and only Fletcher had been cleverer than Ridley when it came to military strategy. He had excelled in everything Cormack had thrown at him, but he hadn't looked forward to any of it as much as combat drilling.

Sayben had done well in his match up. He landed three strikes on his opponent in less than a minute, for which he had received fifteen points. That put him only five behind Ridley, who had yet to fight. He and a red-haired boy called Dax were the last pair to go. Dax was over six feet tall and had muscles much larger than Ridley's, but his form was all wrong. His back was hunched, and his feet were spread so wide he looked like he was riding a horse. He held onto his long-staff with a white-knuckled grip that was sure to make his fingers and forearms tire after a few hard strikes. The pair circled each other while the other boys watched, whooping and hollering for their favorite of the two contenders.

"Come on Dax!"

"Show him how it's done, Ridley!"

"You can beat him, Dax!"

Dax swung at Ridley's head with the long-staff. Ridley ducked under it with ease and landed a blow under Dax's left arm. The crowd roared louder. They didn't really care who won, Ridley realized, just that there was a good fight to watch. Ridley backed up and let Dax recollect himself. Dax made the first move again, running forward and jabbing straight at Ridley's chest. Ridley parried and sidestepped, sending Dax running past him. He went on the offensive, quickly stepping around and hitting Dax on the back of the head. The boy fell forward and rushed to return to his feet. He spit blood onto the ground and swung at Ridley again. Ridley turned his staff sideways and blocked it, then struck down hard on Dax's hand. Dax dropped the staff and stumbled backwards. He grabbed at his throbbing hand with the other.

"I think you broke it!" he yelled.

Ridley held the staff to Dax's neck. If it were a reaper, the sharp metal point would have been poking at his throat. Ridley wiped sweat from his forehead with the back of his hand. "You're lucky we're only using long-staffs," he said. "Otherwise, I would have cut your hand clean off. I don't think I've trained with one of these since I was ten." Ridley reached out a hand, but Dax grimaced and stood up on his own. Ridley scrunched up his face and shrugged. He stretched out his arms in a show of victory, the boys around him cheered for their champion.

"Way to go, Ambersen!"

"Yeah, Ridley!"

"Dax, go get that hand looked at," Cormack called from across the yard. "Ambersen, get over here." The rumble of the crowd died out at hearing Cormack's tone.

"Oh gods, this can't be good," Ridley muttered to no one in particular. Cormack had been particularly hard on Ridley ever since he heard it was Ridley's goal to steal the title of youngest senior officer from him.

"Nice fight," he said evenly as Ridley approached. He wore his standard scowl that reminded Ridley so much of his father. "Your stance was off on that last attack, though. You should have had your left foot forward more."

"Normally you would, if you knew your opponent was going to strike again from the same side," Ridley said, "but I think it's best to assume they're going to counter with something different. I kept my foot in close so that I could switch my front hand and block an attack from the other side if I needed to, without losing any balance. It's a move I learned from—"

"There's news from your father," Cormack said, cutting him off. Ridley wanted to tell Cormack off, but he wanted to hear the news from his father more.

"What is it?" Cormack held out a small slip of parchment to Ridley. Ridley took it and turned it over in his hands. It was rolled up with his father's seal, but the seal had since been broken. "You read it?" Ridley said sharply.

"I have to know what information is getting sent to and from my recruits," Cormack replied with equal venom. "The Legion is your family now, not the Ambersens."

Ridley unrolled the note and read it to himself. It was not his father's writing after all. Ridley recognized the smooth quill strokes as belonging to Elma.

Ridley,

Your father has returned from his trip. I expect he'd like to see you. Stop by the house if you can get away for a while.

Ridley looked up from the letter to Cormack. "Uh, thanks," he said anxiously. "Is that all?"

"One more thing," Cormack said. "You're on mess duty tonight."

"You had me on mess duty last night and the night before! Can't someone else do it?"

"Nope."

"Cormack, please. I haven't seen my father since before the ceremony. He's been gone for weeks."

"What did I just tell you, Ridley? The Legion is your family now. Your brothers have to come before your father. All of them have to work their hides off in drill to keep up with you, so you get to work yours off in the kitchen."

The next few hours crept by more slowly than Ridley thought possible. The kitchens were hot and held the stench of meals from days before. He cooked with three other recruits in the kitchens, not saying a word to any of them the whole time. All he could think of was what his father would say when he returned home. Ridley was the top of his class in all aspects. He was going to be the greatest legionnaire anyone had ever seen. Finally, his father would be proud of him.

When their classmates had finished eating their dinners, Ridley and the others collected the dining ware and took it back to the kitchen. They scrubbed pots, pans, plates, and cups until they sparkled before calling Cormack to do his final inspections. Cormack looked over the dishes slowly and carefully. Ridley was sure he would find a reason for their duties to not be over, anything to make him stay longer. Cormack turned a cup over in his hand and then looked up at Ridley.

"Dismissed," he said finally. A rush of relief came over Ridley. He practically sprinted out of the kitchens so as to not give Cormack a chance to change his mind. He jogged down the long corridor that led to the yard outside, out the front gates, and through the winding streets that ran between the Legionnaire Academy and his home. He burst in the back door to find Elma standing in the kitchen. Looking around, it appeared to Ridley that his family's dinner had not been touched. There were mashed potatoes that filled their bowl to the brim, a pot full of green beans, and a roast hog that had not been cut.

"Elma?" he asked.

"Oh, Ridley, you made it," she said, looking up. Ridley heard his father talking loudly in the other room.

"What's going on?" he asked.

"Now might not be a good time," Elma said regretfully. "I'm sorry, but your father's a bit stressed at the moment. Perhaps it would be best if you spoke with him another day."

Ridley found a certain resolve growing in his chest. "No," he said. "I'm going to see him now." Elma began to stop him, but Ridley shot her a look that told her to back off. He marched into the front room where his mother was sitting on the sofa. His father paced about the room, waving his hands as he spoke.

"I followed the river for miles! She wasn't there, Alana! I don't know where else to look for the poor girl!"

"What's going on?" Ridley asked. His father looked up.

"Oh, Ridley," he said, distractedly. "It's, uh, it's good to see you son."

"It's good to see you too, Father," Ridley replied. They looked at each other without speaking for a moment.

"I'm sorry, but now's just not a great time to talk," his father broke the silence.

"Is something wrong?"

"Yes, I'm afraid something is very wrong." Ridley could tell from the look on his father's face that he was expected to take this information and leave, but he hadn't seen his father in weeks. He was determined not to give up so easily.

"Anything I can help with?" he asked.

"No. It's something with…work."

"Well, maybe I can then. I am a legionnaire now, you know. Well, legionnaire in training, but I'm the top of my class! I'm the best at combat drilling, strategy, survival tests, riding."

"Damn it, Ridley!" his father yelled. He backhanded Ridley across the face. "I told you, I haven't got the time for this! My friends were just killed, and their daughters whom I swore to protect are missing! I've got to get my men searching for them at once! I can't be bothered by any of your silly distractions!"

Ridley did not know what to say. He froze on the spot, holding a hand to his throbbing cheek and staring at his father with his mouth still half open.

"Perhaps you should return to the Academy, Ridley. I'm sure they're hardly getting on without their star pupil," his mother said patronizingly. Ridley turned and stepped out of the room, not making eye contact with either of his parents.

"Ridley," Elma said, stopping him in the doorway. She looked at him with tears in her eyes and without words, uttered her apologies. He had never appreciated Elma enough, he thought. She caressed his face with her fingers before he pulled away, running out the back door and letting it slam shut behind him.

CHAPTER SIX
LIVIAH

The river stretched on for miles and miles. Liviah had been walking for three days now, only stopping to rest briefly at night. The foliage was thicker and harder to navigate in this part of the forest. It seemed as though all the plants had forgotten it was autumn and decided to keep their leaves healthy and green. A brisk wind swept through the forest periodically, and Liviah almost thought she could hear it whisper to her as she walked. She always looked straight ahead, never stopping to appreciate the beauty of the forest around her or the warmth of the sun on her skin. She didn't skip stones the way she and Juliana had so enjoyed doing back home. Those were things of her past now, memories of a time when all was good in the world. Her only focus from here on out was finding out how the Legion was connected to the attack on her family, and with that, learning what had happened to Juliana. She kept on silently and steadily, with only her thoughts to keep her company as she went.

"The walls around Maldenney are tall enough to touch the clouds!" she could practically hear her father saying in her head. He had always marveled at that fact when describing the city to her. She could remember a time when Juliana was just a baby, and Liviah would sit on her father's lap for hours upon hours, listening to his exciting and ridiculous stories. He told her of merchants with magical plants and herbs, or mystical creatures that roamed the woods. She wondered if she would ever hear stories like that again, or even hear her father's voice again at all...

Liviah shook the thought out of her mind and forced out the small bit of hope that she had remaining for her parents. There was no question that they were dead. They had burned down with the Riverside Cottage. The sooner she accepted that fact, the better off she would be.

Next to enter her mind was Ramsey. What had happened to him after she left Glassfall, and why hadn't he shown up in the woods like he had promised? There were a thousand possibilities, only a handful of them good ones. She hoped more than anything that he was alright, that he hadn't been killed while trying to protect her. The thought was unbearable. Liviah didn't know what she would do if she was the cause of Ramsey's death.

She wished her sister was there to cheer her up. That's what Juliana did—make people feel better. Liviah had always thought it was silly to care about other people's feelings as much as Juliana did, but she could use some of her sister's empathy right about now.

Liviah continued walking, wondering what she would even do when she reached Maldenney. Ramsey lived in the city, she knew, but she had never been to Maldenney, and finding Ramsey's house in a city of ten thousand people would be next to impossible. Getting into the city was another issue altogether. She had no identification, no papers to grant her access into the city. Those had been lost when her house had burned. She supposed they would let her into the city if she explained that her house had burned down and she was seeking refuge, but Liviah didn't know whom she could trust. If word got back to the wrong person that the escaped girl from Glassfall had come to Maldenney, she might need saving just as much as Juliana did.

Hunger pangs gnawed at Liviah's stomach, and she felt guilty that all she could think about was food. She hadn't eaten in nearly two days, and dusk was rapidly approaching. She had looked around the river for some berries or nuts to eat, but her searches had been unsuccessful. She knelt at the water's edge and slurped from the clear, flowing current. At the very least, this would fill the emptiness in her stomach for a short time. A river bug landed on Liviah's arm as she drank. She smacked it with her other hand and then held it up to examine it. Her stomach growled again, and before she even knew what she was doing, she had popped the bug into her mouth, chewed it twice, and swallowed it. Immediately, she felt the pain in her stomach lessen slightly, and Liviah speculated at how such a small bug could make such a noticeable difference.

A cold wind blew through the forest as the sun began to set. It rushed through the trees, rustling their branches so that they creaked and moaned under its force. Liviah was walking far slower now than before.

Now that she had acknowledged how tired and hungry she was, she had lost her grit to push on through the discomfort. She watched miserably as the sun finally disappeared and the moon illuminated the blackness of the sky. Her eyelids were growing heavier with each step, and her legs ached with soreness. She sat next to a nearby tree and leaned her back against its trunk.

When exactly she had fallen asleep, Liviah wasn't sure. She woke with a gasping breath, her eyes darting frantically around to remind her of where she was. She shivered in the cold night air. The weather was turning, and she was not dressed for it, as it had been rather warm on the night she had fled her home.

The winds seemed to whisper words to her as they blew by. Liviah ignored the forest's taunts. She had been out in the wilderness so long that her mind was playing tricks on her. Looking to the horizon, there was no sign of light, so Liviah leaned her head up against the tree again and closed her eyes for a second time.

"*Leeeeeave,*" the forest called to her in a low, rasping voice. Liviah's eyes shot open. This time she was certain it was really there.

"Who's there?" she called back.

"*Leeeeeave! Leeeeeave!*"

"Hello?" Liviah yelled as she jumped to her feet with blistering speed. "Who's there?" The trees crackled and moaned even louder than before, as a thousand leaves rustled at once. Liviah looked around furiously, searching for the source of the voice. Everywhere she turned she thought she caught a glimpse of movement, but she could hardly see in all the darkness.

"*Go!*" the voice said. "*Go awaaaaay!*"

"Stay back!" Liviah said. She did her best to keep her voice from trembling. "I'm warning you! Whoever you are, stay back! I don't want to hurt you!"

A huge gust of cold wind rushed over the forest. There was a loud *crack* of wood breaking, and suddenly a massive branch was plummeting down towards Liviah. She screamed and jumped out of the way, coming down hard on her side.

"*Leave now!*" the voice said again. "*Leave now!*"

Liviah heard another *crack* and took off sprinting downstream. It was too dark to bother trying to stay along the banks. Instead, she splashed straight through the water, soaking her clothes as she ran. Branches continued to fall behind her, each one landing in the spot where she had been just moments before. Up ahead there seemed to be light. Liviah squinted her eyes and saw that there was a break in the trees, opening the forest up into some sort of clearing. She ran as fast and as hard as she could. Suddenly, she came bursting out from trees, and there it was—the city of Maldenney.

Liviah turned back to look at the river. It was clear and peaceful, with no sign of any fallen branches or disturbances of any kind. She peered deeper into the forest, but still she saw nothing. Had she been imagining it all? She couldn't understand where the branches had all gone so quickly. Out of sheer curiosity, Liviah began back in the direction from which she came, but another bone-chilling gust of wind made her decide otherwise.

Liviah followed the river with her eyes. It ran straight towards the city wall, where an opening grated with thick iron bars allowed it to flow through. She felt strangely sad as she watched it go. The river had provided her with direction and security, and now for the first time since she left home, she and her guide would have to part ways.

There must have been at least a thousand torches lining Maldenney's borders, illuminating the city with a fiery glow. The walls towered high over the forest's trees, reaching up to the stars that glimmered in the sky. Just north of her position, Liviah could see multiple legionnaires standing guard by the city's gates. She knew they would not let her in without identification, the Legion was strict about keeping track of those entering and leaving its capital. Clinging close to the foliage for cover, Liviah traveled south along the clearing's perimeter. The farther she was from the gate, the fewer guards she saw patrolling the wall. Eventually, she reached a point where it was altogether empty, and the clearing between the city and forest narrowed so that the trees were almost touching the wall.

Liviah found a good tree to climb near the wall and began her ascent up its thick, bark-covered surface. She must have climbed dozens of different trees back home, but none of them were like this one. Its branches were thicker and harder to get ahold of, but they were stronger and sturdier too. The higher she climbed, the more her arms began to burn. Her hands became scraped and bloody from grasping at the rough bark. As she neared the top of the tree, the branches became thin and flimsy. She reached up for one, and it snapped under the force of her weight. For only a second, Liviah was falling, tumbling down towards the forest floor. Before she had gone too far, her arms found another branch and wrapped themselves around it.

She swung her legs up sideways onto it and pulled herself up, then leaned her back against the trunk to rest for just a moment. She was panting heavily, and her entire body ached. Looking down now, the ground seemed miles away.

She climbed up to the top again, this time careful to test each branch before placing her weight on it. When she had gone as high as she could, she sat down on one of the thicker branches and edged herself out onto it so that she was closer to the wall. Finally, when she could go no farther without the branch sagging, Liviah rose tentatively to stand. Even on one of the tallest trees, she was at least ten feet below the top of the wall. The only way to reach it was by magic. She had never tried to float herself before, but she expected it would work just the same as with any other object.

"No hesitation," she whispered to herself. She could feel the power that coursed through her. She closed her eyes and pushed off hard from the branch. For a brief time, Liviah became weightless. She opened her eyes to see the world shrink away beneath her. A moment later, she dropped onto the top of the wall. She doubled over and put her hands on her knees, nearly collapsing from exhaustion. Her head pounded, but she couldn't help but smile. She had never performed such a large spell before.

She wanted to lie down and fall asleep where she was, but she couldn't risk someone coming along and spotting her. Liviah stood upright and her head spun. Her vision was blurry and unfocused. She squinted down to the ground below her. It was a grimy alley full of litter and a large building that looked very abandoned. It was no wonder the legionnaires were not patrolling this part of the city. Liviah took a deep breath in and began slowly walking. She had made it into Maldenney at last. She was one step closer to finding Juliana.

She traveled east along the top of the wall, away from the gate where she had seen the guards before. As time went by, she felt her strength coming back. Soon the land inside the walls became nothing except wide-open fields where crops were being grown, with a few scattered houses and stables amongst them. Near the southeast corner was a winding staircase that Liviah took to the ground. The stairs turned back and forth so many times that she started to become dizzy. She stumbled against the railing for support, her head still hurting terribly. She was so dazed that she almost didn't notice the legionnaire sitting on the last step.

The threat of danger masked Liviah's exhausted state. Suddenly her eyes were focused, and her mind was clear of any thoughts except the man in front of her. She expected him to turn around before she had a chance to retreat back up the steps, but he did not move. He sat with his reaper in his lap, and his head leaned up against the wall. There was a soft whistling sound as air flowed between his lips, and Liviah realized that he was sleeping.

She tip-toed around him and looked him in the face. He didn't look particularly threatening; he was just an average man. Liviah pulled the pendant from her pocket. Now was her chance to get some answers. She removed a torch from the sconce by the stairs, then with a flick of her fingers sent the legionnaire's reaper flying off into the nearby field.

"Huh! What?" the man stuttered as he jumped awake. He looked up at Liviah. "Who are you?" She shoved the torch towards him, and he leaned back against the stairs to avoid the flames.

"Be quiet!" she yelled. "Now, you're going to tell me what I want to know, and then I'll let you go." He tried to reach for the torch, but his hand froze mid-reach. Liviah's eyes narrowed at him as he resisted. Her head was crying out in pain, but she did not let up. "I said, you're going to tell me what I want to know."

"What are you doing to me?"

"Who ordered the attack in Glassfall?"

"What are you?"

"WHO ORDERED THE ATTACK?" Liviah pushed the torch closer to his face.

"I don't know what you're talking about! There was no attack!"

"What do you know about a girl who was kidnapped? Where did they take her?"

"I don't know anything! If I did, I would tell you. I swear!"

Liviah held up the pendant so that he could see. The crescent moon shape shimmered in the torchlight. "Do you know who this belongs to?"

"No idea!"

"You're sure? It doesn't belong to someone specific?"

"Yes - I mean, no! Maybe! I don't know! It's just a necklace, it could be anyone's!"

"Who would know?"

"There's a jeweler in Lucila Square! Maybe she would know!"

Liviah pulled the torch back and released his hand so that it was free to move.

"Don't try to follow me," she instructed him. "If you know what's good for you, you'll forget you ever saw me here." The legionnaire nodded his understanding, and Liviah took off into the fields.

CHAPTER SEVEN
OLIVER

Oliver's eyes must have been playing tricks on him. It looked as if someone had *appeared* atop the city wall. He wanted to sink down under his blanket and hide himself from view, but he was frozen in place, flat on his back. If the person looked down, they would see straight into the shack through the hole in the roof. Oliver was only able to see a silhouette, but he could tell it was no legionnaire. It was the figure of a girl, small and slender. Her hair blew in the wind as she stood there, looking out over the alley.

For a moment, the figure disappeared from his vision, and Oliver found himself wanting her to return. He got up and strained his neck, but it was no use. Immense curiosity overcame him. Who was she, and how did she get up on the wall? A few moments later, the girl rose to her feet and Oliver could see her again. She began walking down the length of the wall, and Oliver ran to his shack door. He opened it silently, careful not to wake Nan.

When he had gotten outside, the girl on the wall had already traveled halfway down the length of the alley. Oliver ran after her from down below. The moonlight shimmered on her dark, curly hair. She was hardly the first person Oliver had seen in his life, but there was something about *this* girl that was infatuating to him.

A familiar feeling welled up inside Oliver. It was the one he had when he saw the kids playing with the dog, the one he had every time he saw someone his age. It was rare, but he knew it better than any other, and he hated it every time it happened. He wanted to never feel it again, but still it consumed his entire body. He wanted to forget caution and reason. He wanted to forget what he was. He wanted to call out to the girl, to say anything and everything he could think of to make her stay and talk with him. He wanted, more than he had ever wanted anything in his life, to make her be his friend.

He cursed himself, and anger took over as Oliver reminded himself of the truth. He was a grudder. He was born a grudder, he would live a grudder, and he would die a grudder. If he said something to the girl, she might turn him in. He wasn't ever going to have any friends, and that was something he would have to accept. He had Nan and that was it. When she was gone...he'd be alone. That's just the way it was. That's the way it had to be.

Then, just as quickly as she had arrived, the girl was gone. She had turned and continued eastward along the top of the wall. Oliver watched her as she disappeared into the night. Who was that girl, he wondered, and what was she doing there?

He wanted to follow her more than anything in the world. It was the middle of the night, and no one would be out at this time. The streets were probably empty except for a few late-night tavern goers. Surely it wouldn't be too dangerous. Oliver imagined running after her. He doubted she would turn him in. What reason would she have to do so? And besides, as far as he could tell, she had just climbed the wall and entered Maldenney illegally herself. He imagined the two of them stepping out into the city, exploring it together. His heart felt light as air, yet pounded with a level of excitement he had never experienced before.

Oliver followed her from the ground below until he had reached the end of the alley. The threshold of the Blights beckoned for him, but he was stuck. It was as if there was an invisible barrier keeping him from leaving Hawthorne Alley. A whole new rush of scenarios flooded his imagination — the girl turning him in, being spotted by a legionnaire, Nan left helpless in the shack, wondering until her last day what had happened to Oliver. He turned to look back at the shack with an all-too-familiar fear filling his chest. He couldn't go out there no matter how badly he wanted to. He just couldn't.

Oliver trudged back through the alley and returned to his shack. He did his best to close his eyes, but thoughts of the mystery girl swirled through his mind. He wondered what she was like. Was she quiet or did she like to talk? Did she enjoy reading books like he did? Where was she from? She was probably a traveler, he assumed — someone brave and adventurous who had been across all of Omnios and seen everything. He tossed and turned for the rest of the night, unable to shake the thought of her from his mind.

After several restless hours, morning had finally struck. Oliver welcomed it as an end to his temptation, for in the day Maldenney was full of people, and was no place for a grudder to go wandering.

"Ollie," Nan called to him from her cot. She tried to sit up, but a coughing fit stopped her.

"Easy, Nan," Oliver said as he jumped up from his bed and helped her back down to a reclined position. "You've got to be careful."

"Oh, I'm fine," she said stubbornly, but she did not try to sit up again.

Oliver sat back down on his cot, his eyes narrowed, staring at the door of the shack. For a while, neither he nor Nan said a word. The only sound was of her ragged breathing.

"How come you've never told me how you found me, Nan?" Oliver said finally. He continued to stare at the door, not turning to look at Nan for a reply.

"The same reason you've never asked," she said softly.

"You weren't sure if I wanted to know?"

"Do you?"

"I think so," he said resolutely.

"Well, then help me sit up. It's no good telling a story lying down."

Oliver crawled over and helped Nan raise herself into a seated position. He stuffed his blanket behind her back for cushioning, then sat against the wall next to her, fixating his gaze on the hole in the ceiling.

"I suppose the best place to start is the beginning," Nan said. "When I was a little girl, I lived in a city called Wilteport. I was *so* happy there. It was the capital of Omnios at the time, where King Talmund Lucila reigned. Talmund came from a long line of Lucila rulers, and the family had been in power for over three hundred years before him. He was adored by the common people, and Omnios was peaceful and prosperous.

"Then, when I was twelve, a plague hit a town far up north. It turned the people's skin gray, and they began to slowly crumble away as if they were made of ash. The *Withering Black*, they called it. It was a nasty, vile thing to see. It swept all over the country like a wildfire, taking town after town. The healers at the hospital here in Maldenney were working tirelessly on finding a cure. They had almost come up with one when the Withering

Black hit Wilteport. It wasn't long before Talmund and his wife caught it, and within weeks they were dead."

"The King died?" Oliver asked, astounded. It made sense, he supposed, that a king could get sick just as well as any other man, yet still, he was surprised.

"He did, and the Lucila dynasty died with him."

"Just like that? Didn't he have an heir or something?"

"He had no children or brothers, only a sister, Cicely."

"What happened to her?"

"Some speculated that she had died as well, but others thought she went into hiding. As the last Lucila who could lay claim to the crown, she would have been a great threat to anyone seeking to take power."

"Well, which was it?"

Nan laughed. "I'm afraid no one really knew, Ollie. But either way, the Lucila family was gone."

"What happened to you then? After the Withering Black hit Wilteport?"

"My mother caught it rather quickly. Within a few weeks, I was left on my own."

"What about your father?"

"He died in an accident shortly after I was born," Nan said, dismissing the topic with a wave of her hand. "I knew it was only a matter of time before I caught the black as well, so I packed up a few belongings and traveled with a group of other survivors to Maldenney, hoping that they would soon find a cure. Even before it was the capital, Maldenney was where all the great minds and scholars of Omnios did their work. We arrived at the city gates more than a week later, but they wouldn't let us in. We were all beginning to show signs of the plague, and they told us they couldn't risk any infected coming in and spreading it."

"Nan, I had no idea…"

"It wasn't all bad. It was just life back then. A man bringing barrels of grain into Maldenney agreed to smuggle me into the city. He emptied one of the barrels, and I climbed inside. When he finally let me out, I went straight to the hospital, but it was overflowing with patients. People were crowding around the front of the building. It was impossible to get inside, so I came around to the back, and that's where I found this shack. It was completely empty, like no one knew it existed. I waited back here for days, thinking maybe someone would come out the back door and I could sneak inside. The plague was getting worse by that point and I didn't have much time left. I had almost given up hope entirely when one day a healer named Lyla came out the back door and spotted me rifling through the garbage. I was so thin, and my skin was turning gray; she could tell immediately that I had the Withering Black. She told me if I stayed in the shack, she would come back the next day with a dose of the cure. I didn't know if she was telling the truth or if she was going to report me to the city guards, but I stayed. The next day, she showed up with a small vile of medicine."

"And it worked?" Oliver asked.

"I didn't know at first. The cure was five doses, each given one day apart. So, the next day Lyla came back with another dose, and the day after that and the day after that. I started feeling stronger, and my skin regained its color. The cure was really working, but when Lyla showed up on the fifth day, I could tell she had been crying. Her eyes were red and puffy, and her hands were trembling as she handed me the last vile. I asked her what was wrong, and at first, she refused to tell me. Eventually, I got it out of her that her newborn son had caught the plague. I assumed she could just give him the cure too, but she said that the vile she was giving me was the last one she had been able to get her hands on. She was going to save me instead of her own child."

"But it didn't matter anyway, did it?" Oliver asked. "Her baby would need five doses, and she only had one left."

"No, they hadn't figured out how to make the cure for infants yet. Five doses would have been too much. It would have made him sick. He only needed one, but even then, there was no guarantee that it would work. Lyla insisted that I take it, that she would feel better if I did. That way at least one of us would be sure to live."

"So, you took it?"

Nan shook her head. "I gave it back. I told her I felt like the first four doses had been enough, I didn't need the fifth. I don't know if she really believed that was true, but we both allowed her to pretend that she did. She took the cure back and gave it to her son. I can still see the look in her eyes as I handed her back the vile."

Nan's milky white eyes stared blankly at the wall ahead, as a thin smile stretched across her face. Oliver wondered what it was like to be blind. Did Nan always see old memories in her mind's eye, or did she spend her days picturing nothing at all?

"What happened to Lyla's son?" he asked.

"I don't know. Lyla never came back. I think she was afraid of what she might find."

"What she might find?"

"Imagine the guilt she would have felt, Ollie, if she returned one day to learn that I wasn't alive. Not knowing one way or the other was probably easier than finding out that she had let me die. I think that would have been too much for her to bear."

"So, what did you do then?"

"I stayed in the shack, living off scraps of food people threw away in the alley, just like you have all your life."

"You just stayed here?"

"I was a grudder Ollie, I snuck into the city illegally. There was nowhere else in Maldenney for me to go."

"But I don't understand why you didn't just go back home to Wilteport?"

"Once they got the cure working, the plague died as quickly as it had come, but by that time the world outside Maldenney was mostly controlled by criminals. The King had died, remember, and there was no one to enforce order with all that had been going on. I knew I would have been better off living in here than going out into the world alone as a young girl. So, I stayed in this shack, accepting that I would live out the rest of my days as a grudder. Many decades later, the Legion formed and took control of Omnios. They toppled the warlords and outlaws, and they gave protection to the innocent. I know you may have strong opinions about the Legion, Ollie—and you have a right to feel that way, growing up as you have—but the Legion isn't all bad. The world was in far worse shape before it came along. It saved a great many people."

Oliver could feel the blood rushing to his cheeks and his ears getting hot. He had always hated the Legion. How could he not? He had been forced to live like an animal, alone in a shack at the end of a dirty alley, all because of the Legion's laws.

"If the Legion was so great and fixed everything, then why didn't you go home once they started to take control?" Oliver said. He was unable to hide the tone of anger in his voice.

"Old habits," Nan chuckled, which turned into a cough. "I had lived my whole life here in this shack, and nothing was waiting for me on the outside...But I suppose I was mostly just afraid."

"Afraid of what? Having a life?"

- 72 -

"I had been living in this shack for forty-five years, Ollie. The world changes a lot in that amount of time. The life I had wasn't one anyone would choose, but I kept it because it was familiar."

Oliver turned away from Nan. How could she possibly choose to continue living like this when she had any other option? He would give anything to not be a grudder.

"What does all of this even have to do with me?" he asked angrily.

"Well, after the Legion took power the Lord Commander established Maldenney as the new capital of Omnios, and several new families with ties to the Legion moved here. That was when I started hearing the haunting noises from inside the hospital. It wasn't long before it shut down. Almost a year later, it reached its worst. On top of the usual sounds, I heard people screaming. The next morning, I was walking down the alley and I heard a baby crying. I followed the sound as it grew louder, until eventually, at the mouth of the alley, I found a beautiful newborn baby boy. You had the brightest blue eyes, with a gold ring around your pupils. That was the very first thing I noticed about you." Nan paused to smile, and even though she couldn't see them, Oliver felt a little embarrassed at the tears welling up in his eyes. "It was so cold out and no one was around. Your skin was blue like you had been out there all night, so I picked you up and carried you back to my shack. I thought you must have been my good luck charm because I never heard another noise from the hospital after I found you. Each day for a week, I sat with you near the mouth of the alley to see if anyone would come back for you, but no one ever did. After that, I decided I would raise you. I named you Oliver, after Lyla's son, and Hawthorne, after the alley that I found you in."

Part of Oliver wanted to cry, and another part of him wanted to scream. He had always imagined that his parents were grudders like him, and that they had died and given him to Nan to take care of. Now he knew the truth, though. His parents weren't grudders. They just didn't want him. They dropped him off in some alley so that he would freeze or starve. They never cared about him at all. He sniffed loudly and wiped his nose.

"Are you alright, Ollie?" Nan said.

"I just really thought they would have wanted me…"

"Oh, Ollie…I'm sure they did. There could be so many reasons why they had to leave you there."

"It doesn't matter what their reason was! They had to have realized I was going to die there, and they left me anyway!"

"You don't know that, Oliver."

"Yes, I do," he said evenly. He got up before Nan had a chance to get another word in. Walking out of the shack, he slammed the door behind him.

CHAPTER EIGHT
RIDLEY

"What do you think Cormack's got planned for us today?" Fletcher asked Ridley over a bowl of oatmeal and some boiled eggs. They sat across from each other at the end of a long wooden table. The mess hall was a poorly lit building with rows and rows of tables, which were just beginning to fill as the recruits made their way from the barracks. They came in groggily and slowly, each of them worn down from the rigorous day to day training. Only Ridley and, much to his disdain, Sayben, seemed cut out for this lifestyle. They did not tire nearly as easily as the other boys and welcomed each new day's task as an opportunity to beat the other.

"I don't know," Ridley said. "I don't care." He stared down at his oatmeal, poking at it with his spoon.

"What's the matter with you?" Fletcher asked.

"Nothing's the matter."

"Yes, there is. Did something happen when you went home last night?"

"What's that got to do with anything?" Ridley said, dropping his spoon.

"You've been acting weird ever since you got back."

"No, I haven't," Ridley snapped. "You don't know what you're talking about, Fletcher. You met me a week ago. You hardly even know me."

"Take it easy, mate. I was just trying to make sure you were alright."

"Well, don't next time! I can take care of myself."

"Alright, alright, I'll drop it."

Ridley looked back down at his bowl, fuming with anger. Who did Fletcher think he was?

"Trouble in paradise?" Sayben said as he sat down next to Fletcher.

"Not now," Ridley groaned at him. "Don't you have someone else you can bother?"

"Yes, I do, but my favorite person to bother is you," Sayben replied. "Which reminds me, did you know that I'm winning?"

Ridley raised his eyebrows. "What are you talking about?" he asked.

"You know, our little competition we have going on where I end your future as a legionnaire? Yeah, I'm winning."

"But that's impossible, I was beating you eighty points to seventy at the end of yesterday."

"You were...until I did Cormack a favor in exchange for twenty points."

"You did what?" Ridley nearly choked on his oatmeal.

"I happened to overhear him talking about how he needed to get out of guard duty on the gate last night, so I volunteered to take it for him."

"He can't just give you points for that!"

"Oh, but he did, little Prodigy, and now I am beating you by ten. Better be careful."

"I wouldn't get your hopes up, Sayben," Fletcher said. "Ridley has beaten you in everything so far. He's not going to stop now. If anything, you've just given him more motivation to stomp you into the ground."

"Impressive," Sayben said. He looked from Fletcher to Ridley, "You have him trained so well." Fletcher's cheeks flushed red.

"Shut up," Ridley said. "And go sit somewhere else! It's bad enough I have to live with you, I don't want to see you while I eat."

"Alright I'm going," Sayben said defensively. He stood up and pointed at Ridley. "But I'm coming for you, Prodigy."

"Don't mind him," Fletcher said. "He's not worth the trouble."

"Yeah...uh, thanks," Ridley said awkwardly.

"Don't mention it," Fletcher said with a smile.

Finished with their breakfast, Ridley and Fletcher were just preparing to leave the mess hall when Cormack walked in.

"Recruits! Listen up!" he yelled. An instant hush fell over the room as twenty-four pairs of eyes looked up at him. "A legionnaire was attacked last night while patrolling the wall. The assailant was a girl, young, from what our man reported, and we have reason to believe she entered the city illegally."

"Oh no...a little girl has invaded Maldenney!" Dax called sarcastically. The recruits joined together in laughter.

"This is not a joke!" Cormack bellowed. The noise ceased without a moment of hesitation, and Dax looked down solemnly at his feet. "Young girl or not, this grudder is considered very dangerous and will be regarded as a serious threat to the safety of our city. I have spoken with the Lord Commander, and he and I have decided that it is in the best interest of Maldenney that we initiate a city-wide curfew until the grudder is caught.

"This means that starting tonight, a few of you will be placed on patrol duty each night to help our legionnaires search the city for the grudder. If you find her, you bring her directly to me! No one else! Understood? Good...Drill yard in fifteen." There was a murmur of voices as the recruits contemplated Cormack's words.

"Something was off about that," Fletcher said.

"A little girl attack shuts down the city? Yeah, that one's new," Ridley agreed.

"This isn't the first grudder the Legion has known about in Maldenney. Since when do we go out of our way to find them?"

"I guess since they started attacking us on patrol and getting away with it."

"Maybe...but still, it seems weird. Why wouldn't we bring her to Captain Landal if we find her? He is in charge of the City Watch. Grudder catching seems like his area of authority."

Ridley shook his head. "Cormack just wants all the glory."

"I don't know, it could be something else."

"Like what?"

"You heard the way he was talking about it. It's obviously really important to him that no one else gets their hands on her before he does. Seems like he's after something more than just recognition."

"Either way, I'm betting that catching her would be worth a lot of points. Which I could use right about now."

Cormack was waiting for them when they arrived at the drill yard. He was not dressed for sparring with long-staffs like the recruits were, however. He was wearing only woven pants and a white, waist-length tunic.

"We'll be practicing hand to hand combat today boys. Go on, get out of that armor."

"Oh great," Fletcher groaned.

"What?" Ridley asked.

"My uncle used to practice his hand to hand combat on me. He'd pummel me to the ground every time."

"Don't worry, I'm sure you'll do fine."

"No, really. I'm awful at it."

Ridley said nothing, but he didn't doubt what Fletcher said was true. Fletcher's strong suits were less physical. He had a mind for tactics and strategy. He was good at thinking things through and problem-solving. Ridley had no doubt that Fletcher would be one of the best minds in the Legion one day, but combat was far from his area of expertise.

The recruits removed their armor and dropped their long-staffs to the ground. It was beginning to get colder with each passing day, and chilling winds bit at their skin without the extra layer to protect them. Ridley didn't let it bother him, however. The other recruits may have suffered in the cold, but he was far more resilient than they were.

"Who's up first?" Cormack asked.

"Me," Sayben said immediately. He turned and smiled at Ridley as he stepped out of the crowd, challenging him to a rematch. Sayben's eyes seemed to taunt Ridley, but it was not enough to make him speak up. He wouldn't give Sayben the satisfaction of controlling him.

"Do we have any other takers?" Cormack asked. Every recruit shied away from his gaze as he scanned the group. "No one is brave enough?" he said, astounded. His eyes fell on Ridley last. "How about...Oswood?" Ridley looked to Fletcher, whose eyes were wide with fear at hearing his name. "Come on, Oswood," Cormack said. "Get out here." Fletcher had hardly taken half of a step before Ridley spoke up.

"I want to fight Sayben," he said.

"It's too late for that, Ambersen. Fletcher has already been picked."

"But I want to challenge him."

"I *said* Oswood is fighting him."

Ridley huffed loudly out his nose, but there was no changing Cormack's mind. Fletcher stepped out into the dirt ring with all the tenacity of a field mouse, meanwhile Sayben smiled malevolently. They each assumed fighting stances, neither of which looked very correct to Ridley, and Sayben cracked his knuckles into his palms.

"Oh, this'll be fun," he said.

"Ready!" Cormack said with a hand in the air. He dropped his arm. "Fight!"

Immediately, Sayben lunged at Fletcher with a punch, which Fletcher caught perfectly in the nose. The recruits laughed as he wiped the blood away with the back of his finger. Sayben swung again, and this time Fletcher had the foresight to at least duck. The boys looking on cheered sarcastically at the move, making Ridley even angrier than he was before. Sayben swung low with his left hand, and then hit Fletcher in the face with his right hand when he tried to block. He was toying with him, Ridley realized. To Sayben, this wasn't a fight at all.

"Keep your hands up, Fletcher!" Ridley yelled. Fletcher met Ridley's eyes and did just that. Sayben swung again, but Fletcher's hand blocked the blow. He swung his leg around and kicked Sayben in the side of the ribs, and the boys went wild. They cheered and hollered for Fletcher the underdog, and the scrawny recruit allowed a smile to spread across his face. Sayben looked at the other recruits and back to Fletcher. The look in his eyes was one of pure enjoyment.

He leapt at Fletcher with his shoulder down. Fletcher's back collided with the ground and suddenly it was Sayben's fight again. Punch after punch landed on Fletcher's face, quickly rendering him bruised and bloody.

"Stop it!" Ridley yelled as Sayben drew back his arm for another blow. Ridley looked at Cormack, who was stoic and uncaring as ever. "Cormack, call him off!"

Ridley ran out into the ring and tackled Sayben. The pair rolled in the dirt, falling onto their backs beside one another, both coughing from dust in their lungs.

"Ambersen!" Cormack bellowed. "Stand! Now!" Ridley rose to his feet and turned to look his instructor in the eye. "Who told you to interfere with the fight?"

"Look at Fletcher!" Ridley said.

"He looks a lot better than I've seen others after combat. A legionnaire needs to be able to hold his own. Are you going to be standing beside him to protect him every time you face an enemy?"

"No."

"No what?"

"No, sir."

"Good. Now, because you've insisted on becoming involved in the training exercise, I want you to fight Fletcher." Ridley looked at his friend who had now risen and was holding a hand over half of his battered face.

"Look at him, Cormack. He's done."

"He's done when I say he's done!"

"I'm not going to fight him."

"You will fight! Unless you want me to set you back to zero points."

Ridley heard a laugh from Sayben. Between his roommate and his instructor, they seemed determined to get Ridley kicked out of the Academy.

"It's okay, Rid," Fletcher sputtered through his own blood. He struggled to his feet. "Fight me Rid."

"You want me to fight so bad, let me fight you," Ridley said to Cormack.

"No. I said Fletcher," Cormack answered.

"Are you scared or something?"

There was a collective *oooh* from the other boys.

"Scared?" Cormack huffed. "I'll fight both of you." Ridley and Fletcher looked at each other in surprise. "Well, let's go, Ambersen! Let me show you how real men fight!" Cormack took off his shirt revealing his muscular arms and torso. None of the recruits realized just how well built he was under all the armor they normally saw him in. Ridley glanced over at Fletcher, who looked even more frightened than before.

"Just try to distract him," Ridley whispered. "Leave the rest to me."

The pair squared off against their instructor. Before either of them even realized the fight had begun, Cormack had run at Fletcher and grabbed him around his waist. He picked the recruit up and slammed him onto his back. Ridley reacted as fast as he could, grabbing Cormack's wrist just as it was drawing back to punch. Cormack turned his attention away from Fletcher and began swinging at Ridley.

This was nothing like Ridley's fight with Sayben. Cormack's attacks were swift, precise, and calculated. Each one targeted Ridley's weakest point of defense. He blocked high right; Cormack struck low left.

Cormack jabbed straight forward, and Ridley was just fast enough to step sideways and grab the senior legionnaire's arm. Cormack dropped to his knees and spun to face Ridley, turning his elbow over his head as he did. With his free hand, Cormack jabbed at Ridley's legs, causing him to stumble back. Cormack jumped to his feet, but Fletcher was back up. He jumped onto Cormack's back and wrapped his arms around his neck. Cormack elbowed him in the gut, but Fletcher didn't release his grip. Cormack let out a monstrous scream, then flipped Fletcher over his shoulder onto the ground again. Fletcher landed on his back, the impact knocking him out. Cormack grabbed the recruit by the collar and punched him hard in the face

"Cormack, he's unconscious!" Ridley yelled. Cormack punched Fletcher again. "Cormack!"

Their instructor wasn't letting up. He pounded on Fletcher's bloody face over and over again. Ridley grabbed Cormack and pulled him off Fletcher's limp body. The pair stumbled over each other and went rolling onto the ground in a cloud of dust. Ridley rolled on top, and he landed his fist solidly on Cormack's nose. There was a loud *crack* as the bone broke, and blood began to pour from it. Ridley drew back and felt blood on his hand as it contacted Cormack's face again. He wasn't sure who's blood it was, but he didn't care.

"That's enough," a commanding voice roared. Ridley looked over his shoulder. Lord Commander Kaeno stood behind the recruits, watching. None of them knew how long he had been there. Ridley released his grip and stepped away from Cormack. "Pick that one up and take him inside," Kaeno commanded. Dax and another boy hurried out to grab Fletcher's hands and feet, then swiftly carried him off towards the infirmary. Cormack and Ridley stood and faced the Lord Commander with full attention.

"You'll have the rest of the day off," Kaeno said to the recruits' great satisfaction. He turned and glared at Cormack. "Your instructor and I have things to discuss." He left the drill yard with Cormack following behind him.

"You just cost yourself fifty points, Ambersen," Cormack said quietly as he passed Ridley. He wiped the blood from his nose. "Hope it was worth it."

Ridley returned to the barracks feeling very defeated. He sat on his cot and stared at the ceiling for nearly an hour, poking lightly at the bruises that Cormack had left him and thinking about how he was possibly going to win his competition against Sayben if their instructor was working against him. A short time later the door opened. Ridley didn't so much as turn his head.

"You know, you've done some pretty stupid things, but breaking Cormack's face in front of the Lord Commander like that...Not your best move," Sayben laughed.

"Shut up, alright? Things are bad enough as it is. I don't need you gloating and making it worse."

"How's Fletcher?" Sayben asked rather seriously. Ridley sat up in his bed and looked curiously at his bunkmate. "What?" Sayben said. "You think just because I hate you that means I have to hate him too?"

"I don't know how he is. I haven't gone to see him," Ridley answered.

"You haven't?" Sayben said with surprise.

"My being there doesn't help him get better."

"Well, well...I may have underestimated you, Prodigy. You can be heartless after all."

The truth was Ridley did care, but how could he go and look Fletcher in the eye when he had failed to protect him? What was the proper thing to say to a mate when you had let them down?

"Since when do you care about Fletcher anyway?" he asked.

"Oh, I don't. In fact, Cormack beating him to a pulp and making you lose it is the best thing that's happened to me since I got here. Not much of a chance for you to catch up to me now, is there?"

"Cormack has it out for me."

"Probably shouldn't have made him mad then."

"You know the reason he hates me is that I'm a threat to him, right? Why doesn't he hate you?"

"Watch it there, Prodigy."

"Maybe it's because he knows you'll only win if he cheats for you."

Sayben's smug grin faded from his face, and a fierce scowl replaced it. "Don't make the mistake of thinking I need Cormack's help to win this little bet, Ambersen. I *always* win. Now come on, get up."

"What?"

"We're going to see your friend."

"Why?"

"Because I heard you two talking earlier. Fletcher think's Cormack is up to something, and I want to know what it is."

"Why would you bring me with you?"

"Because Fletcher is *annoyingly* loyal to you and he won't tell me anything if you're not there."

"Forget it, I'm not helping you beat me."

"Come on, Ambersen. I have other ways of figuring this out. Either we can both go to Fletcher and see what he thinks right now, or I can go by myself and get it out of him the hard way. Between you and me, I don't have a problem with Fletcher. I think he's been through enough today, don't you?"

"Fine," Ridley said.

When they reached the infirmary, Fletcher was asleep under layers of heavy blankets. He had a blackened eye, busted lower lip, and broken nose, as well as purple bruising on his cheeks. On the table next to him was a bottle labeled *Bruiser Remover.*

"Look," said Ridley, "he's asleep."

"Do you see the healer anywhere?" Sayben asked, looking around the room and through the connecting doorways.

"No."

"Good." He uncorked the bottle of Bruiser Remover and splashed Fletcher in the face with the clear purple liquid. Fletcher sputtered awake, spitting medicine.

"What?" he called as he sat up and wiped his face.

"You didn't have to do that!" Ridley said.

"Oh good, you're awake," Sayben exclaimed. Fletcher looked from Sayben to Ridley, and then back to Sayben.

"What are you doing here?" he asked. His words were somewhat slurred with his swollen lip, and his left eye seemed unable to open all the way.

"Oh, the roommate and I just wanted to come check in and see how you were doing." Sayben sat on the edge of the bed and patted Fletcher's leg as he spoke. Fletcher looked at him, unconvinced.

"Uh, how are you doing?" Ridley asked.

"Been better," Fletcher said, but a smile came through as he said it. Sayben narrowed his eyes.

"The reason we're really here," he said, "is we want to know what you think Cormack wants with the grudder girl."

"Both of you were wondering that? Together?"

Sayben looked at Ridley expectantly. "Um…yeah," Ridley said. "Sayben wanted to know, and I guess I did too."

"Alright," Fletcher said puzzledly. "Well, I'm guessing he's got a reason that he wants to be the first one to get to her. It wasn't just about getting the credit. If it was, he wouldn't have told all of us to be on the lookout for her. He wants her found, just as long as she's brought straight to him. That makes me think he wants something from her. I'll bet he knows something he's not telling us."

"Hold on, what do you mean by 'he wants something from her'?" Sayben asked.

"I don't know, it could be anything. Think about it. He's the one who talked to the Lord Commander about starting the curfew, right? The Legion doesn't usually go on high alert for one random grudder break in, so what if it's not a random grudder? What if she's got a reason for attacking, and Cormack doesn't want anyone to find out what it is?"

"So, you think he's hiding something?" Ridley asked.

"Look who's suddenly all interested," Sayben said.

"He could be hiding something," Fletcher confirmed. "The question is, does the Lord Commander know about it?"

"Fletcher, you've been a gem," Sayben said patronizingly as he hopped off the bed and walked out of the room.

"Where are you going?" Ridley asked.

"I'm going to find out where the grudder is," Sayben said in a tone that made it sound as though the answer was obvious.

"So, you two are mates now?" Fletcher asked once Sayben was gone.

"No," Ridley said. "But he had a point. If Cormack is up to something, I want to find out what it is."

"Be careful, Ridley. I know why you want to find out what Cormack is up to, but why does Sayben? Make sure he's not playing you."

"I will." Ridley paused. "Did the, uh, healer say how long you would be in here?"

"Just overnight, hopefully. This Bruiser Remover stuff works really fast."

"Oh good, happy to hear it."

They sat quietly for a moment, with all of the things Ridley wanted to say waiting on the tip of his tongue. Finally, Fletcher opened his mouth to talk. "Ridley, I—"

"You should probably get some sleep," Ridley cut in. He went for the door but stopped and turned around just before walking out. "You'll be alright here?"

"Yeah, sure," Fletcher nodded. "See you later, then."

The next day Cormack had returned to his position as stone cold and emotionless as ever. He took no questions and offered little guidance during activity. Ridley was doing his best to avoid him, which was turning out to be rather simple. They had gone out the east city gate that was near the Legionnaire Academy and were attempting to make bows and arrows from materials they found in the forest. Ridley was carving sticks into arrow shafts far away from everyone else when Dax came up behind him.

"Ridley," Dax said as he came stomping through the foliage. He was holding a misshapen bow that Ridley had to stop himself from commenting on. "Cormack wants to see you."

"That can't be good," Ridley replied. "Did he say what it was about?"

"No. But he looked awfully smug, so it's probably not good news for you."

"Great."

Ridley trudged back towards the gate, where Cormack was watching Sayben demonstrate his bow. Ridley watched as an arrow whizzed through the air and sank itself into a tree. Two others were lodged next to it.

"Excellent precision," Cormack said. "Good work."

"You wanted to see me?" Ridley said.

"Ah, Ridley!" Cormack said, smiling. "The Lord Commander would like to speak with you in his quarters. Now."

"Uh oh," Sayben chimed in. "Sounds like Prodigy got himself in trouble."

Ridley sighed. "Alright," he said.

"Oh, and since you aren't finishing the activity, you won't be receiving any points for it," Cormack added. Ridley shook his head and kept on walking. If the Lord Commander was asking to see him after he'd hit his superior officer, points were the least of Ridley's concerns.

* * *

"She attacked two legionnaires in one night? Do you mean to tell me that *neither* of these men who—need I remind you, were hand selected by *you* for the City Watch—were competent enough to catch her?"

The doors of Lord Commander Kaeno's quarters in the Blackfort were shut, but Ridley could still hear him yelling at someone inside. Ridley hoped he was not going to receive the same treatment, but he didn't feel particularly sure about that.

"Th-that is correct, my Lord," the other voice stammered. Ridley recognized the voice at once, it was Bjorn Landal, Captain of the City Watch—the man whose responsibility it was to control crime in Maldenney.

"And who was the other *pathetic* soul?"

"Embry Jarl, my Lord, one of the legionnaires on patrol duty last night in the Farmlands. She targeted him while he was…"

"Spit it out!"

"While he was fertilizing the crops, my Lord…In any case, Jarl reported that she asked questions about the recent attack in the west."

"There has not been an attack in the west!"

"Yes, of course, my Lord, but according to Jarl the girl seemed quite convinced that there was."

"Well, the girl is mistaken! Captain, do you think I called you here because I cared to know what the girl wants?"

"Typically, when there's a…a criminal in the city we try to find the motive in order to—"

"A CRIMINAL, YES! NOT A LITTLE GIRL! I will not give her the satisfaction of elevating her to the status of criminal!"

"Deepest apologies, my Lord!"

"My patience is running thin, Captain. Find the girl, or I'll appoint a Captain of the City Watch who can. Do we understand each other?"

"Yes, of course, my Lord."

"Good. You're dismissed. Send the boy in."

Captain Landal emerged from the room and left without so much as a glance in Ridley's direction. Ridley pushed the door open slightly and walked inside. The Lord Commander sat at his desk and took several large gulps from his cup before addressing Ridley.

"Come, sit down boy," Kaeno said. Ridley sat obligingly, holding his helmet in his lap. "Did you hear that?"

"Yes, my Lord," Ridley said with a nod.

"Good. How is your training going?"

"It's been excellent, my Lord. I've…learned so much already."

"You have, have you? That's rather interesting, because Cormack tells me that the two of you do not see eye to eye."

Ridley gulped. He opened his mouth to speak, but the words were like cotton in his throat. Kaeno picked up a piece of parchment from his desk and began to read it. "'Ridley often strikes his opponents using moves that have not yet been covered when sparring, despite being previously corrected on this matter several times. Ridley is boastful and arrogant because of his advanced knowledge of many of the skills covered, and enjoys making his fellow recruits look bad, despite their continued progress. He has no idea how to be part of a team and cannot comprehend anything beyond himself.' I could go on. Cormack has plenty to say on the topic, but I believe you understand the point."

"Forgive me, my Lord."

"Why is it that you don't listen to Cormack?" Kaeno asked. Ridley looked the Lord Commander in the eyes, unsure if this was a test or not. "Speak freely, Ridley," Kaeno prompted, though his glare sent a completely different message.

"As a boy my father always said to me, 'The world will never understand greatness until you make them see it.' He said that was the whole idea the early Legion was built on. Why should I play by their rules if I'm better than they are? None of the other recruits have had the training I have. I know more than all of them combined, even Cormack. If I know a better way to do something, why shouldn't I do it?"

Ridley looked at the Lord Commander, waiting for any sign of change in the glare. Then, for just a moment, Kaeno smiled.

"Lord Ambersen is a smart man."

Ridley smiled back half-heartedly. "Yes, my father is…quite brilliant, my Lord."

"I have an important job for you to do Ridley, and I'm entrusting that you'll get it done no matter the cost. Can I count on you for that?"

"Of course, my Lord."

"Good. I want you to find the grudder girl."

"What about Captain Landal, my Lord? Isn't he in charge of the City Watch?"

"Yes, he is. But as you no doubt heard, Landal is an incompetent fool. He'll never be able to find her, and if he does, he won't capture her. Besides, Landal will still be publicly in charge. You will be working behind the scenes to find her on your own."

Ridley furrowed his brow. "I'm afraid I don't understand."

"I'm going to tell you something Ridley, something I believe I can trust you to keep to yourself."

"You can, my Lord."

"I mean it when I say this. You must not tell this to a single soul. Not your friends, not even your father."

"Absolutely, Lord Commander."

"According to the report we received of her attack two nights ago, the girl is a magic user."

"Magic user?"

"Aye, you heard me right, son. There's another word for it, but I won't bother you with all that. The point is, she's more dangerous than you think. That's why I have every legionnaire in the city looking for her."

"Why are you telling me all this?"

"You're the best solider we've brought in in a very long time, Ridley. This is your chance to prove yourself."

"I don't know what to say, my Lord."

"Say you'll find her. If anyone can do it, it's Ramsey Ambersen's son."

"Of course, Lord Commander."

Kaeno slid Ridley a piece of parchment. It was the decree for the curfew, warning people about the grudder. "We've embellished some of the details to make sure people take the threat seriously," he said. "If she attacks at night again, she'll be the only person not wearing legionnaire armor. Shouldn't make it too difficult for you to find her."

"I won't let you down, my Lord," Ridley said. This was exactly the type of opportunity he had been waiting for, a chance to show what he was made of, to show his worth to the Lord Commander.

"No, I don't think you will."

Ridley looked down at the parchment in his hand. He had everything he needed to begin forging his legacy, to make a name for himself as a legionnaire. For once in his life, Ridley was finally going to make his father proud. He slid the parchment back to Kaeno and stood. "What shall I do with her when I find her?"

Kaeno suddenly looked very grave, and his dark green eyes seemed to sink even deeper into his head. "That's the most important part," the Lord Commander said. "When you find her, you have to kill her."

"Kill her?" Ridley said, doing his best to keep his composure. "Are—my Lord, are you sure?"

"Aye, I'm sure. She cannot be brought into custody, Ridley. Do you understand me?"

"But I don't know if—"

"You *can* do it, Ambersen. I've chosen you because you can."

"But why not have someone else do it? Cormack—or anyone could."

"No, not Cormack. This has to be you, Ridley. This is what your father has trained you all your life for. He would want you to do it."

Ridley struggled to catch his breath. Kaeno was right. His father would want him to take the opportunity to prove his worth, and Ridley wanted to as well. "Yes, my Lord," he said at last. "Consider it done."

CHAPTER NINE
OLIVER

Things between Oliver and Nan had been uncomfortable in the last few days, to say the least. Of course, she had no idea why he had suddenly become so interested in his history as a grudder, because he hadn't told her about seeing the girl on the wall. Nan didn't know that it was because of her that he decided not to call out to the girl, and she didn't know that Oliver was furious with her for not taking that last vile of the Withering Black cure all those years ago.

Oliver moped up and down the alley, kicking around a small rock and thinking about what kind of lives his parents had before him. Were they too poor to feed him, and that's why they cast him aside? Did he have a single mother who wasn't ready to take care of a baby? Or could they simply not be bothered with a newborn interrupting their young and exciting lives? The rock skidded across the uneven cobblestone as Oliver kicked it and slid under a loose piece of parchment. Out of curiosity, Oliver picked up the paper and read it.

Attention

An unidentified grudder, who has entered Maldenney by unknown means, is wanted on the charges of illegal entry, assault, torture, and murder. For your safety, your Legion will be implementing a mandatory, city-wide curfew from dusk to dawn. If you have any information about the whereabouts of this fugitive, please report to a legionnaire. The curfew will be effective immediately.

Signed,

Kaliculous Kaeno ☾

Lord Commander of the Legion

When he had finished reading, Oliver wasn't sure what to think. Though his heart had skipped a beat reading the word "grudder," he knew exactly who the Legion was looking for, and it wasn't him. It was naïve of him to think he could care about someone he didn't know, yet reading that the girl he had seen on top of the wall was a dangerous criminal broke Oliver's heart. On top of that, the thought of the Legion searching every corner of the city made him worry terribly. Even if he wasn't who they were looking for, he and Nan would still be in trouble if they were found by accident.

Oliver folded the flyer twice and stuffed it in his pocket. He decided it was best not to tell Nan everything that was going on. There was nothing she could do about it, and it was no use making her worry. She had protected Oliver all his life; now it was his turn to protect her.

He headed back to the shack and opened the door softly to not startle her. She was asleep on her cot, and the all-too-familiar sound of her rattled breathing filled the air. Oliver looked down regretfully at his caretaker. He owed her an apology for his horrible behavior. It wasn't her fault that he was a grudder. She wasn't the one who left him in the alley. That fault belonged to his parents.

"Nan," Oliver whispered, gently touching her on the shoulder. She did not stir, so he tried again. "Nan," he said a little louder. Still, nothing.

Oliver began shaking her shoulder, and he said her name time and time again. "Nan, wake up!" he called to her, but she did not respond.

Anxiety seized Oliver. He felt her forehead and knew immediately that her fever had worsened. She looked even thinner than she had a week ago, and her skin was turning a pale gray. He knew what was wrong of course. Nan still had some weak traces of the Withering Black. It had been inside of her all her life, waiting dormant until her body was no longer strong enough to withhold it. She would be its final victim, all because she hadn't taken the last dose of the cure so many years ago.

Oliver grabbed an old cloth and dipped it in the bucket of water that he had placed under the hole in the ceiling to catch the falling rain. He placed the cloth on her head to cool her skin and sat down on his cot, unsure of what else to do. He dropped his head into his hands, feeling completely helpless. The Withering Black had wiped out entire towns of people once. What could Oliver possibly do to stop it from taking Nan?

Suddenly, he remembered the piece of parchment he had stuffed in his pocket. He pulled it out and looked at it again. "Citywide curfew from dawn to dusk..." he read aloud. A glimmer of hope found its way into Oliver's mind. Perhaps this was it. Perhaps this was the way he would be able to save Nan. A curfew meant the city would be empty, *completely* empty. He could go out and find Nan medicine somewhere, without the risk of so many eyes seeing him.

Every fiber of Oliver's being told him not to do it. There were a million reasons to stay put—something would go wrong, he would get caught, Nan wouldn't want him to go, it wasn't worth the risk—but then he looked at Nan, the only person who had ever loved him, and he knew he had to go. She wouldn't last much longer at this rate, and Oliver couldn't live without her.

That night, as darkness settled around Maldenney, Oliver gathered a few belongings into his bag and stepped outside. The air made him shiver. In the distance, he heard bells begin to ring. Oliver was certain of what they meant. The curfew had officially begun. He stood still and counted each chime. One. Two. Three...There were eight in total, and then...silence. He listened closely. There was no rustling in the leaves, no birds chirping, no howling of the wind. It seemed as if the whole world was holding its breath for him, silently encouraging him to continue on. He reached the end of the alley and peeked around the corner. To his right he saw an empty street, dimly lit by a few torch sconces. To his left he saw the boarded-up entrance of the old hospital and an equally vacant street.

He took a deep breath, and Oliver Hawthorne stepped over the threshold of the alley—the line that separated his small part of the world from the rest of it—for the first time in his life.

Across the street was a mob of small dingy houses that were clumped and clustered together in a seemingly random arrangement. Some of them were hardly larger than his shack. He set off north at a jog, winding through the narrow streets and passageways of the Blights. The wind hit his face and blew through his hair. He allowed his legs to pick up speed until he was sprinting, expertly weaving between the unorganized buildings. He felt alive, more alive than he had in his entire life. He didn't stop running until he was panting for air.

Oliver doubled over from exhaustion and put his hands on his knees, while a wide, uneven grin spread across his face. He was finally living. When he stood upright, he realized he had absolutely no idea where he was. All that he knew about the layout of Maldenney was from the few things that Nan had told him. The shack was at the far south end, just below the edge of the Blights. To the east were the Farmlands, and just north of the Blights he would find the Market District.

As he continued north, the buildings grew slightly larger and farther apart. The streets were eerie without anyone on them, but Oliver doubted he would feel any better if they were full of people. The houses in the Blights were rickety old things, but Oliver still thought they were magnificent. Some were made of stone and mortar, others lumber. Lines stretched from roof to roof where clothing hung to dry overnight. Candlelight could be seen through windows—the ones that weren't broken and boarded up with wooden panels, at least. Some of the stones appeared to be crumbling away, and some of the wood seemed slanted unevenly, but despite all that was wrong with them, the homes still seemed quaint and welcoming. Oliver could imagine sitting down at a table and eating supper with his family night after night.

Eventually the houses stopped, and he reached a large stone archway with the words *LUCILA SQUARE* carved into it. On the other side, a ring of shops and vendor stands surrounded a large fountain, decorated with statues of men and women. The buildings were pressed together with four arch-covered walkways between them, leading to the north, south, east, and west. Oliver looked around in amazement at all of the different stores and shops. There was a newsstand, a bakery, a kennel, a hardware shop, a tailor, a jewelry stand, a blacksmith, a butcher, a tavern, and whatever else Oliver could have imagined. One particular building caught his eye on the northeast part of the circle. It was a rectangular, two-story shop with large stained-glass windows comprising of mismatched colorful shapes. A sign above the door with curly letters read:

Elenore's Emporium of Everyday Essentials

Oliver walked to the window and pressed his face up to it. Perhaps medicine would be included in everyday essentials? He reached into his bag and retrieved a small black pick and steel file. On more than a few occasions, Oliver and Nan had found a locked box or chest in the alley, and Oliver had deemed it necessary to teach himself how to pick them open. Kneeling down by the front door, he slid the tools into the lock and fiddled with them. It was not long before a reassuring *click* invited him in.

Tiptoeing into the building, Oliver could see that Elenore really did possess an emporium of goods. The floors themselves were littered with items, which appeared to be thrown randomly about the store. Directly ahead of him was a staircase to the second floor. Left of the staircase, rows of shelves reached to the back of the shop. Oliver walked down the aisles, brushing his hand along the shelves as he perused them. Their contents were miscellaneous, ranging from books such as *Talloway's Advanced Guide to Archery* to silver goblets and eating utensils; from hunting supplies to cheap linens and fancy robes.

Oliver strolled down the aisles admiring the contents of each shelf, until he came to a small section where a wooden sign labeled *Apothecary* was sitting haphazardly on the floor. Quickly he began to rummage through the contents. There was *Miracle Mucus Remedy*; *Burn, Bite, and Boil Oil*; *Nausea-No-More*; *Quick Cough Cure*; and in a small red beaker with slanted writing, *Fiery Fever Fix*. Oliver grabbed the Fever Fix and dropped it in his bag. He scoured the area for more, but he could only find the one.

Just as Oliver was about to leave, he came to the realization that he hadn't seen a single legionnaire. Looking now through the front window of Elenore's Emporium, he was able to make out a body wearing golden armor. Instinctively, he dropped to the floor. His heart raced as he glanced to the door. He had left it ajar when he entered the shop. If the legionnaire noticed, Oliver would be discovered for sure. How could he have been so foolish to make that mistake? He crawled on his hands and knees to the stained-glass window and peered out. The lone solider had his back turned to Oliver and was making his way to the bakery across the street.

A dim light could barely be seen inside when the legionnaire opened the door. Oliver heard some muffled commotion, and moments later, the soldier reemerged from the building. He was dragging a young girl by her tangled, red hair. For a split-second, Oliver pictured the girl on the wall, but he knew immediately that this was not her. He watched as the legionnaire brought her out into the street and threw her to her knees. She began to sob, pleading with him to let her go.

"How did you get into the city?" the legionnaire screamed violently. The girl muttered a reply, but Oliver couldn't make out the words. The legionnaire tore off his helmet and threw it on the ground in a fit of rage. Even in the near-complete darkness, Oliver could see the strain on the soldier's face. Sweat glistened on the tips of his black hair and dripped down onto his armor. His chest was inflating and deflating rapidly, and the veins in his forehead were bulging with blood. The girl tried to get up and run, but the legionnaire grabbed her around the waist and pulled her back to the ground.

"Enough! Tell me what you are doing in Maldenney!" he demanded.

"I—I told you, I *live* h-here," the girl sobbed.

"You've been attacking legionnaires! Why?"

"I h-haven't! I don't know what you're t-talking about!"

"Fine then, if you won't tell me the truth…" Oliver watched from the window as the soldier unsheathed the sword at his side. "By order of Kaliculous Kaeno," the legionnaire began, "Lord Commander of the Legion and Protector of Omnios, I hereby…" His mouth kept moving but the sound was lost, as if he couldn't make the words come out. He stumbled over syllables for a moment before finally finishing, "sentence you to die."

He held the sword straight out with two hands and brought it level to the young girl's neck. The blade trembled in his hands, and Oliver could see him attempting to steady it.

"Please!" The girl pleaded, and for a moment, the legionnaire's muscles relaxed. There was no use begging, though. He drew back the sword, stopping with it at his side. Oliver froze in horror, preparing to witness the fatal swing. The girl shut her eyes in terror, and the legionnaire let out a brutal yell, when—*BANG!*

Oliver slammed the door of Elenore's Emporium so hard the sound echoed throughout Maldenney. He slumped to the ground with his back up against the door, his heart beating out of his chest. Daring to peek out of the window once more, he saw the girl run clumsily out of the Square while the legionnaire's attention was turned on the door. The soldier looked back to the girl and watched motionlessly as she fled, and Oliver knew that he had succeeded in saving her. He let out the briefest sigh of relief before it quickly turned to terror, for the girl was not the legionnaire's target anymore.

Oliver was.

CHAPTER TEN
LIVIAH

"Sorry," the jeweler said as she handed the crescent moon pendant back to Liviah. "It's not one of mine." The jeweler was a woman named Gemma, who was about the age of Liviah's mother. She was draped in colorful, flowing silk garments that hung loosely from her body, and she seemed to be covered in her own creations from head-to-toe. Rings, bracelets, necklaces, piercings—even her hair had jewelry braided into it.

"But do you know who it might belong to?" Liviah questioned. "It's probably a Legion official's or someone like that, right?"

"If it were a Legion official's, it would have come from me. I'm the only jeweler in the city who has contracts with the Legion. Besides that, it's not even the Legion's insignia."

"What?"

"Look here." Gemma brought one of her own Legion necklaces out from behind the counter. "This is a *real* Legion insignia. See? It has the reaper on it. And this smaller circle on yours is silver, not gold—Legion jewelry is always gold. My best guess is that it's some sort of cheap knock off that someone's trying to pass as the real deal."

Liviah looked down at the necklace in her hand. "Thanks," she said softly.

"It's my pleasure. Sorry I couldn't be of more help."

A tiny bell rang as Liviah opened the door to leave Gemma's shop. What in all of Omnios was she going to do now? She had traveled all this way only to learn that the necklace didn't belong to the Legion after all. It probably meant nothing. Liviah had wasted her time.

She slumped down against a cold, stone wall, folded her arms over her stomach, and tried not to think about how hungry she was. Lucila Square was full of people bustling around, all hurrying to get the last of their shopping done before the sun set. Across the street, Liviah spotted a vendor stand selling fresh produce. A juicy purple and green fruit caught her eye, and her mouth began to water. A lylaberry. Those were Liviah's *favorite*. She hadn't eaten anything so sweet in days.

She rose slowly, almost in a trance, and began walking towards the stand. She pushed through the crowded street, smoothly wriggling her way between the mass of people.

"Hullo there, little miss!" the man in the stand said cheerily as she approached. "Can I interest you in any fresh fruit or vegetables today?" He stretched his arms out in display of his goods.

"Just looking," Liviah said. The man smiled kindly and nodded his head. Liviah looked behind him to where crates of more produce were stacked, waiting to be placed out front in the stand. With her hand still down at her side, she flicked her fingers subtly and gave a twist to her wrist. One of the crates came crashing down, causing the vendor to practically jump out of his boots.

"What the!" he exclaimed, turning around to try to collect his fallen produce. While no one was looking, Liviah grabbed two of the larger lylaberries, dropped one into each pocket, and slipped away.

She walked to the edge of a large building with colorful stained-glass windows in the front, then rounded the corner to a narrow alley between two shops. Sitting down, Liviah pulled one of the lylaberries out of her pocket. She held it before her face with both hands, cradling it like a prized egg. With wide eyes, she sunk her teeth into its purple skin. The sweet juice ran down the corners of her mouth, and Liviah's taste buds danced at the flavor.

She closed her eyes, and for a moment it felt like she was back at Riverside Cottage with Juliana and her parents. In her mind's eye she could see her sister running through the house, half screaming and half laughing, while their dad chased her around pretending to be a giant or some sort of other mythological monster. She could see her mum sitting on the sofa smiling at them while she worked on knitting their winter clothing. Liviah could even picture Ramsey there, who would no doubt have some story about his recent adventures to entertain her.

A hand on her shoulder wrenched Liviah from her fantasy. She looked up and saw a legionnaire standing over her. "What do you think you're doing?" he said with a thick-accented voice. He was an older man, and behind his helmet Liviah could see the disdain he held for her in his eyes. "You pay for that there fruit?" Liviah froze. "Damn Blighters...Come with me girl." He yanked Liviah up by the arm and dragged her back to the vendor stand. "I think I've found your culprit, Ned. Let's see your identification papers, girl."

"This one? Oh no, that won't be necessary." Ned said. "She paid for hers!" He smiled and gave Liviah a wink. "In fact, you forgot your change m'lady." He pulled a few small coins out of his pocket and handed them over to Liviah. "There you are."

The legionnaire glared down at Liviah with flared nostrils, seemingly angry that he couldn't punish her. "Hmph," he grunted.

"Guess I'll just have to chalk those berries up as a loss," Ned said. "Thanks for your efforts anyway, Lieutenant." The legionnaire released his grip on Liviah's shirt and shoved her away, then walked off into the crowd without a word. Liviah stared down at the coins in her hand.

"Why did you do that?" she asked Ned.

"Do what?"

"Lie for me."

"I'm afraid I don't know what you're talking about, m'lady."

"Yes, you do. You know I stole those berries from you, but you didn't turn me in...You...gave me money."

Ned put his elbows on the counter and leaned in close. "I find that if you put your trust in people, they'll pay it back one way or another. And I reckon you needed those berries more than I did."

"Thank you," Liviah said, still unable to completely wrap her head around it.

"Now, I suggest you get back home before the legionnaires come back around. Don't want to be caught outside after curfew."

"Curfew?"

"Didn't you hear?" Ned turned around and rummaged through a satchel, retrieving a piece of parchment. He handed it over to Liviah "Whole city is getting shut down tonight so they can look for some grudder. Every night from here on out, I suppose."

Liviah examined the flyer over and over, then handed it back to Ned. She took off running without a word, pushing her way through the crowded marketplace. "Hey! Watch it girl!" the shoppers yelled as she pushed her way through the crowd. Liviah didn't pay them any attention. Her mind was racing too fast. What was she going to do when the curfew started? Where would she go? There was nowhere she could hide that the legionnaires wouldn't find her.

Liviah didn't stop running until she was well out of the Market District and into the Farmlands. The open air of Maldenney's Farmlands reminded her of home. She needed to get away from all the people to clear her mind. Soon her breathing slowed, and she was able to think, but there wasn't enough time to come up with a plan. Before she knew it, the sun had set. The clanging of bells resonated from the city's center, and Liviah knew that sound could only mean one thing—the curfew had begun.

Up ahead was a small farmhouse and stable. The stable had four stalls, each occupied by a horse. The first three seemed unconcerned with Liviah's presence, but the fourth poked his head out curiously as she came by. A wooden sign above the stall indicated his name as York. Liviah put her hand on York's face, and he nuzzled her back affectionately. There was a sudden yell behind her in the distance, so she opened the stall door and slipped inside. Crouching down on the hay-covered ground, Liviah pinched her nose. The remnants of York's lunch were sitting in the corner of the stall, buzzing with flies. The horse regarded her, clearly wondering what she was doing in there, but quickly shrugged it off and went about his business.

Outside there were footsteps and more voices. Liviah stood and risked a peek out to the field. A pack of legionnaires—more than a dozen of them—were roaming around, talking loudly and laughing. One of them called something to the others, and they all stopped and gathered around him. He seemed to be giving instructions, pointing to groups of two or three and sending them off in different directions. Once they were all gone, only the leader and two others remained. They stood around talking for a moment, then slowly wandered away from each other. One came towards the stable, so Liviah ducked back out of sight.

His footsteps drew closer and closer, until finally, they were right outside the stall. He sighed and kicked his feet around in the dirt. York stuck his head out of the stall and eyed the legionnaire. The boy came up and pet the horse's head, then sniffed. "Agh, nasty," he mumbled to himself, pulling his hand back. "Stupid Farmlands...why did I have to get stuck here? I want to be where the *action* is."

After a minute or two, he walked around to the back of the stables. Liviah carefully unlatched the door and crept around to follow him. She looked over both shoulders. As far as she could tell, the other legionnaires had all gone. This one was alone.

A blue glow grew from Liviah's fingertips and palm, then she sent the spell whizzing through the air. The legionnaire gasped as it hit his breastplate, smacking him onto his back. He reached for the reaper he had dropped, but Liviah hoisted it into the air as she ran at him. Before he could sit up, she was standing over him, one hand reaching out towards his torso the other pointed up to where his reaper floated above her head.

"Oh gods!" the legionnaire exclaimed. He squealed like some sort of animal. It reminded Liviah of the sound a scared pig would make. "It's you! Please don't hurt me!"

"What do you mean, *it's me?*" Liviah demanded. She surprised herself at the way her voice sounded. The words were fiery in her throat. It made her feel powerful. It made her feel dangerous.

"You're the one who attacked those two legionnaires. The one they started the curfew for!"

"Why is the Legion looking for me? What do you want?"

"I don't know!" he squealed again, this time accompanying it with a nervous laugh. "I'm just a recruit, they don't tell us anything!" Liviah motioned down with her hand, moving the point of the reaper closer to his face. "Wait! Wait! I-I did hear something though!"

"Talk."

"There've been rumors—going around the Academy. We all thought someone had made it up. As a joke you know, to mess with the recruits."

"Spit it out!"

"W-w-we were told that a girl had broken into the city, right? But no one really got what the big deal was. And then some recruits started saying that they had heard that someone from Glassfall wrote a letter to Lord Commander Kaeno."

"What did the letter say?"

The legionnaire looked at Liviah's hands. "That there was a girl there who could do magic," he said. Liviah did her best to keep any expression from her face, but fear shot through her heart like a blast from one of her own spells. Her worst fears were being confirmed.

"Who wrote the letter?" she asked. "WHO WROTE IT?"

"I-I don't know! I swear! That's everything I know! We just wanted to be the recruits who found the grudder, that's all! They don't tell us anything." Liviah didn't need him to tell her who sent the letter. She already knew; it was Rolan.

"Marrin!" A voice called in the distance.

"Where are you at, Marrin?" said a second.

The legionnaire's head jolted north to where the Farmlands ended and the Imperial District began. He looked back at Liviah with fear in his eyes, and suddenly their expressions became the same.

"Don't," she said, but it was too late.

"Over here!" Marrin yelled. "Hel—"

His last word was cut off. Liviah twisted her wrist and swung her hand down. The reaper followed the motion, turning so that the shaft slammed into his chest and pinned him to the ground. She didn't wait to see how many other legionnaires were coming. She ran away from their voices as quickly as possible, wishing that the fields still had crops for her to hide in.

"Stop! Come back here!" one of them yelled. Liviah shot a spell over her shoulder and kept going.

"Watch it!" another said.

Liviah cast a second spell at them, but the legionnaires didn't let up the chase. They were much faster than she was, and she knew that she wouldn't be able to outrun them much longer. She stopped and turned around to face them. She closed her eyes and began to move her arms back and forth in a swirling motion in front of her body. Slowly, the dirt beneath her feet began to swirl around in the air in front of her. One of the legionnaires held up a fist, and the others stuttered to a halt behind him. A group of five or six was there, watching in awe as Liviah built up a storm of dust around herself. The cloud grew bigger and denser, and a few of the legionnaires began backing away. Soon, it was as thick as a stone wall. Liviah dropped her arms and ran. The cloud began to dissipate, but by the time the legionnaires could see again, she was already gone.

"Where'd she go?" she heard one of them yell.

"Spread out and find her!" another commanded. "She couldn't have made it far."

CHAPTER ELEVEN
OLIVER

Oliver ran as fast as he could to the back of Elenore's Emporium, looking over his shoulder repeatedly for any sign of the legionnaire. He stumbled into a shelf and knocked over a golden candelabra. It clanged on the ground like a crash of thunder. The flash of gold metal nearly made him halt in his tracks, thinking that it was the golden armor of the legionnaire who had come to kill him. By the time he had passed the eighth or ninth row of shelves—he had lost count—the light produced by the torch sconces out on the street was no longer visible. Oliver looked around frantically for a place to hide. He got down on his hands and knees and crawled into the small gap underneath the shelf that was mounted along the back wall. Squishing his body down to take up as little space as possible, he shimmied his way behind a large statue that was surrounded by several smaller ones.

The door of Elenore's Emporium creaked opened, and Oliver heard the unmistakable sound of armored boots hitting the floor.

Thud. Clink!

Thud. Clink!

Thud. Clink!

His knees were practically in his neck, and his head was bent at an awkward angle that sent a twinge down his entire spine, but Oliver wouldn't dare move. He couldn't if he had wanted to—every muscle in his body was locked into position, frozen tight to where they were.

"I know you're in here," the legionnaire said. His tone was calm and collected now, not at all like it had been in the street just moments before. "You can't hide forever. Just come on out and we can talk."

As his eyes began to adjust to the darkness, Oliver realized he was looking out from behind a pair of stone hands. They extended up from a rectangular base, with fingers that were eerily real. They seemed to grasp at the empty air, as if they were the hands of a man trying to claw his way out of his own grave. A moment later, Oliver realized what the larger statue was. It was a pair of men—or boys, he couldn't tell—standing together with swords in their hands. One was slightly taller than the other, and his arm was wrapped around the shoulder of the other. They were wearing armor as well, like they had just been in a battle. Oliver guessed that the larger one was the father or older brother of the smaller one. Either way, he felt somehow better knowing they were guarding his whereabouts.

"Come out, you filthy grudder!" the legionnaire yelled. Oliver nearly screamed at how close it sounded. Something else struck him about the voice, however. There was a familiarity to it. Oliver was almost certain he had heard that voice before, and that wasn't a feeling he was well accustomed to.

Metal scraped against the ground, and there was a light tapping sound on the shelves. Oliver willed his breathing to soften, but no matter what he did, he couldn't make it quiet down. His heartbeat pounded in his head. It bounced off the walls of Elenore's Emporium, banging like a drum.

Thud. Clink!

Thud. Clink!

Thud. Clink!

The legionnaire rounded the corner of the last row of shelves. Oliver put a hand over his mouth. He wanted to close his eyes, but he couldn't look away. He wanted to run, but he couldn't move. The legionnaire's boots grew nearer and nearer. They stepped in the same slow rhythm. Right foot, pause. Left foot, pause. Right foot, pause.

Only there was no left foot this time. The boots stopped before the statue of the two warriors. Oliver watched from the ground in terror as the boots turned towards the wall where he was hiding. It was over. He was caught.

The legionnaire put one knee on the ground. If there was a time to act, it was now. Oliver mustered all of his strength and kicked the statue of the two warriors. It tottered back and forth for a moment, then went crashing down onto the legionnaire. He fell onto his back, just barely getting out of the way in time. The statue shattered into hundreds of pieces as it hit the floor. Oliver didn't waste another moment. He got up and ran towards the front of the shop.

"Come back here!" the legionnaire boomed. Oliver kept running. He reached the door handle and pulled, but the legionnaire's reaper came soaring through the air beside Oliver's head. It sunk deep into the wood between the door and the frame, jamming it shut. Oliver whirled around. The legionnaire was grinning triumphantly. Oliver glanced up to the staircase, and the legionnaire followed his eyes. They took off at the same time, but Oliver was quicker. He was halfway up the stairs when a hand caught his ankle and dragged him down. He kicked the legionnaire square in the nose with his free leg, then finished up the stairs on all fours.

If the first floor of Elenore's Emporium was disorganized, the second floor was chaotic. Everything was thrown into piles that reached the ceiling, with walkways carved out between them. Oliver ran straight into the mess without hesitation. The path wound, curved, and split in a dozen different ways. It was like a maze with walls made up of random, useless items. Oliver could hear the legionnaire running too, but the hordes of objects distorted the sound and made it impossible to tell where it was coming from. Once he thought he'd lost the legionnaire, Oliver stopped to catch his breath. He put his hands on his knees, wheezing for air. There was a muffled crash of something falling on the other side of the building. He walked slowly, careful not to make noise, and began backing away from the sound. A board creaked beneath his foot, but Oliver told himself it wasn't loud enough for the legionnaire to hear. If he could just find his way back to the stairs…

Bam! Oliver spun on his heels to see window shutters blowing in the wind. He ran over to the window and looked down. They were only one story up, but to Oliver it might as well have been ten. The longer he stared, the farther away the ground seemed to get. Another sound inside told him that the legionnaire was getting closer. He looked out the window again and cursed under his breath. Climbing onto the windowsill, Oliver felt his legs suddenly become very wobbly. He stood for a moment, wondering if he could do it, when the legionnaire's footsteps reached his ears again. That was all the motivation Oliver needed. He let go of the walls and allowed himself to drop. It lasted only a second, and then he was on the ground. He cried out as pain shot up his right leg, but he stood on it anyway.

The legionnaire's head appeared in the window and his eyes locked onto Oliver for just a moment before disappearing back into the store. Oliver turned and ran at full speed. He wanted to put as much distance as possible between himself and Lucila Square. When he reached the battered houses that told him he had crossed over into the Blights, he heard the door of Elenore's Emporium burst open behind him.

"Where are you?" the legionnaire roared.

Clutching his bag, Oliver zigged and zagged through the narrow gaps between the houses. He could feel his blood pulsing in his temples. The longer he ran, the more he felt the pain in his leg. Soon he was limping, struggling to keep on.

"Oof!" he cried as he tripped on the uneven cobblestone and smacked the ground. He scrambled to his feet, and his leg erupted in even more agony. Every step felt like a sharp sword was slashing up the length of it. Still, he continued south without stopping or looking back. Soon enough, he could see Hawthorne Alley straight ahead. He was just about to cross the last street that separated his world from the rest of Maldenney when something slammed into the side of him. Oliver fell flat on his back and hit his head on the ground. Terrified and slightly dazed, he sat up as fast as possible. For a moment, he thought he was hallucinating. Could it really be her? Despite the blow to the head, Oliver thought that he could trust his eyes, and standing before him was the girl from the wall—the one he hadn't been able to stop thinking about since the moment he had first seen her. Oliver climbed to his feet once more. "It's you," he breathed. The girl looked surprised at him.

"Who are you?" she asked. Her voice was soft and had an accent that was different than his. That must be what girls sounded like, Oliver thought.

"Oliver!" he said a bit too loudly, shooting his hand out for her to shake. "We haven't met, but I've watched you before."

The girl raised her eyebrows. "You what?"

"No wait, that didn't come out right! I meant—"

"What are you doing out here?" she interrupted.

"I was..." Oliver was about to dive into the whole story of why he had gone out that night, but quickly remembered that he didn't have the time for it, nor any idea if he could trust the girl. "Going for a walk," he said.

"Going for a walk? During curfew?"

"Yeah. That's it! What are you doing out here?" She looked sideways and avoided Oliver's eyes. "You're the one they've been looking for," he said. He had felt happy to see her at first, but his mind drifted to the curfew flyer, and he remembered why the Legion was after her. She narrowed her eyes.

"Do I scare you?" she asked with a slight smile.

"You're wanted for torture and murder."

"The Legion lied about that."

Oliver considered this for a moment, but his caution got the better of him. "Why should I believe you?" he questioned.

"Do I *look* like a murderer to you?" the girl asked, abandoning her dangerous expression.

"Not really...but then why would the Legion say you are?"

"I don't have time to explain right now, but I'm on your side."

"How do you know what side I'm on?"

"It's illegal for you to be out here right now, which means you're probably doing something you shouldn't be. If you're against the Legion, then we're on the same side."

"What are you doing in Maldenney?"

"Gods, you ask a lot of questions."

The sounds of shouting and footsteps in the distance made both Oliver and the girl turn their heads.

"We have to go!" she said, half whispering and half yelling at him. "Come on!" She began walking north, back towards the Market District Oliver had just fled.

"Wait!" he said, completely unsure if what he was about to do was a good idea. Could he trust this girl to keep his secret? He didn't really know, but he was going to have to. "Don't go that way. I know somewhere better we can hide. It's safe."

The girl nodded, and Oliver limped his way towards the shack. She came up behind him and flung his arm over her shoulder, relieving a great deal of pressure from his leg. He felt a surge of gratitude towards her, and together they staggered down the alley, around the corner, and up to the door of the shack.

"Wait a minute...I've seen this place before," the girl said.

"I know," Oliver said with a smile. She looked at him curiously. "I, uh, saw you. Up on the wall," he added.

"You did?"

"Yeah, that's what I meant to say, uh, before." He pushed on the door and it stuck as always. He smiled uncomfortably. "Sorry, it's a bit tricky."

"Let me," the girl said. She pushed on the door with one hand, and it swung open with tremendous ease.

"Oh, uh, wow," Oliver marveled. She walked inside and he followed closely after her. "Sorry about the mess," he said, pushing away the few belongings he had left on the ground. "Oh, and Nan's asleep, but you don't have to worry about being quiet. She won't wake up." He sat down in the chair and put his hands gingerly on his leg. The girl looked around, taking it all in. She scrunched up her face.

"What is this place?" she asked. Oliver looked up from his injury to meet her eyes, and the faintest smile painted itself across his face.

"Home."

CHAPTER TWELVE
LIVIAH

"You're sure we're safe here?" Liviah asked the boy, unconvinced by his stick-through-door-handle security system.

"I've been hiding from the Legion here for thirteen years, and Nan's been here way longer than me," he said, gesturing to an old woman who was asleep on a cot behind him. "They haven't found us yet."

"Oliver, is it?" Liviah asked. The boy smiled the most ridiculous smile she had ever seen in her life. It looked like he was trying to hold it back, but simply couldn't.

"Oliver Hawthorne," he said, and thrust out his hand for her to shake, but he had his palm facing down towards the ground. Liviah looked at Oliver with raised eyebrows.

"Liviah Cain…" she said eventually, slowly grabbing his hand and shaking it oddly.

Liviah looked around the room. There were two cots lying side by side with a few dirty blankets, a small wobbly table with two chairs that had been poorly made, a pile of very worn clothes in the corner, and a wooden crate filled with books, trinkets, and lots of other items that looked rather useless. A bucket of water sat in the middle of the floor under a sizeable hole in the ceiling. Through it, Liviah could see the sky turning from jet black to a deep violet-blue.

"Why do you live here?" Liviah asked.

"Oh!" Oliver said, "Right, I guess that's probably a bit confusing, isn't it? Well, you see, I'm a grudder. Nan and I both are, actually, and when I was a baby, she found me in the alley. So, she brought me here and now this is where I live...Tada!" He stretched out both hands in display of his home.

"You're a...*gretter*?" Liviah asked. Oliver laughed.

"A *grudder*. It's like an illegal citizen, you know? So, I guess technically you are one too now since you're not here legally...with, you know, all the climbing the wall and such...I'm sorry, I feel like I'm rambling, it's just, well I've just never really done this before."

"What do you mean?"

"Well, you're the first person I've talked to besides Nan," he admitted.

"In how long?"

"Um...ever."

"*Ever?*" Liviah could hardly believe it, but the boy smiled in the most uncomfortable way she could have imagined, and it suddenly seemed a little more believable. "So, you're an illegal citizen —"

"A grudder."

"A grudder...right. You're a grudder, and you live at the end of this abandoned alley, and you've never talked to anyone besides this old woman?"

"Pretty much, yep," Oliver said. Liviah wished he would stop staring at her with that ridiculous smile, but she understood now why his behavior was so strange. Just then the old woman stirred in her sleep, letting out a terrible sounding moan and muttering some inaudible words.

"What's wrong with her?" Liviah asked.

"She's sick," Oliver said. He began immediately rummaging through his bag. "That's why I was out there tonight. To find her medicine." He pulled out a small red beaker and unstopped it, then he tilted Nan's head back and poured the liquid down her throat.

"Let me see that," Liviah said, and Oliver handed her the empty beaker. Liviah looked from the bottle to Nan. Anyone seeing her decrepit state would know that this alone could not save her. It would take a miracle to heal her now...a miracle, or Juliana.

Oliver sat down on a cot and set up pillows under his injured leg. He cut open the leg of his pants with a dagger and then placed the blade back in the bag he had been carrying. His face writhed as he tried to move his leg. Just another thing Juliana would be able to fix. It was becoming increasingly difficult for Liviah to keep her emotions at bay.

"You can sit down," Oliver said. Liviah took up a seat at the wobbly table. "So, what are you doing in Maldenney anyway?"

Liviah furrowed her brow. "Looking for answers," she said plainly.

"Answers to what?"

"*Questions.*"

"What kind of questions?"

"That's none of your business."

"Okay, well...where are you from, then?"

"A village," Liviah said, thinking Oliver would get the hint and that would be the end of the discussion, but he was like a child in a candy shop.

"A village?" he said with wide eyes. "Where? What's it like there?"

"It's small and far away and full of horrible people, alright? Just drop it!"

"I'm—sorry," Oliver said, "I didn't mean to upset you."

"It's fine. And nothing personal, but we don't know each other. I'm not about to tell you my whole life story."

"Got it," Oliver said. "Will you at least tell me how you got into the city? I'm guessing you didn't just say 'please.'" He chuckled softly at his own joke, and Liviah groaned. How could one person have so many questions? Didn't he ever want to just be quiet?

"I slipped past the guards by the gate," she said. "Then I climbed a staircase to the wall."

"It was funny. I guess I didn't see you up there at first, and with it being so dark and all, it sort of looked like you just floated up there or something."

"Yeah...funny." Liviah wasn't sure if Oliver believed that was the truth or not, but she certainly wasn't going to admit anything to him about her powers.

"Agh!" Oliver said, wincing as he touched his injured leg. Again, Liviah's mind drifted to Juliana. Her younger sister would have mended his leg before she even bothered asking his name. She could never stand to see anyone in pain. Her heart was too big for it...too big for her own good, it appeared.

"It looks bad," Liviah said, observing how swollen and bruised it had already become.

"No, I'm sure it will be fine," Oliver said, though Liviah could tell he wasn't really that confident.

"I can't believe no one's ever found this place."

"The legionnaires pretty much steer clear of this end of the city. Everyone does, really. Nan says they don't like going by the old hospital."

"The old hospital?"

"That big building just outside. It used to be a hospital. It was fully operational when Nan was a girl. Then, right after the Legion moved into Maldenney, all these weird noises started coming from it. Screams and roars and other sorts of sounds. They shut the hospital down and boarded it up. People think it's haunted now."

Liviah raised her eyebrows. "That sounds ridiculous," she said.

"Oh, uh, yeah, it's dumb. Definitely not true...it's better when Nan tells it, anyway."

Liviah could see his face turning red, but how could she care about his stupid story, or anything other than finding her sister? She was grateful for Oliver hiding her from the legionnaires, but she wasn't there to make friends.

They watched from the hole in Oliver's roof as daylight arrived, bringing with it the end of the curfew.

"I'm going to get some sleep," Liviah said. "I'll be out of your way by nightfall."

"Oh, um, yeah. That's cool. Did you want to sleep here?" Oliver asked, pointing to his own cot.

"I'm good. Thanks," Liviah said, leaning her chair back against the wall and propping both of her feet up on his table. Several hours later Oliver was fast asleep in his cot, but Liviah had hardly slept. "Psst. Oliver. Oliver! wake up!" She stood over him as she shook him awake.

"What? What is it? What's going on?" he said, slightly panicked and confused.

"Is Nan an augur?"

"A what?"

"An augur!"

"You mean like, the people who make prophecies?"

"Yes, exactly."

"No...I thought those were made up for stories and stuff."

"No, they're not made up! They're all over Omnios! My uncle is one. Come here, listen!" Liviah grabbed Oliver by the arm and yanked him from his cot, dragging him over to the other side of Nan, who had rolled in her sleep to face the wall away from him. They stood silently, listening to the faint words Nan was saying.

"Taken… fort…missing…eclipse…" Her words seemed to echo in the shack as if they were being yelled.

"So what?" Oliver said. "She's been talking in her sleep ever since she got sick."

"I don't think she's just sleep-talking. I think she's making a prophecy! My Uncle Philius taught us about this stuff! He said that a lot of augurs' prophecies come in the form of dreams."

"That's amazing!" Oliver said. "I never knew they were real! But I really don't think that's what's going on here. Nan isn't an augur. If she was, she would have told me."

"But what if she didn't know! If she lived here her whole life, she never would have had anyone to tell her that her dreams weren't regular dreams."

"Alright, so, say she is one. Why is that important for us?"

Liviah slumped her shoulders. She supposed if she wanted answers, she had no choice but to tell Oliver the truth. "Alright," she said, "I'm going tell you what I'm doing in the city. But so help me, if you try to turn me in!"

"I won't!" Oliver said. He laughed. "Who do you think I would tell?"

"Good point."

"Okay. The village I'm from is called Glassfall. Ever heard of it?" Liviah started fidgeting her fingers as she spoke, and suddenly it seemed impossible to look Oliver in the eye.

"No," Oliver said, his cheeks flushing red. "I don't know many places."

"It's deep in the woodlands to the west. It's nothing compared to Maldenney. Most of the people there are farmers and fishermen. A few traders come through every now and then, but other than that it's mostly quiet."

"It sounds like a nice place to live."

"It was, until about a week ago."

Liviah recounted to Oliver the story of what had happened when she awoke to flames so many nights ago.

"I guess I'm just still not understanding," he said when she had finished. "Why would someone want to set your house on fire?" he asked.

"Some of the other families in Glassfall hated us. That's why Rolan tried to run us out of town."

"I get that part, but why did they hate you?"

"Because they have brains the size of acorns, and they hate everyone who's different from them."

"How are you different?"

"We're not, really. They just saw us that way. Kind of like you. People see you as different just because you're a grudder, but that doesn't really make you different."

"Oh, that makes sense...So, you came here to find this Ramsey guy?"

"What?"

"Well, you said he lives here in the city, right?"

"No, I—yes, he does, but I—I don't know if Ramsey is here or not. I came here because of this." Liviah pulled out the chain bearing the crescent moon pendant.

Oliver cupped it in his hand and held it closer for inspection. "What is it?"

"One of the people who set my house on fire was wearing it. I thought it was the symbol of the Legion, which is what led me here. I figured Maldenney was the place to find answers if the Legion is connected to whatever is going on."

"Have you found any?"

Liviah shook her head. "Only that I was wrong. I took it to a jeweler in Lucila Square, thinking maybe she made it or knew who it belonged to, and she told me it's not even the symbol of the Legion."

"But it looks just like it!"

"It's missing the reaper. I should have noticed that before. I just got so caught up in trying to find Juliana as quickly as possible. Now I have no leads on who took her or where they took her."

"How do you know she was taken somewhere at all?"

Liviah felt a piercing pain shoot through her heart. That was a possibility that she hadn't allowed herself to consider up to this point. The thought that her sister had been in the house somewhere was too much to bear. Oliver must have noticed too because he quickly spoke again. "I'm sure she's safe wherever she is. They would have to keep her safe if they wanted to use her for ransom or something...I—I read a book once. These bandits kidnapped a King's daughter when she was out traveling to a festival. They demanded all of the King's riches in exchange for her safe return."

"Yeah, maybe…She has nightmares a lot, and fresh air calms her down. If she had gotten up in the middle of the night and gone out on the porch, someone could have gotten their hands on her without my parents or me hearing it."

"I can't believe someone would do that," Oliver said, frowning and shaking his head.

"I followed the river until it brought me here. I've been finding legionnaires off on their own at night, questioning them about what they know, but none of them have told me anything useful yet."

"*You've* been questioning legionnaires?"

"What?" Liviah said. "You believed that I was torturing and murdering people, but you can't believe that I've been questioning them?"

"Well, I didn't really think about it before!" Oliver laughed. "You caught me off guard, you know? I wasn't thinking straight. But it's not like you're particularly…"

"Not particularly what?"

"I-I don't know," Oliver said in a fluster. "Big? I mean how would you get them to tell you anything without them just arresting you?"

"That's not really your concern, is it?"

"Er—alright, sorry." Oliver said. Liviah shifted her weight uncomfortably in the chair, and it squeaked loudly. "You know, I think you're right, Liviah."

"About what?"

"I think the Legion does have something to do with it, and I think they really do want you dead."

"What makes you say that?" she said slowly.

"Before I ran into you, I was in the Market District, at Lucila Square. I saw a legionnaire pull a girl from a bakery. She was scared and crying. I think he thought that she was you, the girl who they were looking for, I mean. I thought he was going to arrest her, but…he was about to kill her, right there. Right in the middle of the street."

"Did he?"

Oliver shook his head. "I distracted him, and she got away."

"You risked your life to save someone you never met?"

"Um, yeah, I guess so," Oliver said. "Anyway, what does all this have to do with Nan?"

"If Nan is an augur, then her prophecy could be about Juliana. She said, 'taken, fort, missing, eclipse.' Well, Juliana is *missing*, so she could have been *taken* to a *fort*, and…"

"And eclipse? What's that one mean?"

In her excitement, Liviah had nearly forgotten that Oliver didn't know she and her sister were Eclipse. "I don't know," she said, "but the other parts could mean something."

"Maybe. But have you considered the possibility that it was just some nonsense that she was muttering in her sleep?"

Liviah rubbed both hands down her face. Why was Oliver so determined to prove her wrong? "Where is that medicine? We need to give her some more," she said.

"That was all of it," Oliver said.

"Then we'll need to get more."

"It doesn't matter."

"Of course it does!"

"No, it doesn't. She hasn't woken up once in the past day, and it doesn't seem like she will again anytime soon. It doesn't matter if it was a prophecy or not because she won't be able to tell us."

"You don't know that."

"Yes, I do."

"If we just get something stronger—"

"I'm telling you she won't wake up! This isn't some everyday sickness, Liviah! She's got the Withering Black!"

"They cured the Withering Black ages ago."

"Nan had the cure when she was a girl, but she didn't take the whole thing. You needed five doses to make it work, and she only took four. She's been living with it her whole life, and she's not strong enough to fight it off anymore. She's not going to get better, Liviah. She's going to die!"

Liviah could see Oliver's chest inflate and deflate as he panted for air. He seemed to be waiting for her to say something. There was something she wanted to say, but she didn't know if she should. After all, she *barely* knew Oliver. She didn't know him at all, actually, but then she remembered what the vendor Ned had said to her in Lucila Square. *If you put your trust in people, they'll pay it back one way or another.* Something about Oliver made her trust him, and she really needed his help if she was going to find out what Nan knew about Juliana.

"My sister can save her," she said simply.

"What are you talking about?" Oliver asked. Liviah bit her lip and creased her eyebrows together.

"Juliana and I can do magic."

"*Magic?*"

"We're something called Eclipse. That's why I think Nan is talking about Juliana. I know it sounds crazy, but it's true. I can't help Nan because our magic is different, but Juliana can heal people. If we find her, she could save Nan."

"You're right. It does sound crazy."

Liviah sighed and raised her hand towards Oliver's bag. A blue glow arose from her palm, and from the bag his dagger soared through the air, nearly grazing his arm as it passed by. It came to a halt in Liviah's grip. Oliver jumped a foot and nearly fell back onto Nan as she slept.

"That just—did *you* do that?" he shouted. Liviah smiled haughtily.

"Believe me now?" she asked.

"You can do magic! *You* can do *magic!*" Oliver repeated, still clearly trying to wrap his head around what had just happened. "And your sister! She could really cure Nan?"

"Yes. As long as we can find her before it's too late."

"But if what you're saying is true, and Nan really could tell us where your sister is, then we'd need Nan to get better first in order for us to find your sister."

Both Oliver and Liviah's smiles faded. They stared at each other, utterly stumped.

"So we find her better medicine," Liviah said. "Even if it doesn't cure her entirely. We just need something that will help her get better enough to wake up and tell us what she dreamt."

"Where are we going to get that? I didn't see anything last night that looked like it would be much more help than the Fever Fix."

"There's another hospital ward up in the northern part of the city, right? I'll bet they'll have something there that's stronger."

"Well, yeah, but we can't exactly just walk her in through the front door. 'Yes, hello, we're two grudders looking for medicine for our third grudder friend. Oh, and by the way, she's the one the Legion has been looking for. Please help us out and don't say anything, even though we have no money to pay you.'"

"Do you think I'm stupid? Of course we can't do that, but we can steal it."

"No way! They would catch us easily!"

"I'm sure there's a back entrance or something. We can wait until nightfall, sneak in, and then force one of the healers to tell us where they keep the medicine."

"Force them how?"

"We just scare them a little, make them think we might do something if they don't help us."

"What about the legionnaires? I'm sure the hospital has guards. What do we do about them?"

"I can handle a few legionnaires." Liviah released Oliver's dagger and let it float suspended in mid-air. Then she whipped around to look at the door, and the dagger flew full speed at her target, sinking an inch deep into the wood. She turned back at him and smiled.

"But you won't hurt anyone?" Oliver asked.

"No, not really hurt them, at least," Liviah said. "Besides, they'll be in a hospital, so they'll be fine. We'll just get in, get the medicine, and get out."

"I guess we don't have any other choice," Oliver said.

CHAPTER THIRTEEN
RIDLEY

Ridley returned to the Academy exhausted and defeated. He had let not one, but two potential grudders slip through his grasp, one of whom could have been the girl he had been looking for. He cursed himself for letting her go, for allowing the other to distract him. They were probably working together, he now realized. Perhaps it was all for the better, though. Now if he found one, he was bound to find the other as well, and catching two grudders was always better than one.

His footsteps echoed in the stairwell as he trudged up to his room on the third floor of the barracks. He could feel the blood pulsing in his nose where the grudder had kicked him. He paused at the top, allowing his legs a moment to recover from the climb. The hall was quiet, even for this early in the morning. The other recruits should have been waking up and getting ready for the day's tasks by now. He pushed open the door to his own room expecting to see Sayben's irritatingly smug grin, but it was empty. Ridley glanced back and forth down the hall.

"Hello?" he called. There was no response. Where *was* everyone?

He returned his reaper to the armory. There was no one there or in the courtyard. He checked the sparring fields, which were equally as uninhabited. It wasn't until he went to the mess hall that Ridley found all the recruits sitting at one large table, surrounding Sayben. Their smell hit Ridley the moment he set foot in the building. They reeked of sweat and grime, and all of their eyes were red and bloodshot, with dark bags underneath them. They looked as though they had been out wrestling pigs all night long, yet every one of them was roaring with laughter and sharing energetic smiles. The revelry died as Ridley approached, and his classmate's eyes fell to his swollen, purple nose.

"You look like you had an interesting night," Sayben said.

"What's going on here?" Ridley asked. The entirety of the recruitment class was there around Sayben, even Fletcher. Fletcher, whom Ridley had thought to be his one true friend; Fletcher, who had defended him to Sayben on more than one occasion, was now sitting and laughing with Ridley's greatest enemy.

"I decided to get the boys together for some good old-fashioned brotherly bonding," Sayben said. "We spent the whole night tracking down that grudder girl for Cormack. Almost got her too, didn't we boys?" The group let out a tumultuous uproar and many of the boys clapped each other on the backs.

"Everyone went?" Ridley asked, now directing his question at Fletcher.

"Well, we would have invited you...honestly, we tried. We just couldn't find you, mate," Fletcher said shyly.

"No hard feelings, right?" Sayben said smiling.

"No hard feelings," Ridley echoed plainly. He turned to walk out of the building.

"Rid, wait!" Fletcher called, but Ridley was already gone. Fletcher came out the door a moment after him.

"You're friends with him now?" Ridley asked. "Even after he sent you to the infirmary? Even after everything he's done to try and get rid of me?"

"Ridley, come on. First of all, Cormack's the one who sent me to the infirmary. Second of all, I know you don't like Sayben, but he's not actually that bad once you get to know him. He organized everything last night so we could all work together. You know, build brotherhood and comradery and all that."

"He was using you all, Fletcher! He just wanted the credit for capturing her without having to do all the work himself. It should be me that everyone is sitting around in there. I'm the best in the class, not him."

"Yeah, it should be you!" Fletcher said. "You think I don't know that? You think they don't know that? It's no secret you're the top recruit, Ridley. I reckon even Sayben knows it. Everyone in that room looks up to you, but you never bother with any of them! You're like some legendary warrior to them, who they only know about from stories that their wet nurses told them as kids. You think you're better than them, so you keep to yourself, and they all know how you feel about them, so they stay out of your way. The only reason it's like that is because you've made it that way. Sayben could have gone out there alone last night and tried to take all the credit for himself, but he didn't."

"You mean like I did?"

"I didn't say that."

"That's what you meant though."

Suddenly, Sayben came bursting out the door. "Hey, Fletch, I—oh, Ambersen, didn't know you were still here."

"I'm sorry to tell you that you all wasted your time," Ridley said.

"What do you mean?" Fletcher asked.

"I found the grudder last night."

"Really? You caught her?"

For once Ridley managed to wipe the smile off Sayben's face. His look of dumbfounded confusion was worth every bit of the exhaustion Ridley was feeling.

"Where?" Sayben asked.

"Hiding out in Lucila Square," Ridley answered.

"She do that to your face?" Sayben nodded to Ridley's nose.

"She had help."

"Glad to hear it. What'd you do with her?"

Ridley looked sideways and clenched his jaw. There was no point in him hiding from the truth. "I was about to execute her—"

"*Execute?*" Fletcher asked.

"—when another grudder distracted me. She got away."

"She got away," Sayben repeated with far too much satisfaction.

"I had to deal with the other one," Ridley said. "By the time I was able to go after her again, the sun was already up. Curfew was over, there was no point trying to locate her. I know where to look for her now, though. She won't get away from me tonight."

"*Very* interesting story, Prodigy. So, let me get this straight. You found her hiding in the Market District, right?"

"If you're trying to get me to tell you where to look for her, you're going to have to do better than that, Sayben."

"Oh no, no, you've got me all wrong. See I don't want your girl because I know that *we* tracked the real grudder to the Farmlands, not the Market."

"What are you talking about?"

"A girl attacked Marrin out by one of the farmhouses and then started doing some freaky magic stuff. I'm sure you've heard about that, right? Oh, who am I kidding? You have no idea what I'm talking about. You don't have any friends! Nobody talks to you except Fletcher here." He clapped Fletcher on the back, and Ridley clenched his jaw.

"Easy, Sayben. Come on," Fletcher said.

"You're right, I'm sorry. Fletcher wants me to be more...what was the word you used, Fletch? *Cordial,* was it? Fun word, cordial. People don't say that where I'm from, you know. Anyway, point is, unless your girl was also attacking legionnaires and doing magic, I'd say you got the wrong one, Prodigy." He gave Ridley a wink and walked back inside.

"We tracked her to the Farmlands," Fletcher explained. "We were right on her heels until early this morning when we lost her heading southeast towards the Blights. There's no way she got anywhere near Lucila Square. Not before the sun was up."

"Well, you were all wrong then. I'll prove it to you. I'm going to the Lord Commander right now to tell him."

"Maybe that's not the best idea," Fletcher said calmly.

"I'm going! Just go back inside with the rest of them."

"Ridley..."

"It's fine, Fletcher. Just go." They would all see soon. He would find her tonight, and this time she wouldn't get away. This time they would see that he was right.

* * *

Ridley walked the long ornate corridor that led to the Lord Commander's quarters and rapped hard with the brass doorknocker. "Come in," the sharp voice inside called.

Ridley stepped inside and approached the desk. Kaeno's hooked nose was pointed down as he wrote furiously on a piece of paper. Ridley said nothing as he waited for the Lord Commander to finish. His steward, a scared looking boy of no more than ten, stood beside his desk with his hands folded behind his back. He stared straight forward at the wall, not looking at Kaeno or Ridley. The Lord Commander signed the paper, folded it in thirds, stamped it with his seal, and handed it to the boy.

"Take this order to Captain Landal," Kaeno said holding it out for the boy to take. Just as the boy reached for it Kaeno snatched it away. "*Only* to Captain Landal," he added. "No one else sees this."

"Yes, my Lord," the boy said and scampered out of the room.

"Obedient young lad," Kaeno observed.

"That he is," Ridley agreed half-heartedly. He was itching to get straight to what was on his mind, to hear what the Lord Commander had to say about it. Kaeno stared deep into his eyes, seeming to read Ridley's thoughts. He wondered if the Lord Commander already knew why he was there.

"Do you have something you'd like to say?"

"I tracked the grudder girl to Lucila Square. She got away this time, but I know where she's hiding now. I'll find her again tonight and...eliminate her, just like you asked."

"Is that so?" Kaeno asked.

"Yes," Ridley replied confidently.

"Who do you think you are, boy?"

"Lord Commander? I'm afraid I don't—"

"If you're about to tell me that you don't know what I'm talking about, I suggest you hold your tongue! I'm quite sure you do know."

"It—I didn't..."

"First thing after the curfew ended this morning, I was greeted by two very emotional and very angry parents waiting to have an audience with me. Aaron and Maris Wood. Ever heard of them, Ambersen?"

Ridley said nothing.

"No, I doubt you would have. Their daughter, Hensley, works in the bakery. The baker left early yesterday so that he could make sure his family was all present and accounted for before the start of the curfew, meaning Hensley was left to close up shop on her own. Before she knew it, the sun was down and the curfew had started, and seeing as this is the first time a curfew has happened in Maldenney and there's no sort of real protocol in place for these things, poor Hensley didn't know if she should go home or stay at work. And rather than being out on the streets after dark, she thought it best to just stay in the bakery until morning. Now I think that was a pretty smart decision of hers, don't you Ambersen?"

"Yes...my Lord." Ridley's voice came out weak and shaky.

"The only thing is, I woke up this morning to find out that one of *my* legionnaires nearly *killed* her last night. Of course, I told them they were mistaken. None of my men would be so reckless! But they were persistent. They even had poor Hensley recount the details to me and well, you just can't make up stories like that!"

"I…I didn't realize—"

"YOU DIDN'T REALIZE?" Kaeno slammed a fist down on the table. "You didn't realize you almost killed the wrong girl? Do you have any idea what that means, Ambersen? I can't have innocent people in my city afraid of being murdered every time they put a single toe out of line! And by the very men who are charged with their protection, no less!"

Ridley suddenly felt very sick. Dizzyingly, he stared at Kaeno. The Lord Commander was still talking, but his words took a lifetime to reach Ridley's ears. "But…she was hiding. She fought me! If she wasn't guilty, she shouldn't have tried to run!"

"She was afraid, Ambersen! A Southern Quarters girl like her gets stuck out after curfew, then sees a legionnaire…what would you expect from her? It would seem she was right to be so scared."

"She was a Blighter?" Ridley asked.

"DO NOT USE THAT TERM IN FRONT OF ME!" Kaeno roared. Ridley sank down into his own shoulders under the Lord Commander's deafening voice. "She was from the Southern Quarters, Ambersen, and no matter what you or your family may think about the Southerners, they are just as much citizens of this city as you and me! She was *not* the damned grudder!"

"But I didn't kill her!" Ridley wept.

"Oh, and why's that? Because from what she told me, you would have if you weren't distracted."

Ridley stared blankly, unable to come up with the words for his defense.

"You've failed me, Ridley, far more than I ever could have imagined was possible. You are a disgrace to the Academy and to the Legion. You will not become a legionnaire."

"No, Lord Commander, please! You can't!"

"I can and I will! I told you in your induction that you would be tested, and now you have failed that test. We all must pay for our failures in this life, Ambersen, and that is a lesson that you will come to learn very soon. Now get out of my sight."

Ridley left the room as fast as he could, nearly stumbling on the steps on his way out. He leaned up against the wall outside the room and squeezed his pulsing head with both hands. He slammed his fist on the wall, and it throbbed with pain against the stone. How had he made such a stupid mistake? He was so thrilled when he thought he had cornered the grudder! Why hadn't he just taken the time to make sure she was the right girl? He could still hear her pleas echoing in his ears.

Ridley felt sick. All he had wanted to do was make his father and the Lord Commander proud. Now look what had become of him. He was nothing but a shame to himself and his family. He thought about the night's events as he walked back to his home in the Northern Quarters. He played them over in his mind until he had grown too numb to think. Off in the distance, he could see his house, and suddenly, he realized he would not be able to return there. How would he bring himself to step foot inside that place? What would he tell his father?

"Are you a legionnaire?" he heard a small voice say. Ridley hadn't seen anyone walk up, but standing before him were two boys who looked years younger than Theo. They were holding toy swords and shields made of wood.

"That's legionnaire armor, isn't it?" the other asked. "Did you just fight a battle?"

Ridley looked down at his golden breastplate. He had forgotten that he hadn't taken the armor off yet. "It is legionnaire armor, but I'm—"

"My dad says that legionnaires are the bravest, most noble men in all of Omnios! I hope one day I can grow up to be a legionnaire like you."

Ridley looked down at the young lad, his eyes beaming brightly. He reminded Ridley of himself once, before he had lost all of the joy in it. He pushed his way between the boys. "I'm not a legionnaire," he said plainly.

Looking up at the two-story structure that was his house, Ridley felt an odd disconnect from it. It was as if it were a stranger's home; it belonged to the old Ridley, not the person he was now.

A fleeting thought crossed Ridley's mind. His parents might disown him and send him away. Then what would he do? In one fatal mistake, the only future he had ever envisioned had been taken away from him.

He looked again at the door. He couldn't go inside; he couldn't face the truth. He started to turn away, to keep on down the street, but then…what was that sound? He had been hearing it the whole time, he now realized, but had been too distracted by his own thoughts to make it out. It was faint, muffled by the walls of the house. He grabbed the handle and thrust the door open to the front room. His mother was sitting on the feather sofa, sobbing as Elma held her.

"It will be all alright, Madame," Elma said reassuringly, stroking Ridley's mother's long, blonde hair. His mother's hands had blood on them, and there was a knife on the ground at her feet.

"First the Cains and now Theodor," Ridley's father was saying. "I will fix this, Alana! You have my word!" He was streaking back and forth across the room collecting his things—legionnaire pin, identification papers, house key, and fur overcoat.

"Mother! Father! What's happened?" Ridley rushed over to them, not taking the time to shut the door behind him as he entered the house.

"It's Theo!" she wailed. "They've taken him! They've taken my baby boy from me! And I couldn't stop them!" She was so hysterical Ridley could hardly make out her words.

"What? Who took him, Mother? Mother, tell me! Who took him?"

"Legionnaires! They just came in the house and—and they just took him!"

"Ridley, I don't want you to worry," his father said urgently as he made his way towards the door. "This is obviously some sort of a huge mistake. I *will* have Theodor back with us in no time."

"When did they come? When did they take him?"

"Just now! Not a quarter hour ago! Why would they do this? Why, why, why? Why did they take my son away from me?"

Ridley nearly fell onto his back. He steadied himself by grabbing his mother's leg. His throat was closing little by little. Soon, he was sure to suffocate. Kaeno's voice echoed in Ridley's mind, telling him he would pay for his crimes. *This* was it, Ridley realized. *This* is how he would pay.

"Ridley, sit down, take a moment," Elma instructed. Poor Elma was trying so hard to help, but Ridley could tell that she was simply at a loss for what to do.

"This is *your* fault, Ramsey!" Ridley's mother yelled through her tears. "Your *precious* Legion did this! What did you let them do with my boy? What did you let them do?"

"I—I don't know what's going on! Alana, please," Ridley's father said helplessly. "It's just a misunderstanding, I'm sure! If I had been here…" He headed towards the door. "I'll go and see Kaliculous at once. We'll get this all straightened out and—"

"It's not his fault," Ridley said. The room seemed to freeze in time, with every head turning to him. "It's my fault."

"Ridley!" Elma gasped. His mother only continued her sobbing.

"What are you talking about?" his father demanded.

"Kaeno did this because of me. He's taken Theo because of me. He's punishing me because I failed him." His father slammed the door fast and hard.

"You have sixty seconds to explain yourself," he told Ridley.

"He wanted me to find that stupid grudder they've all been looking for! He told me to find her before the City Watch did, and I thought I had found her, but I got the wrong girl!"

Elma looked as though she might faint any moment. She began fanning herself with her hand.

"What did you do with her?" she asked.

"It was some stupid Blighter!" A few tears were streaking down his cheeks. "She shouldn't have been out after curfew! I could have kept searching, anyway. I still would have found the right girl! I don't see why I—"

Suddenly, Ridley froze, staring off at the wall behind his father.

"What?" his father asked. "Spit it out!"

"He wants me to find her anyway."

"What?"

"Kaeno is testing me."

"Ridley listen to yourself! You're not making any sense!"

"I am! It's the only thing that makes sense! He told me he was testing me, right to my face! He said my limits would be tested. This is the test! He took Theo to see if I would finish the mission, no matter what, even if the Legion had taken my own family! Think about it, Father. You're one of the highest-ranking Legion officials in all of Omnios. Who other than the Lord Commander himself has the authority to send legionnaires to take *your* son?"

"Ridley, I've known Kaliculous all my life! He wouldn't hurt Theodor."

"That's exactly the point! He's not going to hurt him. He would never hurt your son. He's just holding him to see what I'll do. Theo's not in any danger, I just have to finish the mission and he'll be returned to us."

"Ridley I—"

"I can do this, Father! You just have to let me!"

His father hesitated. "You have until tomorrow."

"Oh sure! Throw more soldiers at the problem," Ridley's mother said, her words layered with venom. "That's your solution to everything, isn't it?"

"Alana, we have no idea what the situation is! Ridley thinks he does! If he hasn't handled it by daybreak, I'll take matters into my own hands."

"Thank you, Father!" Ridley said as he took off towards the door.

"He's not going to find her!" Ridley's mother said.

"I will find her," Ridley said defiantly. "I know exactly where she's hiding."

"And how is it you just *happen* to know that?"

"Actually, Theo figured that one out for me."

Ridley ran out of the house in a flurry and mounted one of his father's steeds. He whinnied as Ridley surged him forward, hooves clattering down the cobblestone street.

* * *

Ridley pulled on the reins just as they approached the Legionnaire Academy. He tied the horse up at the stables outside and fed him two sugar cubes. He nuzzled his face on Ridley's hand in thanks. The horse was palomino in coat with a magnificently white mane and tail. Ridley smiled ever so slightly. At least he hadn't let everyone down, it seemed.

He could hear the recruits' voices from outside the courtyard's walls. The sounds of metal clanking together told him they were at combat practice. He snuck around the gate where he saw the group standing in a circle as they always did around the fighting pair. Fletcher stood near the back, watching and cheering with the others.

"Fletcher!" Ridley whispered to him. "*Psst!* Fletcher!"

There was too much going on for his friend to notice him, so he picked up a small stone and threw it at Fletcher's back. It clunked against his sparring armor, and Fletcher turned around.

"What the...Ridley?" he said.

"*Shh!*" Ridley replied with a finger pressed to his lips. He motioned for Fletcher to come over, and Fletcher snuck off from the pack of recruits and out of the courtyard.

"What are you doing here? We all heard you got kicked out!"

"I did."

"You can't be here, Rid. If Cormack sees you —"

"I know, I know, but I need your help."

"With what?"

"Finding the grudder. The real grudder this time."

"Come on, Rid, enough with the grudder. You don't have to prove anything, alright? Just leave it to the City Watch."

"No, you don't understand!"

"What then? Tell me why it's so important *you* have to be the one to find her."

"Kaeno kidnapped my brother."

"The Lord Commander *kidnapped* your brother? You've got to be joking. I mean really. This is some sort of joke that I don't get, right?"

"Not a joke."

"Why would Kaeno do that?"

"Look, I don't have time to explain it all, but I have to find the grudder to get Theo back."

"Fletcher!" a voice called from inside the courtyard.

"Cormack's coming," Fletcher exclaimed. "You have to go!"

There wasn't enough time for Ridley to sneak away. Before he knew it, his old training instructor was rounding the corner. Ridley looked from Cormack to Fletcher and did the only thing he could think of to keep his mate out of trouble. He sank his fist hard into Fletcher's stomach, who stumbled backwards as he gasped for air. Cormack came sprinting over to pull Ridley away.

"Well, well, well, look who we have here!" he said. He glanced at Fletcher, who was clutching at his stomach. "Running low on friends there, aren't you, Ambersen?"

Ridley locked eyes with Fletcher and knew that they both understood. "I told you that you can't be here," Fletcher said, playing along.

"Get off me!" Ridley said to Cormack.

"I don't think so. You're coming with me. Fletcher, get back to practice."

"Yes, sir," Fletcher said.

Cormack led Ridley off to the building beside the armory. The recruits stopped to gawk as he was paraded through the courtyard. The building was unmarked and looked dark inside. Ridley had never known what was in there, nor had he ever really noticed it, for that matter. Cormack unlatched the door and pushed Ridley inside. A set of six cells with iron bars lined the back wall, with bits of straw and hay thrown about the floor.

"Cormack, please don't do this," Ridley pleaded.

"Shut up! You've been a pain in my side for far too long. Not anymore."

"You'll never have to see me again. I'll go and never come back."

Cormack shoved him into a cell and locked the iron door. "That's a tempting offer, Ambersen, but I think I'll have more fun with you here." He left the building and shut Ridley in the dark.

* * *

It was several hours before anyone came by. The light that came from the open door blinded Ridley.

"Look at you...*pathetic*," a low, menacing voice said.

"Who's there?" Ridley said. He sat up from the ground and shielded his eyes with his hand. A silhouetted figure was walking towards the bars. The high-pitched sound of metal blades scraping together filled the air.

"You think you know what pain is?"

"Who are you?"

"You don't know anything about real pain...*yet*."

Ridley scrambled to his feet. "If you let me go, my father will pay you!" he said. A deep cackle filled the room, and then it turned into a hearty laugh.

"'*My father will pay you!*' That's the most perfect thing you could have said, Prodigy!"

"*Sayben?*" As his eyes adjusted to the light, Ridley was able to make out the face of his former roommate.

"Oh boy, you should have seen the look on your face."

"What's the matter with you?" Ridley scoffed.

"Relax! I was just having a little bit of fun."

"What are you even doing here?"

"Okay, so here's the deal. Fletcher came to me and told me about your little hiatus from the law. You like that? *Hiatus!* Fletch has been teaching me all the fancy-folk words."

"Fletcher talked to you?"

"Don't be mad at him. He just wanted to help you."

"And?"

- 130 -

"I'm here to do that, of course."

"*You're* going to help *me*?"

"I could be coerced into releasing you from this cell."

"What's the catch?"

"What? A guy can't just help his old roommate out of the kindness of his heart?"

"Come on, Sayben."

"Gods, you were never any fun. I want in on it."

"In on what?"

"The grudder, Ambersen, keep up! You need her caught, and I want to catch her. You claim to know where she is, and I'm not locked in a cell. Seems to me like we need each other."

"Why do you want to catch her so badly? You don't need the points. I'm already gone."

"Wow, you are even more arrogant than I thought. Believe it or not, my life doesn't revolve around you, Prodigy. Sure, it was mostly about getting rid of you at first, but not anymore. I want to be the best to prove it to myself, not to prove it to anyone else. I don't care what you, Cormack, Kaeno, or anyone else thinks of me. All I care about is what I know about myself."

"Well, you can forget it. I have to be the one to catch her if I want to get my brother back."

"Yeah. Fletcher said you'd say that. Alright, well, it was nice catching up then, roomie. Let me know how that whole 'saving your brother' thing goes for you." Sayben smiled and turned away from the cell. He had barely placed a hand on the door to leave when Ridley called after him.

"Wait! Fine...I'll let you come along."

"How very generous of you to allow that from your place of power."

"Just get me out of here."

Sayben took the two knives in his hands and jammed them into the large iron keyhole.

"You know how to pick that?" Ridley asked. Sayben raised his eyebrows.

"I grew up in the Blights; I know how to pick a lock. Honestly, I'm surprised you don't." A moment later, there was a loud *click*, and Ridley was free. He started to push open the door, but Sayben held it shut. "I'm warning you right now, Ambersen, double cross me and you'll wish you hadn't."

"I won't," Ridley said.

"You better not."

"I won't. Just get Fletcher and meet me in the Blights at midnight tonight."

"The crossing of Mills and Fairlane."

"What?"

"They're streets, Prodigy."

"I don't know them."

"Then buy a map and look them up. I know you can afford it."

"Alright, whatever. Mills and Fairlane. Midnight."

"See you then, roomie."

Sayben stepped aside and Ridley left his cell.

CHAPTER FOURTEEN
OLIVER

"I can do this," Oliver said to himself. "I can do this. I can do this."

"You ready to go?" Liviah asked. Oliver gulped.

"Nope," he said. "I can't do this. This is a bad idea. We shouldn't go." Over time, he found himself increasingly unsure of Liviah's plan.

"*What?*"

Oliver shook his head back and forth insistently. "Something'll go wrong. Something *always* goes wrong!"

"No way...No way are you backing out on me now, Oliver. What about Nan? She needs the medicine!" Oliver said nothing. "Look at me," Liviah said. Her eyes were focused and commanding. "We are going to go get that medicine, and we're going to bring it back here so she will wake up. Now get up."

"You go on. I'll stay here. In case Nan needs something, you know? She probably shouldn't be left alone for too long."

"Oliver, Nan is asleep! You said yourself, she's been asleep for days and she'll still be asleep when we get back."

"I can't go!" Oliver snapped. His voice was trembling uncontrollably.

"Why not?"

"I've never...gone out there before," he conceded.

"What are you talking about? You were out there when we met!"

"Not during the day! I've never gone out to where people are. I've never been to a hospital, or even an inn or a shop. I've never talked to anyone besides you and Nan! I can't do this."

Liviah sat down across from him at the table. Oliver wouldn't look at her. He was embarrassed. He was worse than embarrassed...he was ashamed. Why had he ever agreed to her plan? He knew he wouldn't be able to do it. He was a grudder, the lowest of the low, worse than Blighters. No matter how hard he tried, he would never be able to run away from that fact.

"Fine," Liviah said. She stood up and walked to the door, then paused for a moment to look back at him. "You know, all of your life, the world has been happening around you, and the reason you've been missing out isn't that you're a grudder. It's that you're too afraid to go out and live in it. One day you're going to have to wake up, Oliver. Otherwise," Liviah gestured to Nan, "you're going to end up just like her, dying in this shack. Only, you'll be alone."

Liviah walked out into the alley. Oliver knew that she was right. He had always known it. Truth be told, he didn't even know how often things like birth documents came up in the real world. For all he knew, the legionnaires never checked. He looked over at Nan, breathing slowly and scratchily. She needed his help, and Liviah needed his help.

"Wait!" he called after her, running out the door of the shack and down the alley. Liviah was nearly at the end of it, but she heard him well enough. She stopped and waited for him. "I'm coming with you," he said, panting by the time he reached her.

Liviah smiled the faintest of smiles. "Good," she said.

It was late afternoon in Maldenney as they approached the edge of the Blights. Oliver looked up to see the old wooden sign that stood over him reading, *Hawthorne Alley*. There was no one in either direction, but he could hear the far-off sounds of people talking and children playing with barking dogs. Liviah looked at Oliver in anticipation, no doubt wondering if he would turn back again. Oliver gave the alley sign one last glance, then stepped into the cross street.

They walked through the Blights for some time. Only a few people looked at them funny or paid them any sort of attention at all. Oliver could feel himself gawking all around him. He knew he probably looked like some sort of idiot, but he just couldn't help it. There were people everywhere. More people than he had ever seen, more than he had even dreamt of. A group of small children ran by playing some sort of game of chase. A woman rinsed linens in a tub and hung them on a line. A man and young boy threw a wooden stick while their dog chased after it. People ate and drank and talked, and none of them realized how amazing it all was.

They walked clear through the afternoon as it turned into evening. Oliver's injured leg ached under the pressure of each step, but he kept on trying to walk with as normal of a stride as possible. They traveled through Lucila Square to avoid the Imperial District. The shops were emptying out as the nightly curfew approached. Suddenly, Oliver felt Liviah's hand grab his.

"Don't freak out," she whispered in his ear, "but there are legionnaires up ahead."

Oliver tensed up and his hands became suddenly sweaty. Two gold-plated figures were walking down the street, checking in with people and sending them towards their homes. Oliver's eyes darted all around the square, instinctively searching for an escape route.

"Veer left," Liviah told him. "If we look like we're leaving, they won't talk to us."

Oliver did as she instructed and walked at a slight angle away from the soldiers. He watched out of the corner of his eye as the two entered his peripheral and then were gone.

"Hey you," he heard a voice say, and he hoped beyond all hope that it wasn't directed at him. He and Liviah did not look back to see who was speaking. "You there. Girl!"

Liviah stopped in her tracks, and Oliver was forced to do the same. "Let me do the talking." Her voice was so quiet it was hardly audible. She spun around to face the legionnaires and spoke with a sweetness that had even Oliver convinced. "Oh, were you talking to us?"

"We were," the first said. He was grown, unlike the other who was just a boy. Oliver could see the lines of his face through the gaps in his helmet. His voice was tight and pretentious. He had black bars on his shoulder plate, so Oliver assumed he was some sort of officer. "It's getting awfully late. You should be heading back to your homes before the curfew starts."

"Oh, we are," Liviah said with a smile. The officer nodded slowly.

"I just couldn't help but notice that you were traveling north..." He eyed Oliver and Liviah's dirty, tattered clothing. They may as well have had *Blights* written across their foreheads in ink. Liviah faked a laugh.

"Oh, well, we aren't going to *our* home. My brother and I work on a night staff, and our patron lives in the Northern Quarters."

"Your brother?" the officer questioned. Oliver and Liviah were reminded just then how very different they looked from each other.

"Half-brother," she corrected. "We have the same father."

"I see. And which Lord is it that you work for?"

Liviah glanced at Oliver sideways. It was all over. The legionnaire would ask for their documentation as soon as they couldn't come up with an answer. When they had nothing to show him, he would arrest them on the spot.

"Etzra," Liviah said suddenly. Oliver was sure he looked shocked, but he did his best to maintain his composure. The legionnaire chuckled.

"You poor kids," he said. "That old man is a nightmare."

"So much talk of politics," Liviah replied. "I think he gets grouchier by the day." The two snickered as though they had just shared some inside joke, and Oliver did his best to laugh like he understood.

"Well, you best be off. Don't want to keep Lord Etzra waiting."

"Thank you, sir," Liviah said. She curtsied respectfully to the officer and then she and Oliver began to walk off.

"You know what!" the officer called after them. "It's getting late and Etzra's place is a decent walk away. Why don't I have Dax here escort you, so you don't have any trouble if you're out past curfew."

"Oh...thank you," Liviah said. "That would be great."

"Dax," the officer said, gesturing for the other legionnaire to step forward.

"Yes, Captain Landal," the boy replied oafishly. "Follow me." Dax stepped slowly and heavily towards the Northern Quarters, and Oliver and Liviah trailed a few paces behind.

"You kids have a good night," Captain Landal called after them.

"Thank you again, sir," Liviah replied. They walked behind Dax without a word. Oliver looked over at Liviah periodically, but she offered him no reassurance.

"So, you two work for Lord Etzra?" Dax said after walking in silence for some time.

"Yes," Liviah answered.

"I've heard he's something, but I bet it beats working for Captain Landal," Dax complained. "That man is such an arrogant little...*ugh*. I hate patrolling with him. I mean, you met him."

"Sounds awfully bad," Liviah said. "You know, we don't need you to escort us. Really, it's alright."

"It's no problem, miss."

"But I'm sure you have more important things…"

"Trust me, any reason to get away from Landal is a good one. I'm in no hurry to get back to him." It was all Oliver could do not to overcome with panic. Soon they would reach Etzra's home, whoever he was, and the game would be up.

The farther they traveled into the Northern Quarters, the larger the houses were. At first, they seemed relatively modest, but soon enough they had grown into large, multi-floored mansions. They walked past one house that was three stories tall with several smaller wings and towers jutting out from it. Outside, there was a large fountain of a mermaid spitting water, and beside the fountain was a flower garden. Oliver's shack would have fit inside that house at least three or four dozen times over. He wondered how many people lived there. Easily, it would fit twenty or thirty.

"Do you know who lives in that house?" Oliver asked. Liviah looked at him in surprise. Those were the first words he had uttered since they left Hawthorne Alley.

"Which one?" Dax said.

"The big one there, with the fountain."

"I think that's Lord and Madame Kyworth's home."

"Do they have any kids?" Oliver asked, still unable to take his eyes off the massive building.

"Two girls and two boys, I think, but I don't remember their names. Why?"

"Just wondering," Oliver said, and then he realized how suspicious his questions must have seemed. "It looked familiar, is all. I didn't know if maybe my father had worked there once."

Dax simply groaned in understanding. Another few minutes of walking went by and suddenly they came to a halt. "This is it, right?" the legionnaire asked, looking up at a thin, three-tiered building. "I can never keep all these houses straight."

"Yes," Liviah said, "this is it."

"Just in time. Curfew is about to start. You'd better get inside before the old man throws a fit." Neither Oliver nor Liviah moved.

"Well, thanks," Oliver said in hopes that Dax would go.

"We can take it from here," Liviah added, but the legionnaire was not persuaded. Oliver watched as his expression changed from friendly to suspicious. Dax was piecing it all together. He knew they were imposters.

"Get inside," Dax said, his tone suddenly much more malevolent. Oliver could see him tighten his grip around his reaper. Liviah walked up to the front door of Etzra's home and jiggled the knob.

"It's locked," she said.

"Knock then," Dax commanded. "Now."

Liviah knocked on the door three times. Oliver looked to the west. The sun was barely visible over the city now, in less than a half hour it would be curfew. The door swung open, revealing a hunch-backed old man in a nightgown.

"What do you want?" he barked with a voice as rough as gravel.

"Sorry to disturb you, Lord Etzra. We came to work, but we forgot our key and the door was locked," Liviah said.

"Work?" he said, stepping forward so that he was inches from Liviah's face.

"Lord Etzra, these two are claiming that they're a part of your night staff," Dax told the man. "Is that true? Do they work for you?"

Etzra looked from Liviah to Oliver. His long beard brushed his legs as he swung his head back and forth. Oliver could smell the man's supper still on his breath.

"Yes," he said at last. "They do. Now run along and leave me and my staff be before I tell your officer!"

"Oh...of course. Terribly sorry, sir. Good evening."

Oliver looked on in disbelief as Dax scurried off back towards the Market District. When he looked back at the house, Etzra was already making his way back inside with minuscule steps. He paused for a moment to look back.

"Well, come inside," he said to Oliver and Liviah. "I don't pay my staff to stand out in the cold gawking all night." Oliver and Liviah looked at each other, both wondering what in all the heavens had just happened. Liviah shrugged and walked inside.

Just through the door was an entryway with rooms branching off to the left and right. Straight ahead was a massive staircase leading to the second floor. The entryway was well lit with candle sconces, and stone statues of armored men protected its walls. Etzra turned left into what Oliver assumed must have been a drawing room. A long, wooden table sat in the middle of the floor, with silverware set at each of the chairs. Etzra's joints creaked and crackled as he sat down at the head of the table.

"Come, sit," he instructed. Liviah came to sit at the end beside him, and Oliver sat across from her. The wooden chair was heavier than it looked, and it screeched noisily on the floor as Oliver pulled it out. "Now tell me," Etzra said, "why is it you two want so badly to work for me that you're lying to legionnaires on the street about it? I hardly believe it's because I'm just that popular of an employer." He cackled by himself.

"I'm sorry, Lord Etzra," Liviah said, "but we were—"

"Save it, child," Etzra said with a wave of his hand. "I know what this is all about."

"You do?" Oliver asked.

"You lost track of time and ended up a little too far away from home, a little too late in the day. You didn't have time to make it back before curfew, so you told that legionnaire boy that you were supposed to be heading here instead."

"Yes," Liviah said, "that's exactly what happened."

"Well, I'm not an unkind man, whatever people may say about me. You can stay until you're allowed to leave in the morning. The curfew is a nonsense decree anyhow. Freedom being taken away is all that it is. If you asked me, I'd say the Legion is taking too much authority on this matter."

"Thank you," Liviah said. The old man stood up, and a pendant around his neck caught Oliver's eye as it reflected the torchlight. Oliver strained to see it more clearly. When the pendant stopped swinging, he was able to make out the shape of a golden crescent moon, inside of which was a smaller, silver ring.

"Sir!" Oliver said. Liviah kicked him under the table. "Er—my Lord."

"Yes?" Etzra said shortly.

"I was just wondering...your pendant. Where would someone get one of those?"

Etzra looked down at his chain and then quickly stuffed it in his shirt. "What's it matter, boy?" he snapped.

"I'm sorry. I didn't mean to offend you, sir—my Lord. It's just—"

"I have the same one," Liviah said. She felt around in her pocket and pulled out the pendant that her attacker had been wearing in Glassfall. She held it out so that Etzra could see. The old man placed his nose an inch away from the pendant as he examined it.

"Where did you get this?" he whispered.

"Tell me what it means first."

"Ah...I see."

"See what?

"It's not yours then?"

"No."

"Then its meaning is not any of your concern."

"Please, Lord Etzra," Oliver said. "People are in danger. We just want to find out who this could have belonged to."

The old man considered Oliver for a second, contemplating whether or not to trust this strange boy. Etzra sat down at the table again. "What is your name?"

"Oliver Hawthorne," Oliver answered nervously. He hoped Etzra wasn't going to look him up somewhere and find that he wasn't a citizen, but Etzra only looked to Liviah.

"Liviah Cain," she said.

"Cain..." Etzra said the name slowly, mulling it over. "I knew a Cain once."

"I know. Jonathon Cain. He's my dad."

"He give you that?" Etzra nodded to the pendant.

"No," Liviah said. "I took it from the man who killed him."

Etzra chewed on his tongue, taking in the words. "I'm sorry to hear that. Your father was a good man."

"My family was attacked, Lord Etzra. My house was burned to the ground, my parents are dead, my sister is missing...The man who did it was wearing this around his neck, and I have to find out who he was if I want to find my sister!" Lord Etzra clutched at his neck. He pulled his own pendant out of his shirt and turned it over in his hand. The silver circle spun independently of the crescent. "I thought it was connected to the Legion," Liviah said, "but it's not, is it?"

"Actually, it is," Etzra replied matter-of-factly.

"But it doesn't have the reaper!" Oliver said.

"I said it was connected to the Legion, I didn't say it was the Legion's insignia."

"So, what is it then?" Liviah asked.

Etzra picked up the teacup that was sitting on the table and brought it slowly to his mouth. He took a long slow drink, making a slurping sound as the tea passed through his lips. "This symbol," he said, pointing to his own necklace, "is not the insignia of the Legion, but the two are connected. This represents an ancient order that exists *within* the Legion."

"An order?" Oliver asked. "Like someone gave you that symbol to tell you what to do?"

Etzra shook his head. "Don't they teach you anything in schools? An order, boy—a group, a brotherhood. There is a small, selective order within the Legion that is made up of those who believe in its oldest tenants."

"Its oldest tenants?" Liviah asked.

"How much do you know about the start of the Legion?"

"Nothing," Oliver said in unison with Liviah's, "A fair bit." Etzra looked at the two of them, no doubt wondering where in the world two people so different had found each other.

"Nearly four hundred years ago," Etzra began, "there existed a group known as the Vanguard."

"The Vanguard? I've never heard of that," Liviah said.

"You wouldn't have," Etzra said. "The Vanguard was an underground society, created for the purpose of protecting the secrets of a group of magic users known as the Eclipse." Oliver glanced at Liviah, but she remained stoic as ever.

"The world existed in chaos," Etzra carried on. "There was no order, no peace. In this time, a select few individuals, who came to be known as the Eclipse, were given power by the heavens to see peace restored. They served their part in the wars that came, and in time, they achieved their goal. There were those, however, who wished to destroy the Eclipse—warlords and false kings, even dark, magical beasts—anyone who sought dominion over others or who thrived when the world was in chaos. The Eclipse were in danger, so a group came together and devoted themselves to protecting their identities and whereabouts."

"And that was the Vanguard?" Oliver asked.

"Yes. Over the centuries, however, the Eclipse slowly disappeared, until even the members of the Vanguard didn't know who they were anymore. Omnios began falling back into the chaos that they had saved it from in the first place. One Vanguard, a man called Baymore, decided it was no use waiting around for the Eclipse to show up and save us again, so he and his comrades developed a new group—one that was made up of ordinary men who wanted to make a difference in the world. They adopted a new symbol—the eclipsed sun seen on this pendant became a crescent moon, and the reaper was placed through it to represent the power of common men rather than magical. They became the new opposing force against the chaos, and they called themselves the Legion."

"So, what happened to the Vanguard?" Liviah asked.

"No, no, no. You're thinking of it all wrong," Eztra chided. "The Vanguard *is* the Legion. They simply changed the name and developed a new purpose. Only those who have been told the secrets of the Eclipse and sworn to protect them are a part of the Vanguard, but *all* Vanguards are a part of the Legion."

"Like squares and rectangles." Oliver muttered. Both Eztra and Liviah looked at him curiously. "You know, like how all squares are rectangles but not all rectangles are squares? It's the same thing, right? All Vanguards are legionnaires, but not all legionnaires are Vanguards."

"I suppose…" Etzra said, sounding somewhat annoyed. "I suppose that is correct. In any case, the number of Vanguards dwindled as the Eclipse disappeared. There simply wasn't anyone to protect anymore. But a group remained within the Legion, ready to serve should the Eclipse ever come back."

"And it still exists today?" Liviah asked. Etzra stroked his chin in thought.

"I know of only one member, other than myself, of course."

"And who would that be?"

"The Lord Commander, Kaliculous Kaeno."

CHAPTER FIFTEEN
LIVIAH

Liviah's jaw nearly fell to the floor. She sat back in her chair, soaking in what Etzra had told her.

"The Lord Commander..." Oliver said in disbelief. "Does that mean?"

"Yes," Liviah said. Her most horrible suspicions were now confirmed. "It's Kaeno. He's been behind everything." The corners of her eyebrows drooped as she spoke. Etzra regarded them curiously, but Liviah took no time to explain. She grabbed Oliver by the arm and pulled him away from the table.

"What do we do now?" Oliver asked in a hushed voice.

"We have to get to him. He may be the only one who knows where Juliana is."

"It's not that simple, Liviah. He's the Lord Commander! How do you suggest we just 'get to him'?"

"I don't know, alright! We just have to! He took my sister from me and killed my parents! I can't let him get away with that."

Oliver shook his head. "It will never work, Liviah. We'd be arrested or killed before we could get anywhere near him."

Liviah's lips trembled as she scowled at Oliver. He was so happy to help as long as it suited him, as long as he never put himself at risk. "If you don't want to, I'll just do it myself! I don't need you to help me, Oliver!"

"That's not what I'm saying."

"It's fine, Oliver! Just go back home to Nan. Juliana was never your problem anyway."

"We don't have to get Kaeno though!" Oliver said. "If you're right about Nan, then she'll know where Juliana is. We should just stick to the plan we had."

"But now I *know* that it was him! And he's just sitting there in his stupid palace getting away with it! Don't you see that he has to pay?"

"Don't you see that what you're talking about doing is insane? It's a suicide mission, Liviah."

They had raised their voices without realizing it, and now were both looking at Eztra, who had stood up from his chair and walked over to them. "I don't know what it is you're planning, Miss Cain—and I fear I do not want to—but you can't save your sister if you're in need of saving yourself."

"Come on, Oliver," Liviah said. "We should go."

"Wait," he said. "Lord Etzra, you're familiar with Withering Black, right?"

"Familiar? I lived through it! Terrible plague. Why do you speak of it?"

"I hate to ask any more of you, but…you wouldn't happen to know where we could get the cure for it, would you?"

"Of course I don't. Am I a healer?"

"Do you have anything that might help though?" Liviah asked.

"I might. But what possible need would you have for something like that?"

"An old friend," Oliver said nervously. Etzra seemed to consider him for a moment.

"I believe my hospitality has gone far enough," he said at last. "I'm afraid I must ask you to leave at once."

"No," Liviah said.

"I beg your pardon?" Etzra scoffed.

"You must help us. As a sworn member of the Vanguard you are obligated to help an Eclipse, and I am one."

"My girl, don't think you can fool me with…" Suddenly every piece of china on the table began to float, and Lord Etzra marveled at Liviah. She turned her hands around her body, emitting streaks of blue light that sent the china spinning around the room. The china moved faster and faster with each passing second and then suddenly, dropped to the floor. "In all my years…I had my doubts at times, of course, but to see you in real life!"

"Help us this one last time and you'll never see us or hear from us again," Liviah promised. "We can't save my sister without the cure."

Etzra nodded slowly, then hobbled out of the room. He returned quite some time later with a beaker full of some thick, bluish-colored liquid. "This works well for most symptoms, but if, gods forbid, your friend really has Withering Black…Well, this will not be enough to truly cure it."

"I understand," Oliver said as he took the beaker. Liviah flicked her hand and the china that was scattered about the room replaced itself neatly on the table.

"Thank you, Lord Etzra," she said as they left his home. "We appreciate all that you've done for us."

"I will forget all that you have said here tonight, Miss Cain, for the love I bore your father and my honor as a Vanguard. But do not think that you may call upon me for your every need and I will blindly obey. I am loyal to the Legion above all other things."

Liviah straightened her back. "I understand," she said. "Goodnight, Lord Etzra."

* * *

The moment they were back inside the shack, Oliver unstopped the medicine and poured it into Nan's mouth. "I suppose now we wait," he said and slumped down onto his cot. "Are you okay, Liviah?"

Liviah shot him a quick look. "Of course I am. We got the medicine, didn't we?"

"I know, but, with everything Etzra told us…"

"I'm fine, Oliver. I'm glad that I know who's really behind it all."

"All that Eclipse stuff was pretty cool though, huh? 'Created by the heavens to protect the world from chaos.'"

"You didn't really believe all of that, did you?"

"Didn't you?"

"There's no such thing as the gods or the heavens or whatever you want to call them, Oliver. The universe didn't give me the power to protect people. I wasn't chosen to do something special. I was just born this way."

"I don't know. I think people are born for a reason."

"Then you're even more naïve than I thought you were."

"What is your problem with me?" Oliver said. "I've done nothing but be nice to you since the moment we met. I've done everything I could to help you, and all you do is snap at me whenever I say something you don't like."

"Forgive me if I'm not in the best mood, Oliver! I just found out that the Lord Commander of the bloody *Legion* is after me and my sister!"

"Well, you weren't really all that nice to me before we knew that either!"

"You're just so...*much*. Acting like everything is so great. It's not!"

"I just wanted us to be friends, Liviah. That's all I ever wanted."

"Well I didn't come here to make friends! I came here to get Juliana back."

The two did not speak for quite a while after that. They sat in silence, waiting for Nan to wake. Liviah had no idea how much time had passed since they had returned with the medicine. It felt like hours, days even, but the sun had not risen, and Nan had not stirred.

"*Ugh*, how long is this going to take?" Liviah griped. Oliver shot her a dirty look. What was his problem? Didn't he understand that she was desperate to find out where Juliana was? Why wasn't he just as anxious for Nan to wake up?

"You don't even know for sure if she is an augur," Oliver said. Whatever Oliver might think, Liviah was certain that he was wrong. She had been around her Uncle Philius enough times to recognize the mumblings of an augur having a vision when she heard them, and that's exactly what Nan had been doing.

Liviah opened her mouth to respond when the look on Oliver's face made her stop. She looked down to where he was holding Nan's hand in his own.

"Her fingers moved," he whispered, and suddenly Nan's soft breath grew much louder.

"Ollie...is that... you?" Nan said weakly.

"Nan!" Oliver said, "It's me, Nan! I'm here!"

"Where are we, Ollie?

"You're in the shack Nan. You're home. Everything's alright. You've been sick, but you're better...for now, at least."

"You said something about Eclipse," Liviah interjected, unable to wait any longer. "Do you remember that?"

"Who's that?" Nan asked.

"That's Liviah," Oliver said.

"Liviah?"

"She's my, uh—she helped me get you some medicine."

"Come here, sweet girl, let me see you." Liviah looked doubtfully at Oliver, who only gestured towards Nan and nodded his insistence. Reluctantly, Liviah leaned down and guided Nan's outstretched hand to her face. "My, oh my..." Nan said as she felt Liviah's features. "You are a true beauty."

Discomfort crept across Liviah's face, and she felt blood rush to her cheeks. She quickly pulled away from Nan. She was thankful to have a dark enough complexion that Oliver couldn't see her blushing.

"About what you said..." Liviah asked again, "*Taken, missing, fort,* and *eclipse.* Do you remember anything like that?"

Nan took in a deep, shaky breath. "Faintly, my dear. It feels like a dream, except it's as if it were one I had years and years ago."

"Can you tell it to me?"

"There was a fort, yes. I do remember that. But it wasn't complete, like it was still being built. It was full of Legion soldiers and...children. Yes, children, seven or eight of them, I believe. In fact, I think you were there, dear...It was so strange to see again. I haven't seen in quite some time." Silence filled the tiny shack as Liviah took in the words of Nan's dream. She knew it now more than ever—Nan was an augur.

"Do you know where the fort was? Does it exist in Omnios?"

"Let me think...It was north I believe...Yes, north of Maldenney."

"Wait a minute," Liviah said. "I know what you're talking about! I remember Ramsey saying something about a fort called the Bastion that the Lord Commander was having built north of the city! He said it was just two days travel. That's got to be it!" She jumped to her feet without a moment's hesitation.

"Hold on a second," Oliver said. "The what?"

"The Bastion! Ramsey said the Lord Commander sent him there to check on its construction progress, and that was just before Juliana went missing. I'm sure that's where they're holding her. I've got to go before it's too late!" Liviah flicked her hand towards the door and it swung open. Oliver jumped as it slammed against the wall.

"Wait!" he called after her as she ran out into the alley. "You can't just go! How can you even be sure that's where she is? We need to come up with a plan first!" Liviah didn't stop to listen. She was sprinting down the cobblestone, on her way to Juliana. She didn't have the time or the patience to wait and explain to Oliver, and he would only slow her down.

She came out of the alley and took a sharp left turn, heading west through the Blights. Her heart had never beat so fast in her entire life. Juliana was miles away, two days' journey, but the small sliver of hope she had just been given made Liviah feel as though her sister was right in front of her. Over the wall of the city, Liviah could see the first glimpse of sunlight rising. If she could reach the front gates before curfew ended, she should be able to make it out of the city without much trouble.

Liviah rounded a corner and skidded to a halt. Just in front of her were three figures, huddled in a group around a lantern. She back-peddled slowly so that she was hidden in the shadows cast by the houses around her. Two of the figures were legionnaires, but the third had on plain steel armor.

"Where have you been? We've been looking for you all night!" one of the legionnaires said. His skin was dark, darker even then Liviah's, while the other was as pale as moonlight.

"I couldn't find the streets," the non-legionnaire whispered back. He held his helmet at his side, revealing his strong jawline and dark, swooping hair. His features flickered in the light of the lantern. He was quite attractive.

"Curfew is almost over, Prodigy!"

"We'll just have to move quickly then."

"Where are we going?"

"Just a bit farther south. When I was there with Theo, the door was locked."

"So we'll break it down, no problem."

"What if we run into one of the curfew patrols?" the other legionnaire asked. He was lankier and more awkward than the others, and there was a tone of fear in his voice.

"Then you'll have to cover for me," the non-legionnaire said. "This will only work if you're *both* with me. If I can't count on you…"

"You know I'm with you, Ridley," the lanky one said quickly. The boy named Ridley nodded and looked to the other legionnaire.

"Sayben?" he asked.

"Oh, would you relax? I'm not gonna do anything."

"Good. Now, once we reach the alley we have to be on full alert. This girl has put up a fight with plenty of legionnaires so far. Don't underestimate her."

"We don't need a lecture from the guy who's never seen her before. We know what to expect."

Liviah covered her mouth to silence her breathing and shrank deeper into the shadows as the boys walked past her. They must have figured out she had been hiding in the alley somehow. Only she wasn't there now. Instead of her, they would find Oliver and Nan.

She shook it out of her head. Liviah couldn't let *anything* get in the way of her saving Juliana. She knew Oliver wouldn't stand a chance against the legionnaires, but there was nothing she could do to save him. The legionnaires were between her and him. If she went back now they would both be captured, and then who would save Juliana?

The thought of her sister pained Liviah as it always did in times like this—times when she knew exactly what choice Juliana would make, no matter what it may cost her. But Liviah had never been the caring one of the pair. Juliana was the lover and look at where it had gotten her. Liviah was the fighter; she could make the tough choices.

The bell tower struck again. There was one hour until dawn and the end of the curfew. It was enough time to reach the front gates before the crowds came out. Liviah looked back at the legionnaires as they made their way to Hawthorne Alley.

"I'm sorry," she whispered, "but it's now or never."

CHAPTER SIXTEEN
OLIVER

Oliver knew the moment she left the shack that Liviah was never going to come back. Why would she? She had her answers. Oliver was just a means to an end, he realized. He had been foolish to believe he meant anything more her than that. She wasn't so desperate for friendship like he was. She still had friends, a family even. She never needed him, not the way he needed her, anyway. He stepped back inside the shack where Nan was lying quietly on her cot.

"What was all that fuss about, Ollie?"

"Nothing," Oliver said as he helped Nan prop herself up into a seated position. "Liviah left is all."

"Oh, Ollie, it's alright to be upset."

"I'm not upset. I'm glad to be rid of her, really. I'm just happy to see that you're doing better."

"Much better. Though I am wondering where you managed to find this medicine…"

Oliver smiled half-heartedly. "It's a long story. I'll tell you another time." He pushed his cot up beside Nan's and curled up next to her. "There's something I wanted to ask you, actually."

"What's that?"

"Well, it's probably stupid, but your dream…Liviah thinks it was about where her sister is being held captive."

"Why would she think that?"

"She thought you were an augur, but that's ridiculous, right? I mean, you wouldn't have kept that a secret from me, would you?

"Oh, Ollie, people have been putting their faith into dreams long before you and I were born. I don't know that it means they ever come true. Besides, what good would there be in me keeping secrets from you?"

Oliver smiled. "You're right, Nan. I'm sorry. I just had to ask."

"Oh, it's alright, Ollie." Suddenly, Nan's expression intensified. Her hand moved to grab Oliver's.

"What?" he asked.

"*Shh...*Do you hear that?" she whispered.

"Hear what?"

"Listen."

The sound of armor clinking outside the shack answered Oliver's question. His eyes shot to the handle of the door. He had been so preoccupied with Liviah storming out that he had forgotten to place the stick back in to bar it from opening.

"The door," he whispered to Nan. She nodded her understanding and released his hand. As quietly as he could, Oliver rose and reached for the table where her old cane was sitting. He wrapped his fingers around the wooden stick and took a hesitant step towards the door. Gradually, he reached towards the handle and slid the cane between it and the wall. It was almost there.

BANG! The door of his shack burst open, knocking Oliver back and causing him to drop the cane. Before he could even begin to comprehend what was happening, he was yanked violently off the ground and dragged through the door.

When he entered the alleyway, he was blinded by the light of the just-rising sun. He was placed on his knees, and his hands were bound with rope behind his head. He heard Nan wail in pain as she too was dragged into the alley and flung to the ground beside him.

After a moment, Oliver gained his bearings and made sense of what was going on. One legionnaire stood looking down on him, and another pulled down on the back of his hair, forcing him to look up. Their armor gleamed in the sun, reflecting its light onto the walls of the abandoned hospital. The metal was unscathed and shiny as if it was brand new. The symbol of the Legion decorated their breastplates. Their helmets covered all but a T-shape of their faces, revealing their eyes, nose, and a strip stretching down to their chins. There was a third boy there, wearing steel armor that did not match the others.

"I knew you were working with her!" the boy said. Something about him struck Oliver. Why did he feel like he knew this boy somehow? It was an odd phenomenon for someone like Oliver, who did not meet many new people. Perhaps he had seen him on their way to Etzra's house? In the Market District? Oliver racked his brain. Where, where?

As if on cue, the boy removed his helmet, revealing his broken nose. "Remember me?" he snarled. Oliver recognized him immediately as the legionnaire from Elenore's Emporium. He punched Oliver in the face. Blood began to spill out of his nose. "I can't believe you were here all along," the boy laughed. "I had been angry at Theo for dragging me down this disgusting alley before, but I guess now I owe him my thanks. Where is the girl?"

"I-I don't know what you're talking about," Oliver said woozily. His head was spinning from the punch.

"I won't hesitate to kill you, you filthy grudder! Now tell me where you've hidden her!"

"*Ridley*," the legionnaire behind Oliver said with wide eyes.

"What? What else have I got to lose? What else can Kaeno take from me? Now I'll ask you again, grudder, where is the girl?"

And there she was! Down the alley, ducked behind a pile of garbage. Liviah nodded slowly to Oliver and pressed a finger to her lips. He dropped his gaze to the ground. "Alright," he said to Ridley. "Alright, I'll tell you where she is. Please just don't hurt us. We don't have anything to do with her."

Ridley hoisted Oliver up by the shirt collar. "Tell me!"

"She's in there," Oliver lied, nodding towards the back door of the abandoned hospital.

"You're lying!"

"I'm not! I promise!"

"The doors are still boarded up. How did she get inside without undoing them?"

"One of the windows."

Just then a loose cobblestone came flying through the air, straight into the side of one of the legionnaires. "Agh!" the soldier yelled.

The two other boys spiraled around in search of the flying stone's origin. A dozen other stones soared at them out of nowhere, and the boys dove to the ground to avoid them. Oliver saw his chance and took it. He leapt onto the back of the second legionnaire and wrapped the rope that

- 152 -

bound his hands around the soldier's neck. The boy collapsed to his knees and rolled on the ground as he tried to get Oliver off.

"Ridley—help!" he gasped.

* * *

RIDLEY

Ridley glanced quickly at Fletcher. "Get him off you!" he yelled, keeping his attention focused on the alley. The girl was down there somewhere—his ticket back into the Legion was down there somewhere. She *had* to be.

A flash of blue came whizzing by Ridley's head. It collided with the wall of the shack and it dispersed into sparks. Ridley held his sword at his side and readied himself. Out of the corner of his eye, he saw Sayben rise and pull the boy off Fletcher.

"Will you handle him, Fletcher?" Sayben said. "We'll get the girl."

"Come out and fight me, you coward!" Ridley yelled down the alley. "You can't hide forever!"

The girl rose from behind a heap of trash and stood tall in the center of the alley. She was not what he had pictured. In his mind the word 'grudder' had always elicited the image of someone frail, dirty, and weak. This girl was very much the opposite. She was strong.

Ridley narrowed his eyes. That didn't matter. He charged at her with the sword, and she ran back at him. Just before they met, the girl jumped up into the air and cleared the top of Ridley's head. He strained his neck to follow her movement. She landed on the ground near Sayben with a powerful crash of blue energy that sent him stumbling backwards. Sayben scrambled to retrieve his reaper, but as he reached for the weapon, it rose into the air. The girl flicked her outstretched hand and the reaper flew up to the top of the wall.

Ridley let out a cry as he charged for the girl again. She sent a blue bolt towards his feet, and they were swept out from under him. Ridley fell onto his stomach. "Sayben!" he yelled as he pushed himself up.

Sayben took the reaper from Fletcher, who was merely holding the grudder boy out of the fight. Ridley and Sayben stood together near the back of the alley, staring down the grudder girl. She shot repeating bursts of blue light from her hands. One caught Ridley in the shoulder plate, and he felt as though he had been hit with a hammer. Sayben dodged them until one came flying at his face. He raised his forearm to block it, and his gauntlet broke into pieces.

Ridley and Sayben advanced on the grudder until they had pushed her back into the wall. Each of them grabbed one of her arms and held her down so that she couldn't cast any more spells at them.

"Liviah!" the grudder boy yelled. He broke free of Fletcher's grip and ran towards them.

"Leave him!" Ridley ordered Fletcher. "It's the girl we need!"

Fletcher grabbed the boy and pulled him down by his shirt. He ran over to help Sayben and Ridley, but the girl, Liviah, aimed her hand at the dagger clipped to Fletcher's belt. Before Ridley realized what had happened, the dagger went flying into Sayben's arm. Sayben screamed as it pierced deep into the muscle, and Liviah broke from his grasp. She raised her free hand to Ridley's chest and shot a spell at him at point-blank range. His armor cracked under the force, and he was thrown back onto the ground.

Sayben pulled the dagger from his arm and swung it at Liviah. She dodged the stroke, but he punched her in the face with his other hand. The grudder boy ran at Sayben and Liviah to help, but Fletcher tackled him before he reached the quarreling pair.

"Stay out of this, Oliver!" Liviah screamed.

"I don't want to have to hurt you," Fletcher told him. "We only want her!"

"No!" the boy named Oliver yelled back. He thrashed around in Fletcher's arms. "Get off me!"

Ridley stood with his sword still in hand and started at Liviah. She was backing towards the shack to avoid strokes from Sayben's blade, occasionally sending spells his way. Ridley let out a yell as he ran at her. She pushed both hands towards Sayben and he was thrown away from her. She turned to do the same to Ridley, but he felt only a small force as the spell hit him. She must have been getting tired, Ridley realized.

Another spell hit Fletcher, who went rolling off Oliver and into a wall. Ridley jumped towards Liviah and chopped down with his sword like an axe. She put up a hand to deflect the blow, and Ridley's attack redirected as if he had hit an invisible shield. He swung again, and again Liviah blocked it. Attack. Deflect. Attack. Deflect. Ridley could feel her resistance growing weaker with each swing of his blade. She stepped back unsteadily as he advanced.

"Oliver!" she called. "Get out of here!"

"I'm not leaving!"

"Oliver, GO!"

"I can't leave Nan!"

Ridley dropped his shoulder and slammed it into Liviah, knocking her to the ground. She looked up at him and spit blood. It splattered onto his face and armor, but he didn't bother wiping it away. With both hands on the hilt of his sword, Ridley swung down. The blade suspended in mid-air, just inches above Liviah's chest. He put one hand on the blade and pushed down. Liviah was pinned to the ground. He could feel her energy fading as he pressed.

"No!" Oliver screamed.

Sayben ran to Ridley's side. This was it. Ridley finally had her.

* * *

LIVIAH

Liviah knew it was over. She could hold off one of them maybe, but not two. The harder she resisted Ridley, the more she felt herself weaken. Her vision started to go hazy, and everything sounded like she was hearing it underwater. She closed her eyes and waited for the final blow.

"Fight them, Liviah!" she heard Oliver's voice say. "Fight them!" She opened her eyes and locked with his. "You're stronger than they are! You can do it!"

"Shut up!" The legionnaire who held him yelled.

"Think of your sister! Juliana needs you."

It was like he had popped a bubble inside of her. Suddenly, a rush of power surged its way through Liviah's entire body. The feeling trickled down to her fingertips and toes until every part of her seemed to buzz with it. It was like an intense emotion, but greater—as if all of the joy, sadness, excitement, and anger she had ever felt was being washed out, and only power was left behind. For a moment, it was almost blissful, but just as quickly as it came, it was gone. Something snapped inside of Liviah, and a deep pain erupted in her head. She let out a tremendous scream. Faintly, she heard Oliver's voice say something. What it was, she couldn't tell. She pushed back against Ridley with all of her strength, and everything went white.

What seemed like hours went by before Liviah could see again. The alley was in shambles. The corner of the hospital had collapsed. Debris flooded the street and dust filled the air. The front of the shack had caved in, and the door was broken in two. The legionnaires had been thrown into the city wall, which had crumbled to less than half its height. Ridley was lying on the rubble and Oliver was hunching over Nan, his back covered in dust and rocks. Liviah felt woozy, and her head pounded with every beat of her heart. Oliver looked at her and called something, but she couldn't hear him.

"What?" she thought she said, but even her own voice wasn't audible.

"Are you alright?" she heard his muffled voice say. He ran over to her and helped her up.

"I'm—I'm fine," she said wearily. "Come on...let's get out of here..."

"Can you walk?"

"Y-yeah..."

"Okay, come on. Let's get Nan."

"You're not going anywhere," Ridley said. He rose from the rubble, standing behind Nan. His face was caked in dirt and blood. His once perfect hair was tangled and matted to his forehead. A wild ferocity loomed in his eyes as he held Nan's body close to his own, a dagger in his hand.

"No!" Oliver yelled. He ran towards Ridley.

"Stop!" Ridley yelled, pressing the dagger close to her throat. "Give yourself up and I won't hurt her," he said to Liviah.

"Take me instead!" Oliver pleaded. *"Please!"* Ridley didn't acknowledge Oliver's plea. Liviah knew it was useless. He only wanted her.

"I'm not...worth it," Nan croaked. Her voice wasn't scared. She sounded calm.

"Shut up!" Ridley said and shook her violently. Liviah gulped. She could feel Oliver's eyes on her, begging her to do something, *anything*. "Well? What will it be?" Ridley demanded.

Liviah looked at Oliver. He was creeping sideways, eyeing something on the ground. What was it? Slowly, he bent down and picked it up—one of the legionnaire's reapers. His eyes met Liviah's. With the slightest shake of her head, she tried to tell him not to do what he was thinking, but it was too late. In a split-second, he had grabbed the reaper and charged at Ridley.

Ridley was so focused on Liviah he almost didn't notice. Her turned at the last second and pointed his knife at Oliver. Without thinking, Liviah leapt forward as hard as she could. She soared towards Oliver, colliding with him as he was mid-stride. Ridley started towards them, but Liviah was too quick. She wrapped one arm around Oliver's torso and shot her free hand towards the ground. They flew into the air, just clearing the collapsed portion of the city wall. Oliver screamed and kicked as she dragged him away.

"No! Nan!" he shouted. "Nan!" They landed in the grass outside the city, and Liviah took off at a shaky run. When she had broken far enough into the foliage, she collapsed onto the dirt. Oliver came sprinting after her. "What are you doing?" he screamed. "We have to go back, now!"

"We would—have died—if we had—stayed there." She was gasping for air as she spoke, hardly able to breathe.

"Now Nan is going to die!"

"Ridley would have—killed you both. There was nothing—I could do for her. It was over. He had us beat."

Oliver shook his head vehemently. "That's not true!" he said. "You just don't care. You *never* cared about helping Nan! You only used her to get what you wanted and then you tossed her aside. You don't care about anyone but yourself!"

Liviah sat upright and glared at Oliver. Suddenly, she had a newfound strength. "Who are you—to say what I care about? You don't know me! We just met!"

"I know you well enough."

"Is that so?"

"Even I can see through the little act you put on, Liviah."

"*Act?* You think I put on an *act?*"

"The tough girl who's not afraid of anything? Yeah, I *know* that's an act. Because I know that deep down, you're just scared. You're scared of being left alone, so you don't let anyone in! Nobody can leave you if you don't have anyone in the first place, right? Now, thanks to you, I'm alone!"

"You think *I'm* scared? You're the one who lived at the end of an alley for your entire life because you were too afraid to leave it. You're scared of everything, Oliver! Of them, of me!"

"I am not scared of you!"

"Well maybe you should be!" Liviah said. Her hands blazed blue and she stepped up into Oliver's face. "Maybe I am a monster! Look at me, Oliver! Maybe I'm everything they said I was! I don't know! But at least I know I'm not like you! I'm *not* afraid to live!"

"I'm not afraid to live!"

"You've watched thirteen years disappear before your eyes because you're afraid of anything that's different from your miserable grudder life!"

"Shut up! You have no idea what that's like!"

"And you have no idea what it's like to have your family taken from you!" Liviah realized what she said and stopped. She stepped back from him and the magic at her fingertips dissipated. "Oliver, I'm—"

"Well, thanks for teaching me what that's like, Liviah. You should just go. You got what you wanted from us. You can find you sister now." He turned and started walking in the direction of the main gate.

"I didn't mean to say that. Oliver, where are you going?"

"I'm going back!" he called over his shoulder. "I'm going to get Nan."

"You can't go back. Oliver, stop!" He kept on walking. "I said stop!" Liviah sent a spell flying in his direction, but it whizzed by him and smacked a tree instead.

"Don't you dare use magic on me!"

"Then stop acting stupid! If you go back there now, Ridley is going to kill you."

"Stop acting like you care, Liviah!"

"Why are you so certain I don't? I came back for you, didn't I? I could have gone on to find Juliana! I could have let the legionnaires take you, but I didn't! I stuck my neck out for you!"

"Why did you come back?" Oliver screamed at her. "You saw them before you left, right? That's how you knew they were there. And you left anyway! So why come back at all?"

"Because if I left you behind, Juliana would never forgive me for it!" Liviah answered. Oliver fell silent and they both stared at each other. "If I find her, she'll want to know how, and if she found out I left someone else behind to save her...she'd blame herself and she'd never forgive me for it." She watched as Oliver's anger dissipated into sadness, and his aggression faded to exhaustion. Tears cut streaks through the dirt on his cheeks despite his clear efforts to hold them back. Liviah and Oliver stared each other in the eyes, neither daring to blink. It was a new look for Oliver, not the same daunted one Liviah had grown so used to seeing in him. "I can't let you go back," she said again.

"Liviah."

"No, Oliver," she said. She charged up a spell in her hand to show him that she meant it. "You're coming with me."

"Fine." Oliver broke the gaze and marched past Liviah. "I just hope your sister's not like you." Liviah watched as he disappeared deeper into the foliage.

"No," she said softly to no one. "She's nothing like me."

CHAPTER SEVENTEEN
RIDLEY

"Where are they going?" Ridley asked. The stench of the Ambersen's moldy old cellar filled his nose. He had been down there only a handful of times in his life. Once to fetch a barrel of ale for his father when they had house guests over, once when he and Theo had broken a vase and were hiding from Elma's wrath, and once during his extensive years of legionnaire training, when his father made him spend a full day and night down there without food or water to strengthen his mental fortitude.

"I'm afraid I don't know," a feeble voice replied. There was a certain brazenness in the tone that infuriated Ridley beyond all reason. Under normal circumstances, he wouldn't have put up with it. He would beat the prisoner in question until they were happy to cooperate, but in this case his prisoner looked to be on her last leg.

"Liar!" Ridley yelled. "You were in that shack with them, which means you heard their plans. Now, I *won't* ask again; where are they going?"

"You're an angry boy," the old woman said. "That much anger is no good for someone your age. Takes all the fun out of being young."

"If you don't tell me what I want to know, I'll—"

"You'll what?" the woman chuckled. "Kill me? I'm well on my way, boy. Old, sick, and blind. Can death really be worse than this?"

Ridley wondered if the woman knew how much her smile angered him. An enemy with nothing to lose was the worst kind to face. He had no leverage he could use against the woman because there was nothing that he could threaten to take from her. He paced across the room, and her milky white eyes seemed to follow him. In fact, they *were* following him. Ridley took a startled step away from the chair she was tied to and walked slowly back to the other side of the room. There it was again! Her eyes, blank and unfocused as they may have been, were following him as he moved. Slowly, Ridley bent in close. He waved his hand in front of her face. Nothing. Ridley curled up his lip in disgust. The old hag was toying with him, listening to his movements and turning her head to follow them.

Ridley walked to a table on the side of the room and picked up a dagger. He unsheathed it slowly, careful to make sure the noise between the sliding metals could be heard. The woman's head jerked towards the sound of the noise. "Know what that sound is?" Ridley asked.

"Sharpening your butter knife?"

"Maybe you're right. Death would be a mercy to you, so perhaps I'll make you beg me for it."

"Oh, hush, child. All that doom and gloom won't be necessary. I'll tell you where they're going, but I'm afraid it won't do you any good."

"Why not?" Ridley snapped. "Where is it?"

"A Legion fort north of here. The Bastion she called it."

"The Bastion? But that's...What are they doing there?"

"The girl believes her sister is being held prisoner there."

"Held by whom?"

The grudder woman leaned in close, too close for Ridley's comfort. The stench of her warm breath swirled around in his face. She was disgusting.

"I think you and I both know the answer to that," she whispered. Ridley stepped back.

"The girl, what kind of power does she have?"

"Far more than she realizes, I think. She has magic greater than you and I could imagine."

"The boy? What about him?"

The woman laughed. "Oliver..." she said, though it seemed to be more to herself than to Ridley. "Oliver is a special boy, more powerful than you'll ever be."

"Quit speaking in riddles, you filthy animal! I want to know if the boy is like *her*."

"No, he's not like her. But I wouldn't underestimate him if I were you."

Ridley looked up and down at the woman. How had this crazy grudder survived so long? He started towards the cellar stairs.

"Ridley," the woman said. Ridley jumped. How had she known his name? He turned slowly to look at her. "I should warn you. You won't like what you find at the Bastion."

"And that is?"

"Yours to discover, if you so choose. Just don't say I didn't warn you. There are fouler things in this world than death."

Ridley didn't want to spend another moment with that old woman. He practically ran up the stairs and shut the cellar door. He glanced into the living room. Sayben and Fletcher were out cold on the two couches, being tended to by Elma.

"Ridley!"

Ridley turned towards the back door. He had hardly noticed his father standing there, still wearing his fur overcoat. "Father? What are you—"

"Your mother just told me that you showed up at the house with two injured friends and some old woman. Now what's all this about?"

"I know where the grudders are going."

"Damn it, Ridley enough with this grudder nonsense! You said that you could get Theo back!"

"I can! I will. I just have to go to the Bastion."

"The Bastion?" A look of surprise spread across his father's face.

"Yes, why? What does that mean, Father?"

"Nothing, nothing. That's good. We have men stationed there. I'll send word to have them find the grudders and return them to us quietly."

"No!" Ridley yelled. His father looked appalled.

"I beg your pardon?" he said with malice in his tone.

"I have to be the one to find the girl."

"Ridley, come now! See reason. I've given you your chance and you failed! Now this is no time for you to play the hero with some foolish act of bravery!"

"That's just it. The Lord Commander took Theo because *I* failed. If I'm not the one who makes it right, we may never see Theo again."

"Ridley, if, as you believe, the Lord Commander took Theodor only to test you, then your brother is not in any real danger."

"But Kaeno wants to see if I'll follow through on his orders!"

His father paused thoughtfully for a moment. "Ah, I see what's going on here," he said. "Your concern is not only returning your brother to us. You want to regain your favor with the Lord Commander. You want back in the Legion." Ridley froze, unable to think of what to say.

"Father, I..."

"Don't apologize, Ridley. You're putting the mission first. That is what I trained you to do. You really are the perfect soldier." His father grabbed him by both shoulders. It almost seemed as if he was finally...proud? But then why did Ridley feel so horrible?

"Thank you, Father."

"But you won't be going."

"But Father!" Suddenly, a hand caught Ridley's face, and he felt the familiar sting that always came when he angered his father.

"Do not talk back to me, Ridley! That is my decision, and my decision is final! I'll send word to the men at the Bastion and to Lord Commander Kaeno. Now go up to your room. I will notify you when we have news of your brother."

Ridley marched up the wooden staircase to his room. He slammed the door behind him. He wanted to go back down the stairs and punch his father in the face. Didn't he understand that this was Ridley's one chance to get his life back? He looked into his mirror. His entire body was still covered in dust and dirt from the events of the early morning. Ridley removed his shirt. His torso was bloody where his damaged breastplate had dug into it. He pressed two fingers to his lower chest, counting his bruised ribs. One, two on the left. One, two, three, four on the right. His body ached with every movement.

Ridley watched through his window as the day passed by. He heard the sounds of the city die down as the curfew grew closer. It was odd that the Lord Commander hadn't ended the curfew now that the girl had left. Perhaps he didn't know yet.

Eventually, night fell, and Ridley collapsed in his bed. He wondered what he was going to do when they had Theo back. The perfect soldier...that's what his father had called him, and he was never going to be a soldier again. The perfect soldier...

Ridley sat up in his bed. A single thought was swirling around in his mind. He *wasn't* the perfect soldier, not if he didn't finish the mission. He was placing the orders of his father over the orders of the Lord Commander. Maybe his father was right; going to fight the girl again was risky. But if Ridley was going to live up to what everyone wanted him to be — what his father thought he was — wouldn't he have to try?

He glanced at the broken breastplate leaning against the wall. He needed new armor and a new weapon. He walked out of his room, went down the hallway, and knocked on the door of his parents' bedroom. "Father?" he said softly. No answer. Ridley glanced down the staircase into the main floor of his house. There was no sign of his father or mother. He reached for the door handle and hoped it wasn't locked.

Twist.

Click.

Open.

Ridley was in. He bolted over to his father's wardrobe and pushed aside his clothes. Behind them, in a glass case, was his father's own legionnaire armor. It was not the same glittering gold that the Legion was so known for now, but an incomparable black. It was so black, in fact, that it looked to Ridley as if the metal itself was radiating darkness.

The glass case creaked as he pulled it open. Careful not to make another sound, Ridley removed each piece of armor and strapped it on. A thin layer of dust coated the metal. How long had it been since his father had worn it last?

Ridley took a few steps around the room, testing his mobility. The armor fit like a glove. His father's reaper leaned up against the back of the wardrobe. Ridley picked it up and twirled it in his hand. Its weight was greater than the reapers that the legionnaires carried now, but the balance was just the same. Mounted on the opposite wall was a shield that matched the armor. Ridley pulled the shield down, doing his best to keep quiet.

He heard his father raise his voice downstairs, and his mother yelled back. They were both on edge, Ridley couldn't imagine what they would do if they caught him sneaking out wearing his father's armor. He pushed the bedroom window open and looked down. Their house sat on a slight hill, and Ridley was on the second story. A jump that far in all this armor could break his legs.

There was no choice but to sneak down the stairs that led from the second floor to the kitchen. Once he was down there, he peeked around the corner to see his father in the living room drafting a message as fast as he could. Not wanting to waste a second of his opportunity, Ridley darted through the kitchen. It wasn't until he was halfway to the door that he noticed Elma there. She watched him in his father's armor, a look of fear in her eyes.

"Elma!" Ridley's father called. Ridley ducked behind the counter where Elma was chopping vegetables just before his father entered the room.

"Yes, Lord Ambersen," she said.

"Send a falcon to the Bastion with this letter at once!"

"Right away."

"And when you've finished, we'll be in need of some supper. It's quite late, and I think a bit of food would do us all good. I'll go and get Ridley from his room."

Elma glanced down at Ridley. Their eyes locked for just a second. "I already offered him something to eat," she said suddenly. "He said he wasn't hungry."

"Nonsense! He hasn't eaten all day."

"That's what I told him. He said he hasn't got much of an appetite."

"Fine, then. If he wants to sit in his room and pout like a child, so be it. It's no wonder the Legion let him go."

"Why don't you join Madame Ambersen in the dining room? I'll bring supper out as soon as I've sent this letter."

"Very, well. Alana, you needn't worry," his father's voice began to trail off. "Theodor will be returned to us very soon."

Ridley held his breath until the sound of his father's footsteps had gone. He rose and looked at Elma, and he could tell that she understood his gratitude. He silently opened the back door and ran out into the night, leaving Elma and his parents behind.

Ridley ran down the streets as fast as the armor would allow, making his way past the Legionnaire Academy. He stopped for a moment as he went by, then ran into the Academy's stables. Waiting for him there was his father's palomino horse that he had left behind the day before. The horse whinnied as Ridley approached, recognizing him as a friend. Ridley patted the horse affectionately and fed him a sugar cube, then saddled the steed up and set off at a gallop towards the east city gate. The legionnaires on guard stopped him as he approached.

"Halt! What are you doing out after curfew? This gate is for Legion officer use only!"

Ridley kept his helmet on. "Who do you think you're addressing?" he called back from atop his horse. He lowered his voice so that it was deeper than normal. "I am Lord Ramsey Ambersen on official business for the Lord Commander."

"Lord Ambersen, my apologies! We didn't recognize you in your armor."

"No matter, just open the gate."

"Right away, my Lord."

The soldiers turned massive iron gears, winding the chains that opened the gate. Ridley didn't wait for them to finish. As soon as the gap was large enough, he leaned forward and sunk his heels into his horse's side, urging the stallion forward as they took off into the forest.

CHAPTER EIGHTEEN
OLIVER

"Keep up!" Liviah called back. Oliver was walking some twenty paces behind—close enough that he could see her, but far enough that they didn't have to speak. "If you fall behind, I'm not going to wait for you!"

Oliver scoffed under his breath. Liviah had taken on a particularly defensive stance towards him ever since they left Maldenney, treating him as if *he* was the one who had messed up her life, or *he* had abandoned someone she loved.

They had been walking all day and eaten nothing but a handful of dry nuts, each. To be honest, Oliver didn't mind that part. He had spent so much of his life hungry that he was much more accustomed to the feeling than Liviah was. While she groaned and complained about the pains in her stomach, Oliver remained resilient and focused. It was so nice to not feel like the weaker link for once. He had been so lost in his own thoughts that he didn't notice Liviah had stopped until he walked right into the back of her.

"Ouch!" she said as he stepped on her heels. "Watch it."

"What'd you stop for?" Oliver asked. "Legionnaires?"

"No, look." She pointed towards a clearing in the trees up ahead, where a road intercepted their path and led to a stout little building. Next to it, there was a stable where one chestnut colored horse was tied up, enjoying a lunch of oats and hay. Smoke billowed out of the chimney, and a sweet aroma filled the air. Oliver inhaled as deeply as he could. It was honeyed chicken, perhaps, or maybe a fresh beef stew. His sense of smell was so overwhelmed that it was making things up. Oliver's stomach seemed to twist in on itself, and suddenly he found it far more difficult to handle his hunger. He glanced at Liviah and almost thought he caught her licking her lips. "Do you think it's an inn?"

"Dunno," Oliver replied. "Looks like there's a sign on the door. What's it say?" They continued out into the clearing at a slightly quicker pace than before. "The Sleeping Giant Tavern," Oliver read aloud.

"Thank heavens! I'm starving," Liviah said. She started to push the door open when Oliver grabbed her by the arm.

"Wait. We can't go in there. We haven't got any money."

"So?" Liviah wrenched her arm free.

"So, how are we going to pay for it?"

"We won't. I don't know about you, but I don't plan on ever coming back to the Sleeping Giant Tavern. We'll run out before they can stop us, and we'll never see them again."

"We can't do that!"

"Why not? You didn't have any problem stealing when it was to save Nan." Liviah bit her lip as she uttered the words. Neither she nor Oliver had mentioned Nan since they left Maldenney.

"No," he said, "I didn't have a problem with it." Bringing Nan up made Oliver feel the hurt of his loss all over again. He glared at Liviah, but she refused to meet his gaze. She pushed open the door and went inside without another word. He had half a mind to stay outside and prove his point to Liviah, but the rumbling in his stomach and the smell of fresh bread made him think otherwise.

The Tavern was dimly lit inside. Most of the tables were empty. One gaunt-looking man with wispy white hair sat alone at a corner table, nursing a steaming mug. Oliver followed Liviah up to the counter, where a plump woman was polishing the wood furiously. They stood at the counter some time while the woman continued to work.

"Ahem," Liviah said at last. The woman nearly jumped.

"Oh, sorry dear! I...didn't see you walk in." Her smile turned down just long enough for Oliver to notice, and just as fast perked right back up. "What can I get for you?" she asked. Oliver studied the woman's face. She had rosy cheeks and a warm demeanor, but she seemed rather distant. It was as if her mind was occupied in another world entirely.

"Cider for each of us," Liviah said. "And whatever that is that I can smell cooking."

"Coming right up!" Her voice was cheery, but her smile was pained and unconvincing. She stepped back through a door that led to what Oliver assumed was the kitchen. "Two pot pies, Torin, and rolls!" She returned to the counter where Oliver and Liviah were still waiting. The three looked at each other in silence for an uncomfortably long time. "Sit anywhere you like," she said awkwardly. "I'll bring your tea."

"Cider," Liviah corrected.

"Right, cider."

Oliver and Liviah made their way to a booth. The table was splintering, and the wooden bench was hard. Nevertheless, it felt good to be inside and out of the elements. They sat facing each other, and Liviah continued to avoid Oliver's eyes.

"There's something off about that woman," he said in attempt to break the tension. He was furious with Liviah, but he preferred talking to silence. He also needed something to keep his mind off the fact that they were stealing their food.

Liviah raised an eyebrow. "What do you mean?" she asked.

"She was acting...weird. Like there's something that's really bothering her."

"Maybe there is," Liviah shrugged. It was clear she didn't have any interest in whatever was plaguing the tavern keeper, but Oliver just couldn't seem to shake the feeling that something was wrong.

A burly man in a stained apron came out of the kitchen carrying a tray with two bowls and a plate of bread. He set the tray down and Oliver and Liviah immediately began shoveling the food into their mouths. Peas, carrots, lentils, and chicken, all covered in a delicious gravy and surrounded by a thick crust. It burned Oliver's mouth and throat, but he kept on eating anyway. He could feel it in his stomach, soothing his hunger pangs.

"Oh! Well..." the man said, startled. His voice was deep and throaty, and his thick black mustache muffled his words. "Two pot pies; they're the house special, you know."

"Really good," Oliver said through another steaming mouthful.

"Anything else I can get you?"

"The hostess was supposed to be bringing us cider," Liviah said.

"Oh!" His face grew concerned as he turned to look at the woman at the counter. She was staring back at them, though somewhat absentmindedly. "She must have forgotten. You'll forgive her, I hope. Let me go remind her."

Oliver had almost finished his pot pie as the cook took his leave. He shoved the last spoonful into his mouth, then threw his elbow up on the table and rested his head on his hand. "I always wondered what it would be like to eat at one of these places," he said.

"At a dusty, old tavern in the middle of nowhere?" Liviah asked.

"At a real inn. With a cook and a hostess, and hot food that they bring to your table."

"And? How is it?"

Oliver looked around the room at the cobwebs, rickety furniture, and dim lanterns. He laughed. "It's a lot less...fancy...than I had imagined," he admitted. Liviah giggled down at her pot pie.

"You got that right, grudder."

"At least the food is good," he said as he reached for a warm roll.

"Maybe," Liviah said, and then dropping her voice to a whisper, added, "or maybe it only tastes good because you haven't eaten properly in a long time."

Oliver laughed. "I don't think I've ever eaten properly."

"My friend Addi's dad used to make the best candies," Liviah said reminiscently. "Lylaberry taffy, sugarbean tarts, and turtlenut truffles! Oh, I loved those."

"Wow, I've never even heard of any of those things. I hope I'll get to try them sometime."

Liviah's smile fell. "Yeah, well...I don't suppose I'll be getting them anytime soon. I don't know if I'll ever see anyone from home again."

"You'll get to go back there someday."

"Addi was my best friend. The first time Juliana used magic was on her twelfth birthday. We had invited Addi over, and mum made a cake to celebrate. Juliana went to blow out the candles and instead, every lantern in the house went out. Seemed sort of silly to make up an explanation, so we told Addi about our magic."

"What did she say?"

"She lost her mind at first," Liviah said. "But she got used to it pretty fast. I was so happy we told her. It was nice, you know? Having someone on the outside to talk to about it." Oliver smiled. "Oliver," Liviah said.

"Yeah?"

"I just wanted to say, about back in the city..."

"Cider's here!" The hostess said loudly as she appeared with a tray holding two glasses. She looked down at Oliver and Liviah for a while before placing a glass down on the table. She grabbed for the second, but it slipped out of her hand and shattered on the floor.

"Terribly sorry!" she exclaimed. She bent down to pick up the broken shards and without warning, began to cry. She covered her face with her hands and sobbed noisily.

"Enid, dear!" The cook came hustling out of the kitchen. "I'm sorry," he told Oliver and Liviah. "Excuse us a moment. I'll come back and clean this up." He stood Enid up and walked her out of the room.

"See! What was that?" Oliver said when the pair was safely out of earshot. "I told you something weird was going on."

"Yeah, let's get out of here," Liviah said. "I don't want to stick around any longer."

"Don't be so hard on them," the man at the corner table said with a gruff, scratchy voice. He picked up his mug and strode over to where they sat. Oliver could see his rotting, yellowed teeth. "I imagine seeing the two of you made Enid think of them boys of hers an awful lot."

"Her boys?"

"They lost them not long ago. Will and Gus."

"No wonder," Oliver said. "She must feel terrible."

"Their sons died?" Liviah asked seriously.

"Well, I assume," the man said. "I come here almost every day. One day the boys are running around, the next day—gone."

"How long ago was it?"

"Maybe a fortnight? Hard to remember exactly."

"Oliver! That would have been right before Juliana."

"You don't think?" Oliver questioned.

"That it was related? Could be. Come on." Liviah pushed past the old man and Oliver hurried to follow her. They stepped behind the counter and crept up to the kitchen door. Liviah pushed it open just a crack so that they could hear.

"I don't know how much longer I can handle it, Torin," Enid sobbed. "My poor boys! What if they're hurting them?"

"We have to stay strong, my love," Torin said. "You remember what they told us. We don't breathe a word of it to anyone, and they'll return the boys to us unharmed."

"But what do they want with them?"

"Just to study their magic. I'm sure the Legion is curious about the Eclipse. They want to learn more, is all."

"Did you hear that?" Liviah whispered. "He said *Eclipse*!"

"So, what do we do?" Oliver asked. Liviah opened the door into the kitchen, causing Torin and Enid to jump at the sight of her.

"Sorry!" Torin said quickly. "Your cider!"

Liviah didn't waste any time. "Your sons are Eclipse?" she asked. The couple exchanged a furtive glance.

"Sorry?" Torin said. "They're what?"

"I heard you talking. You said that they're Eclipse."

"I'm afraid you must have heard incorrectly…"

"I'm an Eclipse too, and so is my sister. She was taken from our home, just like your boys were."

Oliver could see the thoughts firing through Enid and Torin's minds. The husband and wife seemed to communicate telepathically.

"What are your names?" Torin asked.

"Liviah Cain, and this is Oliver Hawthorne."

"Come with me." Torin walked to the back of the kitchen and opened a cellar hatch to reveal a ladder. He climbed down, while Enid stayed behind. Liviah went closely behind Torin, so Oliver was left with no choice but to follow.

The cellar was cold and dark. Twice Oliver stepped on Liviah's foot, to which he was met with disgruntled looks. Torin held a single lantern up ahead as he led the party down a winding passage. The ground was uneven, and Oliver had to be careful not to trip and fall on the slippery wet stone. No one said a word as they walked, and Oliver grew wearier with each passing step. Liviah was as resolute and focused as always. When they reached the back of the cellar they stopped in a room containing dozens of barrels.

"What do you know about the Eclipse?" Torin asked.

"Only that I can do magic, and apparently some Eclipse saved the world from chaos before disappearing," Liviah said.

Torin nodded. From behind one of the barrels he pulled out a large, heavy book. He brushed the dust off the top to reveal the same symbol that was on Etzra's pendant—a golden sun being eclipsed by a silver moon.

"That's the symbol of the Vanguard," Liviah said.

"The symbol of the Vanguard because it was first the symbol of the Eclipse. This is the *Obscuratus Aeterna*. It has all the information about the Eclipse you would ever need." He handed the book over to Liviah, and she immediately began pouring through its pages.

"They're blank," Oliver said as Liviah stared intently at empty pages.

"What are you talking about?" Liviah asked.

"The pages. There's nothing on them."

"Are you going mad? There's clearly writing all over them. Look." She pushed the book towards Oliver and still, he saw nothing.

"I'm no expert on the Aeterna," Torin said. "Some spend their whole lives studying it only to come up with more questions than they started with. But if I may speculate, perhaps only an Eclipse can read from its pages," Torin said. Oliver frowned and looked away from the book.

"Can you and your wife read it?" he asked.

"Well, of course we can."

"So, you're both Eclipse too, then?" Liviah asked.

"Well, yes. How else would my sons be?"

"Hold on...Are you saying that my parents were Eclipse?"

"I—well, surely you knew that, right?" Torin's muffled voice said through his thick mustache.

"My parents weren't Eclipse. They couldn't have been. They didn't have any magic."

"Ah, yes. As confusing as that may seem, magic is not an essential condition of being an Eclipse. One may choose to give up their magic, as Enid and I have, but we remain Eclipse nonetheless."

"Why would someone want to give that up?" Oliver asked. He would give anything to have the abilities Liviah had. He couldn't imagine choosing to let that go.

"Many choose to rid themselves of their curse."

"Curse? What curse?" Liviah asked.

"Unfortunately, magic does not come without a price. There's the physical toll that it takes on our bodies, which can be overcome with practice and time, but there is also a second, deeper burden. Each Eclipse bears a curse that is specific to him or herself."

"So, you can give up your magic to get rid of your curse?" Liviah asked.

"Yes. The more an Eclipse uses magic, the more severe their curse becomes. Some choose to stop using magic all together until, eventually, they are no longer able to."

"But I don't have a curse."

"You're still young. It's possible your curse has not manifested enough to be noticed yet."

"What sort of things would a curse be?" Oliver asked.

"Oh, anything my boy. Anything that could be considered undesirable."

"What was yours?"

Torin stroked his mustache and looked away. "An Eclipse's curse is very personal business."

"Oh, I'm sorry! I didn't know."

"No matter," Torin said with a wave of the hand. "An honest mistake."

"That's what you did, then?" Liviah asked. "Gave up your magic to get rid of your curse?"

"No, actually. There's one other reason an Eclipse would choose to relinquish the gift."

"Which is?"

"To have children."

"Children?"

"Yes. The gift of the Eclipse is passed down through the generations. In order to have children, the parents must be willing to give it up."

"Does that mean that Liviah's parents could do the...floating thing...too?" Oliver asked.

"Possibly," Torin said. "The gift works like any other trait that is passed down. A child may have eyes like his father's or a nose like his mother's, but his features are not completely identical to either. The same applies to magic. While it is likely that one of Liviah's parents had an ability similar to her own, a child developing entirely new magic is not unheard of."

"You're saying that my parents gave up their magic to have me and my sister," Liviah said, "and they never even told us?" She turned away, hiding her face in the darkness of the cellar. Oliver placed a hand stiffly on her shoulder.

"I'm sure they planned to tell you," he said in a feeble attempt to comfort her.

"No," Liviah said through a sniffle. "They wouldn't have. That was just like them. They sacrificed so much for Juliana and me, and they never wanted us to see it. They didn't need the credit. They were just good parents. They only wanted us to be happy."

For the first time since they had met, Oliver felt as though he actually understood Liviah. "I know how you must be feeling," he told her. "I never even got to meet my parents, and I still miss them every day."

"I'm terribly sorry for what you both have gone through," Torin said. His deep, strong voice was trembling. "We don't mean to cause you any more pain...but you must understand...we just want our sons back."

"What are you talking about?" Liviah asked.

"Um...Liviah..." Oliver said, tapping her frantically on the arm to get her attention. Two legionnaires in glittering golden armor had just climbed off the ladder, and a third was on his way down.

"Come along now," one said with a high and scratchy voice. "We don't bite."

"You sold us out!" Liviah screamed at Torin.

"I'm sorry!" the tavernkeeper wept. "They threatened to kill our boys if we didn't help them!"

"Torin!" Enid called from atop the cellar door. She was just beginning to make her way down the ladder.

"Enid! What are you doing? Don't come down here!"

Liviah reached up towards Enid with an open palm and pulled the woman off the ladder. She screeched as she fell, crashing onto one of the legionnaires.

"Enid!" Torin screamed.

The second legionnaire swung his reaper at Oliver, who ducked just in time to avoid a blow to the head. Liviah flicked her wrist effortlessly and sent the solider flying into a row of barrels. They came crashing down, spilling wine and ale all over the cellar floor.

The third legionnaire advanced towards Liviah but froze in his tracks just out of reach of her. He looked down at his feet, which Liviah was binding in place. She raised her other hand, and a pained expression painted his face. He dropped his reaper and screamed. Liviah clasped her hands together, and the man collapsed unconscious.

"Your magic..." Torin said, horrified. "It is unlike anything I have seen in a child of your age."

Liviah stepped towards him, her lips curled up in disgust. "I am not a child," she said.

"They threatened us!" Torin said defensively. "Please, I'm begging you—"

"Liviah, come on!" Oliver yelled from the base of the ladder. "Liviah, let's go!"

Liviah left Torin cowering on the ground. She picked up the Obscuratus Aeterna and followed Oliver up the ladder. Once they were back in the kitchen, she shut the cellar door.

"Those sellouts!" she yelled.

"They're just scared, Liviah. They don't know what to do."

"I don't care! They're Eclipse, and they still betrayed us!" She locked the cellar from the outside.

"Liviah."

"Relax, they'll make it out. This will slow them down at least."

The tavern was empty when they went back into the dining room, for which Oliver was grateful. He wasn't in the mood to be around anyone right now. He said nothing when Liviah snatched a bag of coins from behind the front counter as they left.

The forest outside was quiet and calm, unaware that anything significant had taken place inside The Sleeping Giant Tavern. They set off walking again, their journey seeming to resume as quickly as it had paused.

"Oliver, look!" Liviah said. She was holding the Obscuratus Aeterna, which was smoldering away between her fingers. They watched in awe until she was left with nothing but two handfuls of ash. "What happened to it?"

"It belongs to Torin and Enid. Maybe it can't leave them."

"That was supposed to give me answers!" Liviah said, throwing the ashes on the ground.

"Come on," Oliver told her. "We'll worry about that later. Let's go get Juliana."

CHAPTER NINETEEN
LIVIAH

Autumn had turned to winter faster than usual this year. Liviah rubbed her hands together in front of the crackling fire as the first snowfall of the season blanketed the forest floor. They had been lucky to find wood that was dry enough to burn. The heat of the flames was a welcome comfort to her fingers.

Oliver sat on a log across from Liviah. His face flickered in the dancing light of the fire and the night sky above. Neither of them had said much since they left the Sleeping Giant Tavern the day before, and she found herself wondering if Oliver was angry with her for locking Torin and Enid down in the cellar. It was hard for Liviah to be around Oliver sometimes. He always made her feel guilty for the things she had done. Under normal circumstances, they would probably never have been friends, if that's even what they were now. Neither she nor Oliver knew what to call each other. If they were friends, they were not particularly good ones. Liviah didn't think of Oliver the way she thought of Addi, yet there was still something about him that drew her in. Liviah had even told Oliver things she normally would have kept to herself, partly because she had to, but partly because she wanted to as well.

"It's f-f-freezing out h-h-here," he said. Neither one of them was dressed for the weather, as it had been considerably warmer the night they fled Maldenney.

"I'm cold too," Liviah said as she watched her breath leave her mouth.

"It would p-p-probably be w-w-warmer if we sat t-t-together."

"Alright," Liviah said, scooting over on the log and patting beside her. Oliver hurried over and immediately she felt the warmth of his body.

"That's better," he said.

Liviah looked at him out of the corner of her eye so that he couldn't see her gaze on him. What did he think of her, she often wondered? As far as she was concerned, she had given Oliver little reason to like her. Yet here he was, helping her find her sister.

"What are you going to do after you find Juliana?" he asked.

"I don't know," Liviah said, and truth be told, she hadn't once thought about where she and her sister would go once they were reunited. "Maybe try to figure out what all this Eclipse stuff is about."

"Yeah," Oliver said, exhaling sharply. Liviah stared into the flames, watching them dance in the darkness. She hadn't seen fire this close up since her last night in Glassfall, when her home had burned to the ground. She thought about the boy who attacked her. What if he had been the one who took Juliana from the house? What if *he* was the reason all of this had happened, and Liviah had let him go?

"Woah!" Oliver shouted, leaning back away from the flames. Liviah snapped out of her thoughts and the fire immediately shrank back down. She hadn't even noticed that it had been growing. "Did you do that?" he asked.

"I...don't know," Liviah said. She looked down at her hands. They hadn't even been pointed towards the flames. "Back in the alley when Ridley had me pinned down, I thought he was going to kill me, but then..."

"What?"

"You mentioned Juliana, and the thought that those three boys might stop me from finding her... I just got angry, and something happened. It was like some other force took control of me. I felt all of this power, and it didn't feel like it was mine. I didn't even know what I was doing, I just did it."

"Honestly, Liviah, I thought you were going to get us killed. You destroyed the whole alley. It's a miracle we didn't get hurt."

"I barely remember doing that. What if..."

"What if...what?"

"What if I can't control it?"

"You will. You just need practice, and maybe someone who's more familiar with it who can teach you."

"It seems like everyone who knows anything is either dead or can't be trusted."

"You said you had an uncle back home, right? He might not be an Eclipse, but if he was around your parents enough...I'm sure he could help you."

"I have no idea if Philius is still there, or if he's even still alive...Even if I find Juliana, we're going to be completely alone, aren't we?"

"What about your parents' friend, Ramsey? It sounded like he was looking out for you."

"He was, but he lives in Maldenney, where I'm now a wanted criminal."

"Right," Oliver said softly. "You know, when we were in Lucila Square and that legionnaire asked what family we worked for, I thought for sure you would say Ramsey's name."

"I thought about it."

"Why didn't you?"

"I know he would have helped us, it's just...what if Ramsey wasn't there?"

"You think his family would have turned us in?"

"No, not at all, but what if he wasn't there because he never made it back from Glassfall? How could I look at his family and ask for their help if I was the reason he died?"

"Liviah, it wouldn't have been your fault."

"A lot of things are my fault. I think sometimes not knowing the truth at all is better than learning a truth you don't want to hear." They sat there huddled together until the logs of the fire burned out and only embers remained. "I'll go get more wood," Liviah said. She wandered off to where the brush was thicker, and the forest floor was protected from the snow. Leaves crunched under her feet as she collected sticks and small logs in her arms. She was bending over to pick one up when something moved behind her. "Oliver?" Liviah asked. A twig *cracked* behind her, and she whirled around. "You're not being funny, Oliver." The branches of the trees rustled, and a bone-chilling wind met Liviah's skin.

"*Liviaaah,*" she heard the forest whisper.

"Hello? Who's there?"

"*Liviaaah.*"

Liviah dropped the wood in her arms and took off running back towards the fire. She came out into the clearing and saw nothing but the blackened logs. Suddenly someone grabbed her arm from behind.

"Liviah!" Oliver said.

"Oliver! There you are!"

"Did you hear that?"

"You heard the voices too? Where were they coming from?"

"I don't know. They were like whispers from all around. I'm more concerned with how they knew my name."

"*Your* name? I heard my name," Liviah said. "Just like outside Maldenney."

"Outside Maldenney?"

"I heard it then too. Like the trees were talking to me... telling me to leave."

"Liviah...You don't think the forest is...haunted, do you?"

"No, that's ridiculous."

"*Oliver...Liviah...*" the trees whispered again.

"You were saying?" Oliver whimpered. They looked at each other, fear frozen on their faces, both thinking the same word.

"Run!" Liviah screamed. They sprinted through the forest as fast as possible, jumping over roots and rocks. A torrent of wind picked up leaves from the ground and swirled around them.

"*Leave these woods and never return!*" the forest commanded. A branch came plummeting down towards Oliver.

"Watch out!" Liviah called. He looked up too late. There was no time to move. Liviah pointed both hands up at the branch and willed it to stop. It hung suspended above his head for a moment, and then she dropped it beside him on the ground. It was at that moment that the wind seemed to die. The leaves returned to the ground, and the trees did not stir. Oliver and Liviah stood together, their eyes peeled on the forest around them.

"Liviah, look," Oliver whispered, pointing to the base of a large oak. Liviah held up her hands, ready for a fight. In the dim blue glow, she could see the bark shifting and moving. Then it turned, and standing before them was a figure that was half-tree, half-man.

"Wait!" the figure said in a voice as smooth as silk. "You must forgive me for scaring you, Oliver Hawthorne and Liviah Cain. It is often hard to tell the difference between friend and foe."

"What are you?" Liviah asked. "And how do you know our names?" His skin had the ringed texture of wood grain, and he had wooden antlers where his hair would have been. He had a pointed beard and his eyes were the brightest green Liviah had ever seen. He wore no clothes, but leaves sprouted from his skin. He smiled at them kindly.

"My name is Do'hara, and I am an arbrosprite," he said.

"A *what*?"

"A being of the forest. It is my job to defend the forest from those who would wish harm upon it. I make it my business to know those who enter my forest, but I did not realize that you were a guardian of nature yourself."

"I'm not a…tree fairy or whatever it is you are."

Do'hara laughed. "No, you are not a *tree fairy*. But an Eclipse, yes."

Liviah dropped her hands. "How did you know that?"

"You stopped a branch as it fell through the air. This is not an ability most humans have, to my knowledge. As I said, we are both guardians of nature. The sun and moon have given you the powers of the heavens, while the forest grants me the powers of the earth."

"You control the trees?" Oliver asked.

"No, I do not 'control the trees,'" Do'hara said, mocking Oliver's voice. "I merely communicate with them." He placed his hand on the trunk of the oak tree and its branches instantly bloomed perfectly green leaves. "It is the job of arbrosprites to keep those out of the forest who would disrupt the balance of nature."

"We're not trying to disrupt any balance!" Liviah exclaimed. "We're just passing through, so you can let us go!"

"I offer my humble apologies. You are free to leave or stay. So often, mankind causes destruction in our forests. We sprites find it best to keep humans out whenever possible."

"Sorry to intrude," Oliver said. "We'll be on our way."

"Actually," Do'hara said, "I believe I may be able to help you on your journey."

"You can?" Liviah asked.

"I have seen more of your kind in the distance, in a great castle to the north. I assume that is the location to which you travel?"

"The Bastion?" Liviah said. "Juliana really is there, then!"

"She is not alone either. I fear they may all be in danger. You must go to them at once. I can help you travel more quickly, but only so far as the forest will allow."

"Great. How?"

Do'hara touched the base of the tree again, and its branches lowered so that they were a few feet from the ground. He sat on one and patted beside himself. "Climb on."

Liviah and Oliver sat down next to him, and without warning the tree began raising them back up towards the sky. Liviah felt Oliver's hand clutch her arm. His eyes were as wide as could be. "Are you afraid of heights?" she asked. Oliver nodded, unable to form words.

"Do not worry, Oliver Hawthorne," Do'hara called to him over the wind. "The trees will not drop you!"

"How can you be sure?" Oliver called back.

"Because I have asked them not to!" the arbrosprite said with a laugh.

It was not until they were higher than every other tree in the forest that the oak stopped growing. Liviah could see nothing but treetops for miles in every direction. Do'hara snapped his fingers and in a ripple effect, the entire forest turned green. A moment later, the trees were yellow and orange, then the leaves fell, and it was back to normal. Liviah smiled at him in wonder. It was the most beautiful thing she had ever seen.

"That is the location which you seek," Do'hara said. He pointed to a stone fort glowing in the light of orange torches. It looked so small from their perch atop the tree, but it was still miles away. The tree surged into motion and Oliver grabbed onto Liviah again. She grinned at him as she felt the wind in her hair. Somehow the air up here wasn't cold, but warm and sweet smelling. The great oak slid through the forest like it was on ice. The ground trembled as they moved, and before Liviah knew it, the Bastion was no longer a small speck in the distance. The massive fort loomed ever-closer now, and her joy was replaced with both anxiety and fear. The branches of the oak lowered until they were back on the ground.

"What are you doing?" Liviah asked. "We aren't there yet."

"I cannot leave my dominion in the forest," Do'hara said. "The land beyond here is under the sovereignty of men. This is as far as I can take you." Oliver and Liviah jumped off the branch.

"Thanks for your help," Oliver said, "but I'm glad to be off that thing."

Do'hara laughed warmly. "I wish you good fortune, Oliver and Liviah. If you should ever need my services again, you know where you can find me."

"Thank you," Liviah said. Do'hara nodded, and the great oak tree retreated back into the forest.

"We're almost there," Oliver said.

"Yeah...we'd better get going." They traveled the rest of the way on foot while Liviah devised a plan.

"Hold on," Oliver said when she told it to him. "You want me to be bait?"

"Oh, don't call it that. It sounds worse when you say it that way."

"That's what it is!"

"Well, have you got any other ideas?"

"Why can't you be the bait?"

"You're joking right?"

"No," Oliver said. Liviah snickered. "What?" he asked.

"You just can't do what I can, Oliver. You don't have magic and you're not exactly a fighter either, so it only makes sense that we do it this way. The only way we are getting through this without anyone getting hurt is if you do what I say, when I say it." Oliver didn't seem particularly thrilled with this. She supposed he had agreed to the plan though, because when they finally arrived at the Bastion, he got into position without further argument. "Are you ready?" Liviah asked him.

"I guess so."

"Give me a few minutes to sneak around before you go."

"Got it."

Liviah crept around the tree line until she was north of the Bastion's gate, behind where the guards were standing on duty. "Oy, stop right there," she heard one of them say as Oliver approached. He leaned on a walking stick to support his leg. Liviah watched from behind a rosebush as the solider murmured something to his comrade and then walked to meet Oliver.

"Please, help me sir," Oliver said off in the distance. "I was traveling with my father and we were robbed."

"Where are you traveling from?"

Liviah didn't listen to hear what lie Oliver came up with. She tiptoed out from behind the bush and pressed herself up against the fort's stone wall. One legionnaire still stood by the gate. She clenched her fist until she could feel the energy build up in it. Whizzing through the air, her spell collided with the legionnaire's breastplate. He flew back in the air and collapsed on the ground.

"What was that?" the other said, turning around to see his comrade on the ground. Liviah raised her hand to cast another spell, but before she could, Oliver had hit the legionnaire over the head with his walking stick. He looked at Liviah matter-of-factly.

"Well," she said as she walked over to them, "I guess I stand corrected." She cast the reaper aside with a wave of her hand. She and Oliver each took one of the legionnaire's arms and dragged him into the tree line. Propping him up against a tree, Liviah patted his face until he came to.

"Ohhh..." the legionnaire groaned as he rubbed the spot on the back of his head where Oliver hit him.

"What is your name?" Liviah asked.

"Nagel...Who are you?"

"Do you know where you are, Nagel?"

"I'm...I'm at the Bastion...Hey...Who are you? You aren't supposed to be here." He tried to stand up, but Liviah's magic made him unable to move from the tree.

"Keep your voice down if you want to live, Nagel. There's a girl being held here. Her name is Juliana. Tell me where she is."

"I'm not telling you anything," Nagel spat. He tried again to stand. "What—what is this? What are you doing to me?"

"Tell me what I want to know, and I won't hurt you!" Liviah growled. She could feel her rage boiling up. Nagle glared back at her, so she pushed her hand down, making him sink into the dirt.

"Agh!" he called out as his back was pressed into the tree. "Head straight into the fort! At the end of the courtyard, go left! That will take you to the Lord's Tower."

"The Lord's Tower?" Liviah questioned. She pressed down harder.

"His personal quarters! That's where they go when they get here!"

"How many others are here?"

"I don't know, I—agh! Four, I think! Maybe five."

"Why did he bring them here?"

"He's going to use them!"

"Use them for what?"

"Their magic! He's going to sacrifice them! He wants to take their magic for himself!" Liviah took the stick from Oliver and whacked Nagel in the side of the head.

"Liviah!"

"He'll be fine," she said. "We couldn't risk leaving him awake. Now come on. Let's go find Juliana." She reached down and grabbed a key ring from Nagel's belt. Then, ducking low, she and Oliver crept towards the gate and let themselves in.

The Bastion was surprisingly barren inside. The wooden scaffolding along the walls and stacks of stone in the courtyard showed that it was still under construction. They ran straight through the courtyard without interference, took a left as Nagel had instructed, and came to the base of a large circular tower. Liviah pushed on the door. It budged slightly but didn't open.

"Can you force it open?" Oliver asked.

Liviah took a few steps back, raised both hands to the door, and made a pushing motion towards it with her arms. The door trembled slightly. She tried again, and still it barely moved. "I can't," she said wearily. "I think I've done too much magic recently. I'm exhausted."

"Let me try," Oliver said. He narrowed his eyebrows and stuck out his tongue in concentration, a look of bravado sweeping across his face. He walked several paces back from the door, turned towards it, and began to charge. Liviah nearly couldn't look. Oliver lowered his shoulder and just as he reached the door, it swung open. Oliver crashed into a table inside, sending silverware tumbling to the ground along with himself.

"Juliana!" Liviah yelled. Her little sister was standing by the door, looking down at Oliver. She wore a pearly satin dress that draped to the floor and her white-blonde hair was done up neatly. She looked beautiful. For a moment, Liviah felt like nothing had changed—like she was the same girl who left Glassfall, and everything was back to normal. She knew that it wasn't, of course, but her sister was here, and that was enough for now.

"Livvy!" Juliana cried. Liviah ran to embrace her sister when suddenly, Juliana's expression changed. "No, Liviah wait!" she shrieked, but Liviah was already inside. Juliana fell to her knees. "No!" she said as tears pooled in her eyes.

"What? Jules, what is it?"

"The door is enchanted to trap Eclipse! Once you come inside, you can't leave!"

CHAPTER TWENTY
OLIVER

For three days, Oliver had been helping Liviah look for her sister. They had both risked their own lives several times in the process. They had spent cold nights hungry in the woods, and now that they were finally here, they needed to be rescued as much as Juliana did.

Liviah didn't seem to care. She squeezed her sister with all her might, and Juliana hugged her back. They looked at each and grinned widely despite Juliana's tears. Oliver wasn't sure what to make of the situation.

"Juliana!" a boy's voice called from up the winding staircase. Liviah's hands began to glow blue.

"Relax, Liviah," Juliana said as she wiped her tears. "He's a friend. I'm down here, Will!"

"Will?" Liviah asked. "You don't happen to know a Gus too, do you?"

"Um, yes...why?"

"I'll tell you later," Liviah said quickly as she saw a boy descend the stairs.

"Who was at the" — the boy paused as he entered the room and saw Oliver and Liviah—"door?" He was tall and beefy, with wavy hair. Following behind him were three others — a shorter boy with a similar face, but who was chubbier and younger; a girl with braided, black hair that went halfway down her back; and a boy with a round face and bowl-cut blonde hair.

"Everyone, this is my sister, Liviah, and..."

Oliver stood up and brushed himself off. "I'm Oliver," he said, waving awkwardly.

"Will," the boy said. "This is Gus and Andromeda." Oliver stared at the young blonde boy. Will hadn't introduced him like he had the others.

"What's your name?" Liviah asked the boy. He shied his face away and said nothing.

"Don't know," Will said. "He just got here a couple days ago. He hasn't said two words to us."

"And you're all Eclipse?"

"Sure are. You too, huh?"

"I didn't expect you all to be our age."

"Did the Legion kidnap *all* of you?" Oliver asked.

"Not exactly," Will said. "At least, it didn't seem like that at the start of it all. Gus and I were here first. The Legion heard we were Eclipse, I guess, so they sent some official to our parents' tavern and told them they were looking for us. They claimed they had experts on Eclipse magic who wanted to help us develop our gifts. Mom and Dad were hesitant at first. They thought something might be up because Gus hasn't even gotten his magic yet, but we were...*heavily encouraged* to cooperate. So, we went along with them, but we didn't do much training when we got here. Didn't do much of anything, really. They treated us real nice, though. People came and brought us food, drinks, new clothes. They told us we never needed to leave the tower; they would bring whatever we wanted right here. After a while of doing nothing, we just started to get bored. Whenever we asked about training or how long we'd be here, they'd find a way to brush it off. Eventually, Gus and I decided this was either really fishy or at least a huge waste of our time. We decided we were going to leave and go home, and that's when we learned about the enchantment on the door."

"So, when you walk up to the door..." Oliver wondered.

"It's like walking into a brick wall. It blocks us from using our magic too."

Liviah reached out with her hand towards a vase in the corner of the room and scrunched up her face. The vase shook but didn't rise. She reached out her other hand, and it lifted maybe an inch or two off the ground. She dropped both arms, panting and sweating from the effort.

"I can't," she mumbled.

"That was right around the time Andromeda here got taken from her family," Will said. "A little after that, Juliana showed up."

"What happened to you, Jules?" Liviah asked. "How did they get you away from home?"

"Honestly, my memory is kind of foggy," Juliana said. "I remember I had another nightmare, so I went and sat outside on the porch to calm myself down. After that...I remember seeing someone walking towards the house. It was dark, and I couldn't see who it was. That's when it gets sort of fuzzy. The next thing I remember is being thrown in a wagon with a cloth over my head. And then I think..."

"What?"

"Well, I thought I remembered hearing Ramsey's voice, but I can't remember what he was saying. I kept going in and out, though, so it's hard to know what was real and what I was dreaming."

Oliver saw the blonde boy perk up at Ramsey's name.

"Ramsey went to look for you..." Liviah said. "I don't know what happened to him after that."

"He didn't come back?"

"He—I—well, I'm not sure. I didn't stay in Glassfall after they took you."

"Why not?"

"Jules...when I woke up...I..." Liviah seemed to be struggling to find the words, which appeared to only be increasing Juliana's apprehension. Oliver wished there was something he could do to help—some way to soften the blow—but Juliana would have to find out the truth eventually. "They set the house on fire after they took you, Jules. Riverside Cottage...it's gone."

"Oh no!" Juliana sobbed. "Our house is gone! You all made it out though, right?" Liviah looked painfully into her sister's eyes. Oliver could see her holding back tears. "Liviah? Mum and Dad made it out alright, didn't they?" Juliana asked again.

"Mum and Dad's room...the ceiling caved in outside the door. I tried to open it, but it was blocked." Liviah's tears were falling now, streaming down her face. Oliver had never seen her cry. She had always been so strong.

"What happened to Mum and Dad, Liviah?"

"I'm sorry, Jules...They're gone."

"No, no, no, no!" Juliana sobbed. She collapsed into her sister's arms, and Liviah held her tightly as they both cried. Gus, whose legs were a bit too short for his body, waddled over to them and rested his hand softly on Juliana's back.

"Come on guys," Will said. "Let's give them a minute." He turned and walked upstairs, the other Eclipse following close behind. Oliver opted to go upstairs with the others, to what he realized was a large bunkroom. Will sat down on one of the beds and cracked his knuckles into his palm. "I feel so bad for them," he said to no one in particular. "I wish there was something we could do."

Oliver stood awkwardly at the top of the stairs. Out of the corner of his eye, he could still see Juliana and Liviah hugging.

"So, Oliver, what's your story?" Will asked. "Did the Legion come after you too?"

"Me? Oh, no. Well, sort of. But I'm not an Eclipse."

"You're not?" the girl named Andromeda said.

"No, I'm just Oliver."

"How did you get involved in all of this mess then?" Will asked.

"It's a bit of a long story. I was a grudder in Maldenney." The blonde boy's head perked up at the mention of Maldenney. Was he from the city too?

"So, how did a grudder from Maldenney and an Eclipse from Glassfall cross paths?"

Oliver was hardly listening anymore. The longer he looked at the blonde boy, the more he thought he recognized him. It just didn't make sense, though. Until a week ago, Oliver had never left the alley, and since then…That was it! The alley!

"I know you," he said to the boy. "Your name is Theo, isn't it? You're Ridley's brother."

Theo gasped. "You know my brother?" he said.

"Would you look at that," Will said. "He speaks!"

Oliver could feel his blood pulsing through his temples. "I know your brother," he confirmed. "He took someone I love from me."

Theo scrunched up his face uncomfortably and sat on his bed. He looked back at Oliver without speaking. Oliver was furious. He wanted Theo to say something, *anything*, so that Oliver could yell at him, curse him, tell him it was his fault that Nan was taken from him. The silence only angered Oliver even more. He walked towards Theo. He didn't know what he was going to do when he reached him, but his legs seemed to move without his brain telling them to. Will placed a massive hand on Oliver's chest.

"Woah hold up there," he said. Oliver turned his stare to meet Will's eyes.

"His brother is a legionnaire," Oliver said. "Did you know that?"

Will turned to look at Theo. "That true?" he asked. Theo nodded, his face full of fear. "And you don't think that was something you should have mentioned?"

"I—I'm sorry," Theo stammered.

"It's *your* fault," Oliver said.

"What's his fault?" Will asked.

"He's the reason Nan is going to die!"

"Who's Nan?"

"She was my family—my *only* family—and now she's gone!"

"I never...I didn't..." Theo stuttered.

"But Ridley did! And you're the one who led him down the alley in the first place! You're the reason he knew to come looking for us there!"

"I didn't mean to hurt anyone," Theo squeaked.

"Why don't you have a seat," Will said. He grabbed Oliver by the shoulders and pushed him effortlessly down into a chair beside his bed. "Everybody just cool off for a second."

"What's going on up here?" Liviah said. She and Juliana had just come up the stairs.

"Your friend Oliver knows Theo here," Will said. "I guess he's someone named Ridley's brother."

"*Ridley's* brother?" Liviah said.

"You know what he's talking about?"

"Ridley tried to kill us!"

"Oh, great. This just keeps getting better," Will said, throwing both hands up in the air.

"And Ramsey," Oliver said. "I saw you look up when Liviah said Ramsey's name! What do you know about him? Where is he?"

"Ramsey Ambersen?" Theo said timidly.

"Yes," Liviah and Juliana said in unison.

"He's my father."

"Your father?" Liviah asked. "*Ramsey* is Ridley's father? Gods, if I had known that it was Ramsey's son after us this whole time—"

"Will somebody explain to me what's going on?" Will asked.

"Theo's dad was our parents' best friend. He saved my life when the people who took Juliana attacked me. And Theo's brother Ridley has been trying to hunt me down ever since I got to Maldenney."

"What?" Will shouted. "You've got to be kidding me! This is absurd! You're telling me that you and Juliana are Theo's dad's best friends' kids, and Theo's brother is trying to kill you because he doesn't know that his dad knows you?"

"Yes, exactly. And I didn't know that Ridley was Ramsey's son."

"Don't you people ever talk about your families?" Will exclaimed.

"That doesn't make any sense," Juliana said, ignoring his question. "If the Legion is behind the kidnappings then how could they possibly get away with kidnapping Ramsey's son?"

"What do you mean?" Will asked.

"Ramsey is a Lord in the Legion," Liviah explained.

"This guy's a *Lord* and they messed with his family?" Will asked. "It's gotta be a corrupt group or something then, right?"

"Worse," Liviah said. "It's not just a group. It's the whole Legion. Oliver and I did some digging, and Kaeno is one of the few people in the world who knows about the Eclipse. He's also the only person in Maldenney with the authority to order legionnaires to kidnap another Lord's son."

"You think the Lord Commander himself is after us?"

"It's the only thing that makes sense."

"Why, though? What does he want from us?"

"Our magic. He's planning on sacrificing us in some sort of ritual to take our powers for himself."

"What?"

"That's what the guard outside said. He also said that Kaeno was planning on doing it soon, so we need to get out of here fast, before he shows up."

"Well, I'm glad we know that, but there's one problem. We can't leave the tower, remember?"

"I can," Oliver said. They all looked at him. "Juliana said the door was enchanted to keep Eclipse inside, right? I'm not an Eclipse."

"He's right!" Will said. "He can get outside!"

"And do what?" Liviah asked. "That doesn't change the fact that we're stuck in here."

"There's got to be a way out of here. The Lord Commander would have to get you all out of the tower eventually, wouldn't he?" Oliver asked.

"Something has to be powering the enchantment," Andromeda said. "Something with magical power tied to it. If you find the object, you could lift the enchantment." Everyone looked at her. "My father does this sort of thing," she said softly.

"It's too risky," Juliana said. "Even if we could get out of the tower, the guards would come after us and kill us."

"Well, we can't just stand around waiting for them to kill us in some weird, magic-stealing ritual either," Liviah said. "We're dead either way."

"Not all of us have to die," Juliana offered.

"What are you talking about?"

"The Legion doesn't know you're here, Liviah. We could wait until they lift the enchantment to let the rest of us out, then you could hide and escape."

"Are you crazy? I came all this way. I'm not leaving you Jules."

"Please...I can't let them hurt you, Liviah. Not for me."

"And I can't let them hurt you! I don't have anyone else, Jules! Mum and Dad are gone! If I lose you..."

"But one of us should get to live."

"What do you expect me to do? Just walk away and let you die? I'm not scared of the Legion!"

"You should be," Will said. "You're stupid if you're not. It's the most powerful force to ever exist."

"No, it's not," Oliver said. He looked to each member of the group around him. "You can all do *magic!* The Lord Commander brought you here because he wants to take your power. *Your* power, not his. He's scared of what you have! Whether he can actually take your magic or not, I don't know, but I do know that you're not going to make it out of this alive unless you try to do something about it! I've lived my whole life as a grudder, scraping by off food that other people threw away. I hated every single day of it, but I never did anything about it because I was too scared. So, yes, maybe the Legion will come after you, and maybe they will find you, but that doesn't mean you should be afraid of them! I've seen Liviah take on three legionnaires at once and beat them. If she can do that, who's to say you all couldn't hold your own against the Legion? Who's to say *you* couldn't be the most powerful force to ever exist?"

"What do you suggest we do?" Will asked.

"Let me go out there. I'll see if I can find another way out of the tower. If I do, then we all escape together. If the Legion comes, let them come! I'm not like the rest of you. I can't do magic, but I believe in you and I'll fight with you if it comes to that."

"They're not fighters," Will said pointing to the rest of the Eclipse.

"Neither am I! But what choice do we have? It's fight or die at this point. No one else is going to do it for you. You're your own best hope."

Will looked at the others, contemplating. "Yeah," he said. "Yeah, okay!"

"I'm with you," said Andromeda. She smiled at Oliver, the corners of her rose-colored lips curling up in perfect crescent shapes. He looked away quickly as he felt his cheeks grow hot.

"Me too!" Gus said. He pumped his fist up in the air.

"Jules?" Liviah asked. Juliana looked around at the group. They were all watching her in anticipation.

"Okay," she said softly. "Okay."

"What do you say?" Oliver asked Theo. The boy smiled nervously and nodded his response.

"Alright," Will said with a grin. "Let's do this, then!"

"Do you have any weapons?" Liviah asked. "We need to be ready to fight when Oliver gets back."

Will looked around the room for something to use. He picked up the chair Oliver had been sitting in and slammed it on the ground. It shattered into several fragments, and Will held up one of the broken legs which now had a sharp, jagged end.

"That'll have to do," Oliver said. "Everyone grab one." Will broke another chair so that all seven of them were armed with wooden shards. They made their way down the staircase, stopping at the door. Oliver turned around to face them. "Any idea what this magical object may be?" he asked Andromeda.

"It could be anything. Probably something small that could be easily protected," Andromeda said.

"Great...I'll just look for all the tiny, well-guarded things."

"Are you sure you want to do this?" Will asked. "You're risking a lot to help us here, and there's no guarantee it'll even work. You could just leave if you wanted."

"I'm sure," Oliver said. He thought about Nan giving up the cure to the Withering Black so that Lyla's baby could have it. If she were in Oliver's position now, this is what she would do.

"Alright. Just play it safe out there." Will stuck out a hand.

"Don't worry. I will." Oliver said, grabbing Will's hand and shaking it. He turned and started out the door.

"Oliver?" Liviah said. She looked at him like she didn't know what to say, with words hanging on her lips that she just couldn't get out. "Be careful," she told him at last. He smiled at her.

"Thanks, Liviah."

Oliver stepped back out into the cold night. He wasn't sure if he had imagined it, but this time he could almost feel himself passing through the enchantment as he crossed the threshold of the door. He had hardly gone a few steps before a figure rounded the corner and began walking towards him. Oliver thought to hide, but it was no use. He had already been seen. He heard the Eclipse behind him making exclamations, but Oliver's attention was fixed on the man approaching. He held a reaper and shield at the ready, blocking Oliver's only path from the tower. The metal of his armor was so black that he was almost invisible in the dim light of the night.

"Stop right there," the figure commanded. Oliver knew immediately who it was. He would never forget that voice. "It's over," Ridley said. "Where's the girl?"

"Where's Nan?" Oliver asked back.

"That's what you call that old hag?" Ridley scoffed. "She was very helpful in telling me where you were going. After that, she surpassed her usefulness to me."

Oliver's heart sank. He had known all along that Nan was as good as dead the moment he and Liviah left Maldenney, but a part of him had been holding onto a small hope that he would still see her again one day.

"Tell me where the girl is now! Unless you want me to cut you down right here," Ridley said.

"She's inside, but there's something you should know."

"Shut up! I don't need to hear anything you have to say, you filthy grudder."

"Rid!" Theo yelled from the door. Ridley's eyes widened and he peered around Oliver.

"*Theo?*"

CHAPTER TWENTY-ONE
RIDLEY

"What are you doing here?" Ridley asked his little brother.

"The Legion kidnapped me," Theo said. "Just like the rest of them."

"They only took you to test me," Ridley reasoned. "You weren't really being kidnapped."

"No, Ridley. I'm just like them...I can do magic. I didn't know until the other day. I found out by accident."

"What? No...you're one of them?"

"They're called Eclipse," the grudder boy from Maldenney said. "And if we don't get them out of here soon, the Lord Commander is going to have them killed."

"The Lord Commander won't kill Theo. My father—"

"Is Ramsey Ambersen?" The grudder girl said. "We know. My name is Liviah Cain. Your father was my parents' best friend. He risked his life to save mine when my sister was kidnapped. We're on the same side."

Ridley looked around at all of the prisoners. "Everyone just shut up!" he said. So much was happening at once that he couldn't make sense of it all. "Theo, come on! I'm getting you out of here!"

"The door is enchanted to keep the Eclipse in the tower," the grudder boy said. "If you want Theo out, you'll have to let them all out."

Ridley gritted his teeth. "How do I break the enchantment?"

"We have to find the object that's powering it and destroy it. We're guessing its somewhere here in the fort."

"I'll handle it," Ridley said.

"I'm coming with you," Oliver added.

"I don't need your help!"

"Probably not, but I don't trust you."

"I could kill you right now if I wanted to."

"You could, and they'd kill you as soon as you broke the enchantment." Ridley looked past the grudder to where the Eclipse stood in the doorway. "You could barely fight off Liviah with help. I don't think you want to try your luck with all of them."

"Fine," Ridley said, "but you follow my lead."

The grudder looked back to his friends for a second. "Alright," he said at last. "You lead the way."

Ridley turned and walked back into the courtyard, the grudder following close behind. They stuck close to the wall, in the shadows cast by stacks of building materials. "A fort like this could easily house over a hundred men," Ridley whispered. "Thank the gods it's not fully manned yet. The only thing I don't understand is, why would you hold prisoners at a fort that's not well guarded?"

"Because they don't need it to be well guarded."

"But if the fort is holding something as valuable as magic users—"

"Eclipse."

Ridley huffed. "If it's holding something as valuable as *Eclipse*, you would want it to be heavily protected."

"They don't need the fort to be heavily protected because the enchantment is preventing any sort of break out. The only thing they need well protected would be—"

"Whatever is powering the enchantment."

"So, what's the most secure part of a fort?" Oliver asked. Ridley thought for a moment. It would be the Lord's Tower, but that wouldn't make any sense; the Eclipse were being held there. The only other place would be...

"The oubliette," he sighed.

"The what?"

"Just follow me. And stick close. If you get caught, I'm not risking my neck to save you." They continued creeping along the wall until they reached a wooden door on the west side of the courtyard. Ridley tried the handle. "Blast, it's locked."

"Give me your knife," the grudder said. Ridley looked at him, disconcerted. "What do you think I'm going to do with it? I just need it to pick the lock."

"Here," Ridley said, reluctantly pulling out his knife and handing it over. The grudder stuck the tip of it into the lock and wiggled it around for a second.

"I need another piece," the grudder said. He looked at Ridley's armor. "Give me that pin." Ridley looked down at the Symbol of the Legion that was welded on to his armor.

"What?"

"Just the spear part." The grudder reached for it and Ridley shoved his hands away.

"Watch it."

"Do you want Theo out or not?"

"Fine." Ridley grabbed onto the miniature reaper that overlaid the crescent moon on his chest and pried it off. It snapped with surprising ease, and he handed it over. The grudder stuck it into the lock and twisted it around with the blade of the knife. "I didn't kill her," Ridley said.

"What?"

"That woman you called Nan. I didn't kill her. She's still alive."

The grudder stopped working on the door and stood up. "Where is she?"

"She's safe. At my home in Maldenney. My maid, Elma, will make sure she's cared for until I return."

"And then what?"

"I'll turn her into the proper authorities. They'll try her for her crimes and then—"

The grudder scoffed. "You don't get it, do you?"

"Get what?"

"Her only crime is existing. We don't do anything wrong. We just live and get punished for it. You know they'll kill her, right?"

"Hey, I don't make the laws, you know."

"No, you just enforce them, right? It doesn't matter, she's going to die soon, anyway."

"What do you mean?"

"She's got this old plague, the Withering Black. She took enough antidote when she was younger to contain it, but now that she's older...she'll die without the cure." He resumed working on the lock.

"I swore to uphold the laws of the Legion," Ridley explained.

"Really, did you? Because right now, you're helping me break the Eclipse out of Legion custody. What? Upholding the law is suddenly less important when it's someone you care about that's in danger?"

Ridley didn't know how to respond, and by the look on his face, the grudder knew he had just won that argument. "Well, I guess it doesn't matter now. I'm not a legionnaire anymore."

"Good. I don't know why you'd want to be. The Legion is evil."

"*Evil?*"

"Yes, evil."

"I shouldn't be surprised," Ridley sneered. "People like you have no appreciation for what the Legion has done for Omnios."

"Really, like what? Kidnapping kids? Killing grudders? Sentencing girls to die for being out after a stupid curfew?" Ridley's eyes shot to meet the grudder's. "You're welcome for that, by the way."

"For what?"

"For stopping you from killing that girl."

"What makes you think I would thank you for that?"

"I saw you. You didn't want to do it. It was eating you up inside." Ridley did not respond. He only watched as the grudder tinkered with the lock. "I'm Oliver, by the way."

"Um…Ridley."

Oliver stuck his hand out. "It's nice to meet you when you aren't trying to kill me, Ridley."

Ridley looked dumbfounded at Oliver, and then at his hand. How, after everything, had they ended up here? He took the grudder's hand and shook it. "Nice to meet you," he said, still somewhat in disbelief.

A moment later, the lock clicked open. Oliver handed Ridley back the knife and broken piece of the pin. Ridley turned the miniature reaper over in his hand. This was the weapon of the legionnaire, something he would likely never be again. He opened his palm and let it fall to the dirt.

"Keep this," he said, handing the knife back to Oliver. "You might need it." They burst open the door with their weapons drawn. Inside was an empty stone staircase, dimly lit by a single torch on either side. "Perfect," Ridley said, strapping his reaper to his back. "This should be the right way." They each pulled a torch from its sconce and began their descent down the stairs.

"So, what is this *ooblit* thing we're looking for?" Oliver asked.

"Oubliette," Ridley corrected. "They're secret dungeons that the Legion puts in forts. You can only get into them by trap door.

"How do you get out of them?"

"You don't."

"Oh…wonderful."

At the bottom of the staircase was a metal cage door. Ridley pushed it open and stepped into a large open room. Chains hung from the walls and ceiling, with wrist clamps on the ends of them. "This is an interrogation room," Ridley said. "Which means the oubliette should be here. Look around on the floor." They held their torches close to the ground, scanning for any sign of a trap door.

"I don't see anything," Oliver said. "Just stone and—oof!" he tripped on the corner of an uneven rock. Ridley brought his torch over and handed it to Oliver. He bent down and pulled on the stone; it must have weighed over fifty pounds. He picked it up and dropped it to the side, revealing a hole that was several feet deep and only wide enough for one person to stand in. Oliver shined the torch down in the hole. A golden lockbox glistened in the light.

"There it is," Ridley said.

"Great. How do we get it out?" Oliver asked. Ridley grabbed his reaper and stuck it down the hole. He tried to use the hooked end to pick up the box, but he couldn't get it to balance. "Let me try," Oliver said. He took the reaper and tried pushing the box up against the wall. It slipped down the wall the moment he picked it up.

"This isn't going to work. We need something we can grab onto it with. Maybe if we can get these chains off the wall…"

"Wait! Stop moving," Oliver said. "Do you hear that?" Ridley froze. He could hear muffled bell chimes coming from outside.

"That's not good…"

"What is it?"

"Either the Lord Commander just arrived…or they know we're here."

"We have to hurry! Let's go!"

"There's no time to get the chains," Ridley said. "You're going to have to go down there."

"You want me to go down into the trap door that you *just* said you can't get out of?"

"You can't get out by yourself, but I'll pull you up!"

"Need I remind you of the time you tried to kill me?"

"But I'm not now! Come on, if I wanted you dead, this is not how I would do it."

"How come you can't go down there?"

"I'm heavier than you, and I'm wearing armor. You won't be able to pull me out. Come on we have to hurry!"

Oliver dragged his hands down his face and groaned. "Alright, fine." Ridley grabbed his hand and lowered him down slowly into the oubliette.

"Have you got it?"

"Got it," Oliver said.

"Here, hand it up to me." Ridley reached down and grabbed the box from Oliver. It was heavier than he had expected.

"Alright, now pull me up," Oliver said. Ridley stood. "Ridley, pull me up!"

"Wait! *Shh.*"

"Ridley!"

"Someone's coming."

"Then get me out of here!"

"There's no time."

"*What?*" Oliver asked. Ridley grabbed the stone and began sliding it back over the hole. "What are you doing?" Oliver demanded.

"Just keep quiet for a second!" Ridley whispered. The stone sank down into the ground, concealing Oliver in the hole. Ridley stood and stepped in front of the box just as a legionnaire came into the room.

"What are you doing down here?" the soldier questioned. The markings on his shoulder plate told Ridley he was a captain, likely the acting commander of the Bastion.

"Sir," Ridley said, standing in attention. "There was word of a rescue attempt for the prisoners. The Lord Commander sent me to relocate the artifact to a more secure location."

"Ah, well, if the Lord Commander sent you," the captain reasoned.

"It was a direct order from Lord Commander Kaeno himself, sir."

"Interesting armor. It's quite old, is it not?"

"It is, sir. The Lord Commander thought it would be a better choice for this mission."

"I see. What is your name, solider?"

Ridley paused. If he gave his real name, the captain was bound to recognize him. "Sayben, sir."

"Sayben…?"

"No family name, sir."

"No?"

"I don't have a father, sir."

"Good. No one to ask questions."

Ridley stepped back just as the captain pulled a knife from his back and swung at Ridley's neck. He bent down and retrieved his reaper from the ground, scooping it up and striking the captain on the side all in one clean motion. The captain jabbed forward with the blade, but Ridley sidestepped and caught his wrist. He slammed the shaft of his reaper down on the captain's hand, disarming him. The captain tackled Ridley onto his back as they wrestled over the reaper. The captain pried it from Ridley's grip and struck him in the head, knocking off his helmet.

The captain stood up. The blow to Ridley's head was dizzying, but out of the corner of his eye, he saw the knife on the ground. He began crawling for it. He had almost reached it when the captain grabbed him by the leg and pulled him back. The next thing Ridley knew, the shaft of the reaper was being pressed down on his neck, suffocating him. Ridley tried to push the captain off himself, but he was losing strength with each passing moment. Ridley looked around for a weapon. The knife was too far out of reach. His shield was across the room.

The lockbox caught Ridley's eye. He reached his fingers out for it, straining his muscles to stretch farther. He could feel his lungs emptying as the captain pressed down on his throat with the reaper. Just a bit farther and he would be able to reach it…

Wham! The captain slumped to the side as Ridley slammed the lockbox into his helmeted head. Ridley gasped for air as the captain released the pressure on the reaper. He dropped the box and rose to his feet. Grabbing the unconscious captain by the arms, he dragged him to the wall and clamped a chain to each of his wrists. Ridley looked down at the lockbox. He had everything he needed to save Theo now.

Wearily, Ridley walked over to the stone that covered the oubliette. He grabbed it with both hands and pulled it away, revealing Oliver inside.

"Ridley," Oliver said, "is that you?"

"Yes," Ridley breathed. "There was a legionnaire. I took care of him." He reached a hand down and used all the strength he had left to hoist Oliver up.

"Thanks," Oliver said as he was lifted out of the hole. He picked up the lockbox. "You know for a second there I thought you were going to leave me down in that thing."

Ridley managed a laugh.

"Yeah, well, for a second there I thought I was too. I guess I owed you one." He grabbed his reaper and clipped it to the strap on his back, then picked up his shield and torch.

"How are we going to get this thing open?" Oliver asked. "I can't pick the lock. It's too small to fit the knife in."

"Give it to me," Ridley said. He took the box from Oliver and looked it over in his hands, then heaved it against the stone wall as hard as he could. It broke apart at the hinges and clattered to the floor.

"That's it?" Oliver asked. "*I* could have done that!" Ridley walked over to the box and pulled out a necklace with a crescent moon pendant on it.

"What is this?" he asked. "That's not the insignia of the Legion."

"It's the symbol of the Vanguard."

"What's the Vanguard?"

"It's an order of people who know about Eclipse. It was created to protect them, but I guess that's not the case anymore. Kaeno is one of the few members left."

"How do you know all that?" Ridley asked incredulously. Oliver smiled ear to ear.

"Wow…So, this is what it feels like to know about something that other people don't, huh?"

Ridley put the pendant around his neck. "We can throw it in the fireplace and melt it," he said as he put his helmet back on. "Let's hurry up and get back to them. We probably don't have much time left." They climbed the stairs with the lockbox in hand. Ridley opened the door just a crack and peeked outside. "There are legionnaires all over the place. We're never going to make it."

"Let me see," Oliver said. He traded places with Ridley and began pointing at various spots as he looked out into the courtyard. "Okay, I've got a path figured out."

"Are you mad? There's no way we can get through there without being spotted."

"I'm not good at a lot of things, but I am good at hiding. Just follow my steps and stay close."

Together, they crept into the courtyard. Oliver led Ridley close along the wall, then they darted out and ducked behind a stack of stones. From there, they waited for a trio of legionnaires to pass, then crawled on their stomachs under a nearby wagon. After confirming the coast was clear, they snuck around the corner and into the corridor leading to the Lord's Tower. They stood up and ran for the door.

"Liviah! It's us. Open up!" Oliver whispered.

The door swung open, and Ridley saw the six Eclipse kneeling on the ground with their hands behind their heads. At least ten legionnaires stood around them with their weapons drawn.

"Lookin' for your friends?" the legionnaire who opened the door asked in a low, gruff voice. A platoon of legionnaires rounded the corner of the corridor behind Ridley and Oliver. Before they knew it, a dozen reapers were trained on them, ready to strike at any moment.

"Drop your weapons!" one of the legionnaires yelled.

"I'm a legionnaire," Ridley said. "I'm here on direct orders from Lord Commander Kaeno and I demand you release me to—"

"I said, drop it!" It was no use. Ridley and Oliver threw their weapons down. They clanked unceremoniously on the ground.

"These two aren't Eclipse," the legionnaire at the door said to the one outside. "Bring out the blocks." He smiled at Ridley with yellow teeth. "We'll take care of them now."

One of the soldiers left the corridor and returned a minute later with two blood-stained slabs of wood. He dropped one in front of Ridley and the other in front of Oliver. Following behind him was a huge man dressed in black, leather armor. He reminded Ridley of the Legion's blacksmith, Villis Cantar. He had a cowl pulled over his head and carried the largest axe Ridley had ever seen—the tool of an executioner. He stopped in front of Ridley, looking him up and down.

"Take off your helmet," he said evenly. Ridley looked to his brother, who was watching through the door. Theo's face was helpless…He knew what was about to happen.

An unblinking stare from Liviah caught Ridley's eye. She looked at him intently, as if to communicate something. He nodded slightly, hoping that he understood what she was trying to say. He raised his hands slowly towards his helmet. With his right hand, he unclasped the strap on his chin, and with his left hand, he gripped the chain around his neck. He hurled his helmet into the face of the executioner, then, before anyone knew what was happening, he yanked the thin chain off his neck and threw the pendant to Liviah. She caught it out of the air and closed her palm around it. A dim, blue light shone through the cracks between her fingers. The executioner yelled violently as he threw Ridley's helmet against the wall. Ridley watched as Liviah struggled to produce the energy to break the pendant. At first nothing happened; the effort was straining her too much. Then a flash of light erupted from the tower. The only sounds Ridley could hear were a scream from Liviah and what sounded like a forge hammer striking hot steel. The light disappeared and Ridley looked to Liviah. She opened her palm and let the shattered pieces of the pendant fall.

"Now!" she yelled to the other Eclipse. She pulled her hands down to the ground and all ten legionnaires in the tower crumpled to their knees. The oldest Eclipse boy grabbed one of their fallen reapers and disappeared right before Ridley's very eyes. He manifested less than a second later behind the executioner and swung hard at the back of the massive man's head. The executioner yelled out in pain, then grabbed the reaper and yanked it from the Eclipse's hand. The boy continued to disappear and reappear behind the other legionnaires, keeping them well distracted if nothing else.

Ridley picked up his own weapon, then barely ducked under a swipe from the executioner's axe. The man swung the axe like there was no weight to it. Ridley quickly deflected a second blow, and then a third. It was too much for Ridley's weapon to take. The shaft of his reaper shattered into pieces as the axe collided with it. A blast of blue energy hit the executioner in the chest, knocking him flat onto his back. Ridley turned around to see Liviah give him a nod before sending two mores spells into the fray of soldiers. The rest of the Eclipse had all joined the fight, uselessly swinging reapers at the legionnaires.

"Come on!" Ridley yelled to everyone. "Let's go!" They ran for the courtyard with the last of the legionnaires chasing behind them. Ridley could see the gate on the other side of the Bastion. If they could only make it there.

The doors around the courtyard seemed to all burst open at once. Hordes of legionnaires poured through them, too many for Ridley to count. The group stopped in the middle of the fort.

"Will! What do we do?" one of the Eclipse said.

"Just...hold your ground!" Will answered. They backed into a circle as the legionnaires surrounded them. Up by the ramparts, Ridley could see archers nocking arrows. They were outnumbered ten to one. Even with magic they wouldn't stand a chance.

The tower bells rang again, breaking the silence that had overcome the Bastion. They rang three times, sharp and loud, echoing eerily throughout the courtyard. "Riders approaching!" one of the archers called from atop the wall. "Riders approaching!"

Without a moment more of warning, the gates burst open and in came a cavalry of at least forty men on horseback. They cut through the crowd of soldiers like a knife through butter, hacking and slashing the legionnaires to the ground as if they were no more than cattle. Mounted archers picked the men off the walls. Ridley ducked low to avoid the blades that swirled overhead. The last of the legionnaires fell dead, and into the fort came riding the very last person whom Ridley wanted to see—Orion Cormack.

Cormack's mount was one of the largest horses Ridley had ever seen. Cormack sat proud and tall, with all the arrogance that Ridley had always despised him for. His glimmering golden armor shined marvelously in contrast with the horse's black coat. In all the disarray, Ridley almost hadn't realized that the riders who saved them were legionnaires themselves.

"What the hell have you done here, Ambersen?" Cormack yelled. Ridley opened his mouth to speak, but something stopped him short. Another rider was entering the Bastion, this one not wearing any armor. Instead, a black cloak trailed behind him, flapping in the wind as he rode. Even from a distance, Ridley recognized the silhouette of his father.

"Ridley! There you are!" his father called to him. He dismounted his horse before it came to a full halt, then sprinted to his son and held him at arm's length to examine him. "I was worried sick. Have you been hurt?"

"Father! No," Ridley said in bewilderment, "I'm—fine. I'm..." What was he? Glad? Ashamed? Angry? No, none of those. He was...surprised. Where was his lecture about what a failure and disappointment he was? Where was the reprimanding for his disobedience? His father was not the type of man to be so easily forgiving, but right now all he seemed to feel was genuine concern.

"Father!" Theo screamed from behind the other Eclipse. He burst through them and ran over to his brother and father, jumping up and wrapping his arms around his father's neck. "You came for us!"

"Theodor?" their father said aghast. "What in the heavens are you doing here of all places?"

"The legionnaires took me," little, round-faced Theo said through tears. "I'm alright now, though."

Ridley could hardly believe his own eyes. This was the greatest display of fatherly affection that he had ever seen out of the man. It was almost unnatural. Why was his father acting so different? He supposed attitudes did often change when people were in danger, but this was extreme.

"I feared I would never see you boys again. We'll head home straight away. I want you both back in Maldenney where it's safe, as soon as possible."

"Ramsey?" Liviah said. Ridley had almost forgotten the others were there. The girl and her sister were huddled together, looking at Ridley's father with timid expressions.

"Girls…" Ramsey said, his eyes growing large and wide as he saw the pair for the first time. "I can't believe…I don't understand. How did you all end up here together?" Liviah and her sister started to run towards him.

"Juliana, wait!" Will said. Both girls stopped. "This is Ramsey?" he asked darkly.

"Yes," Juliana said. "Why?"

Will narrowed his eyes. "He's the one who came to my parents' tavern looking for Eclipse. He's the one who brought us here."

"What? No, that's not possible. You must be mistaken." Liviah said.

"Will's right," the red-haired girl said. "I remember him. He was there when they took me, too."

"Father, what are they talking about?" Ridley asked. His father looked on at the group with a blank stare. He did not move or speak.

"Ramsey?" Liviah said. Still, he offered no explanation. "Why are they saying that, Ramsey? Ramsey, tell me what's going on!" Tears were welling up in her eyes as she screamed. Ramsey inhaled slowly, allowing his expression to fall stone-cold as he released the breath.

"My dear Liviah," he said cynically, "this all would have worked much more smoothly if I had known you were an Eclipse as well."

"*What?*" Ridley said. Theo fell over trying to back away from his father. He scrambled to his feet and ran to hide behind the other prisoners.

"You were in on Kaeno's plan the whole time?" Liviah said. Her lip trembled violently as she tried to keep the hot tears which pooled in her eyes at bay. "You were helping him capture the Eclipse, knowing he was going to try to sacrifice us for our powers?"

"You think that halfwit was behind this?" Ramsey spat. "The Vanguard himself! Please! Kaliculous Kaeno could never come up with something so...*sophisticated*. All he knows is stabbing, cutting, and slashing, but I must say, he makes a very convincing suspect, doesn't he? And using the legionnaires to do my dirty work does make it all the more believable that he's to blame. I suspect people will be outraged when I uncover what the Lord Commander has been up to."

"Even Theo?" Ridley interrupted. "You planned to kill your own son?"

"You must think me heartless, Ridley. I would never sacrifice my own son."

"But you were!"

"No, I wasn't! Theodor is not my son."

"What?" Theo said.

"What are you talking about?" Ridley questioned.

"Haven't you ever wondered why your mother treats the two of you so differently? Why she loves Theodor so much and loathes you, Ridley?"

"What has that got to do with anything?"

"I know Kaeno told you of my brother, Balfour. It was he whom your mother loved; he whom she had planned to marry. But Balfour was *cursed* with the magic of the Eclipse, and he refused to expose her to his vile nature. When he called off their engagement, her parents forced her to marry me instead. I tried to be everything she wanted, but she only craved him. Then, just after his death, I discovered that she had become pregnant with Balfour's child. Your mother and I had been married for years, of course. The scandal of such an affair would have ruined your mother's reputation, so I swore not to tell anyone. I raised Theodor as my own son, always knowing that one day he would turn out to be the same as Balfour— an *Eclipse*, with the same wicked curse as his father."

"I can't believe this…He's still your family!"

"Oh, come now, Ridley. Don't be so noble. You and I both know you didn't come here to save Theodor."

"What are you talking about? Why else would I have come?"

"Because you thought that hunting down Liviah was your ticket to becoming a legionnaire again, didn't you? If it so happened that you could save your brother along the way, then so be it, but you and I both know that you did it for yourself. I can't say I really blame you. That life is all you've ever known, isn't it? You were *made* to be a legionnaire, Ridley. You were practically bred for it, and the opportunity was taken from you before it had even begun. You would have done anything to get that back, wouldn't you? Even when you thought it meant putting your poor brother at greater risk, you put the mission first. You truly are the perfect soldier, Ridley. I couldn't be prouder of you for that."

In fifteen years, Ridley's father had never once told him that he was proud. Now, the only words Ridley had ever wanted to hear were being uttered at the worst time imaginable. He hated himself for how good it made him feel. He shouldn't care what his father thought of him anymore, but he *did*. No matter how hard he tried not to, Ridley still cared. He looked from his father to his brother. Theo was staring at him blankly, not blinking and not moving.

"No, Theo, that's not true," he insisted.

"We never got along, Rid. I know you never liked me much…" Theo reasoned. Ridley couldn't even argue that Theo was wrong. The two of them had never been close. He stood there with his mouth gaping open.

"Come on, Theo! You're my brother!" Ridley said, but it was no use trying to reason. He could feel Theo's gaze grow cold, and his little brother turned away from him. It felt like a dagger slashing through Ridley's heart. He had never been as alone as he was in this moment. His father had betrayed their family, and now his brother hated him.

"I don't believe you," Liviah yelled. "This isn't true!"

"It *is* true, my dear girl. I was the one who sent men to attack your home! I was the one who kidnapped Juliana!" Ramsey said.

"But the necklace! The man who attacked me in Glassfall had a Vanguard necklace!"

"You mean like this one?" Ramsey withdrew a Vanguard pendant from inside his shirt collar. "The Lord Commander has many like this one. Very easy to misplace."

"And the letter...You're the person who sent Kaeno a letter from Glassfall telling him about an Eclipse there, aren't you?"

"Clever girl...I knew if anyone found the clues, they would suspect Kaliculous, but I didn't expect you to be the one to find them. When I heard you had gone to Maldenney, it was almost too good to be true. How foolish I had been to let you go, and then there you were, walking right back into my hands. All I had to do was have Cormack suggest a curfew to search for you, and well...you know the rest."

"You're a murderer!" Liviah screamed. Her hands glowed blue, and the legionnaires on horseback honed their reapers in on her.

"Going to fight them all?" Ramsey said. "You're a child, Liviah. Your magic is shaky, unreliable even at its best, isn't it?"

"You said you would find Juliana!" Liviah yelled. "You said you would protect her! But you were just waiting for the right time to kill us!"

"I must admit, I was devastated when I learned you were an Eclipse, Juliana...I had loved you, I'm afraid. And *you*, Liviah, well you were truly a surprise. My younger brother had the gift, and yet I did not. When your parents told me about Juliana's powers and said nothing about you, well, naturally I assumed it could skip the oldest child. I had so hoped to keep you alive. Your death would have been so unnecessary."

"I hate you!" Liviah screamed.

"That is something I will have to learn to live with, I suppose. Bind them all!" Ramsey yelled to his soldiers. "We'll start the ritual now."

Some of the men dismounted and moved towards them, but none of the Eclipse submitted.

"You watched us grow up!" Liviah screamed at Ramsey. She bore into his eyes with her own as she spoke. Both fists were clenched so hard that her knuckles were turning white. "You - you told me you would protect us! We trusted you! Our parents trusted you to look after us! You were their friend, and—and you killed them!"

An electrifying, blue light radiated from Liviah's fingertips. It swirled up and around her hands and forearms, illuminating the courtyard with the brilliance of a hundred torches. The horses reared and bucked, knocking off their riders and galloping for the Bastion's gates. Only Cormack's giant stallion maintained its composure. The other Eclipse shielded their eyes.

"Stop, Liviah!" Ramsey yelled. "You'll destroy yourself before you kill me!"

Several of the legionnaires ran at Liviah. She shot her hands towards them, and a blast of blue energy sent them flying backwards. Dust and dirt began to swirl around the fort as the winds picked up.

"Liviah!" her sister called to her.

"It's no use!" Oliver shouted over the sound of the wind. "She's lost control again! She can't hear us!"

"We have to get out of here!" Will yelled.

"We can't leave her!" said Oliver.

"She might kill us if we don't!"

Ramsey drew his sword and made his way towards Liviah. His feet skidded backwards in the dirt with each step. She cast a spell in his direction, and he deflected it with the blade's edge as if he were parrying a swing. A dim red light rippled across the metal as each spell came in contact with it. The sword must have been enchanted to deflect magic, Ridley realized. Slowly his father grew closer to Liviah, resisting the force of her magic as it pushed against him.

"Stop, Liviah!" he taunted. "You're not as powerful as you believe!"

Liviah spread her hands out wide and a glowing orb appeared in the space between them. She compressed it down, closing her hands in on each other. Every muscle in her body appeared to be flexed and strained. Her feet rose up off the ground slightly as her body became weightless. Cormack spurred his horse and galloped towards the gate. The remaining legionnaires pursued him on foot, and Ramsey suddenly became panic-stricken.

"Ridley! Please!" he called, pleading for the aid of his son. The orb was no larger than Liviah's fists now. Any moment, it would explode. Ridley cursed himself and ran at them. His body was pushed from side to side as the barrage of wind, dust, and debris spiraled around the Bastion courtyard.

Liviah released the orb, and it shot forward from her hands like a bolt from a crossbow. Ridley dove and tackled his father out of its path. The orb collided with the stone wall behind them, and a sound like a clap of thunder erupted in the fort. Ridley flew back into a wall, and everything went black.

CHAPTER TWENTY-TWO
LIVIAH

Liviah woke to a hand resting on her forehead. Her vision was blurred, but she could tell it belonged to her sister. An excruciating headache threatened to make her black out again, but the longer Juliana's hand remained pressed to her skin, the better Liviah felt. Soon, the pain was gone altogether, and she could clearly see Juliana's face smiling down at her.

"Juliana," she said urgently, trying to sit up. Her sister pressed a hand gently down on her shoulder.

"It's alright, take it easy. The legionnaires are gone. We're safe."

Liviah threw her arms up and wrapped them around Juliana's neck, pulling her sister down on top of her and embracing her in a big bear hug. The two girls laughed together as they lay on the ground. The sun shone brightly down on them from a sky as clear and blue as the ocean, and Liviah could almost forget that anything terrible had ever happened to them.

It took some time before they collected themselves and wiped away the tears that had accompanied their laughter. Liviah abruptly realized there had been others watching them, and she felt embarrassed at her childishness. She got up quickly and brushed the dirt off her clothes. Will, Gus, and Theo said nothing. They only watched as the sisters had the safe reunion they had long been waiting for.

Looking at the fort now, Liviah never would have guessed they were still at the Bastion. It was a mere shadow of the sinister castle it had seemed the night before, now vacant of all legionnaires. The front wall was in ruins, with a large gaping hole where the gate once stood. "What happened?" Liviah asked her sister.

"Well," Juliana began, "after you blew up the wall—"

"After I *what*?"

"You made this little orb thing," Will said. "It was like a little ball of magic. And when you released it, it shot forward and blew a hole in the wall. It was both terrifying and impressive." Will winked.

Liviah sat down. Her head was spinning again. "I don't even remember doing that."

"What do you remember?" Juliana asked.

"I remember learning that Ramsey was behind everything. I still can hardly believe it. I mean he was Mum and Dad's best friend, and he betrayed us!" Theo ran off with his face in his hands. Juliana hit Liviah on the arm with surprising force. "Ow! What was that for?"

"You could be a little more sensitive!"

"About what?"

"Ramsey is his *dad* and he sent him here to be killed. If you think you feel betrayed, imagine how he feels!"

"Sorry," Liviah said defensively, rubbing the spot on her arm. Juliana rolled her eyes and got up to follow Theo. Gus went along with her. Liviah couldn't help but smile to herself as she watched her sister walk off.

"What?" Will asked.

"Nothing, it's just... I don't think Juliana has ever hit me and not immediately tried to heal it and apologize a hundred times."

"And you're happy that she didn't this time?" Will asked with a chuckle.

"She's gotten stronger. She's standing up for herself. That's good for her."

"Yeah, your sister is something," Will said. Both he and Liviah turned and watched as Juliana comforted Theo, with Gus standing fondly nearby. "Before she got here, Gus was terrified. He was crying all the time, constantly saying he wanted to go home. I had no idea what to do with him. Then Juliana showed up, and she just talked him through it. Every day, she kept him strong. I don't want to say I'm glad your sister got kidnapped, but I don't know what we would have done without her."

"She's always been like that. She likes helping people. Hates to see them hurt. I just hope it doesn't get the better of her."

"It won't. That's what big brothers and sisters are for, right? We won't let anything like this happen to them again."

Liviah smiled. She liked talking with Will. He understood what it felt like to be responsible for someone else. "So, do you want to finish telling me what happened last night?" she asked.

"Oh, you know, the basics. You scared off most of the legionnaires with your sparkly blue magic trick, then you blew up the fort and we all got sort of banged up. I woke up and it was daylight. Ramsey and Ridley were both gone."

"Did Juliana have to heal you as well?"

"Just some minor stuff. No broken bones or anything like that."

"That's good."

"There is one thing you should probably know though."

"What?"

"It's Oliver. He hasn't woken up."

"What? Where is he?"

"Inside. Andi's with him."

"Andi?"

"Andromeda, we call her Andi."

Liviah started straight for the tower where they had first found the other Eclipse, but she had only taken a few steps before she was stumbling and sweating.

"Easy!" Will said as he caught her. "You just did a lot of magic. Your body needs time to recover."

"I'm fine," Liviah said, pushing him off her. Will stepped back immediately and she marched forward with determination. When she got inside, she saw Oliver lying unconscious on the table, while Andromeda sat beside him, stroking his sandy brown curls. She moved her hand away as Liviah approached the table.

"What's wrong with him?" Liviah demanded.

"I don't know," Andromeda said. Her voice wavered slightly. "Juliana tried healing him, but…" As if on cue, Liviah's sister entered the room, followed by the others.

"When were you going to tell me that he hadn't woken up?" Liviah asked Juliana.

"I didn't want you to worry."

"Can't you heal him?"

"I tried."

"What do you mean you tried?"

"I mean I tried, and it didn't work. It was like he was…"

"What? He was what?"

"Resisting it. Like his body wouldn't let my magic work."

"Well, try harder!"

"Liviah, I know you're worried about him, but you've got to calm down."

"Calm down? How can you expect me to calm down? I did this to him! If something happens to him, it's my fault!"

"He just needs time, Liviah. He'll wake up soon."

"What if he doesn't?"

"He *will*."

Liviah breathed heavily through her nose. "Well, we can't just wait around here. Ramsey might come back."

"Where should we go?" Will asked.

"Your parents' Tavern?" Juliana suggested.

"No, that's too obvious. They'd suspect it immediately, and I don't want to put my parents in any danger." Liviah's throat closed up at that, knowing full well that she had left Will and Gus's parents locked in a cellar with legionnaires.

"What about where you're from, Andi?" asked Gus. Andi shook her head.

"Everyone's homes are off limits," Liviah said. "It has to be somewhere that Ramsey wouldn't expect."

"Anyone got any ideas?" asked Will. No one said anything for a while, and then someone she had forgotten popped into Liviah's head.

"The forest," she said. "We can go to the forest."

"Are you mad? It's almost winter, we'll freeze to death!"

"Not in this forest we won't. Trust me."

"One thing first—Juliana, come here." Juliana walked over to Will, who raised a hand to block his mouth. He whispered loudly so that everyone could hear. "Your sister's not, you know…crazy, right?" Despite herself, Liviah broke into a smile.

"Just help me get Oliver up," she said. She started to grab Oliver's arm, but Will slung him over his shoulder with surprising ease.

"Lead the way," he said.

They did not have to walk long before they had reached the part of the forest Liviah was looking for. "I think this is far enough," she said as she came to a halt in the front of the line. The others looked around.

"Is there supposed to be something here?" Juliana asked. Liviah looked around at the trees above.

"Not something, someone," she said. The others all followed suit, looking up at the barren trees. "Hello!" Liviah called to them. "Hello! Do'hara!"

"Uh, Juliana," Will said, "would you like to reconsider your answer to my earlier question?" Juliana raised her eyebrows at him in response.

"Liviah, what are you doing?" she questioned.

"He should be able to hear me! Maybe I have to threaten the trees or something."

"I'm a little confused," Gus announced loudly.

"Don't worry, buddy. We all are," Will assured him.

"Hand me that big rock over there!" Liviah said, pointing to a spot beside Juliana's feet. Her sister picked up a rock nearly the size of her head and carried it over. Liviah took it and weighed it in her hand. Once she had decided it was heavy enough, she spread her palm out and the rock floated into the air.

"I'm going to throw this rock at that tree over there!" she said loudly to the forest. "On the count of three! One, two, three!" Liviah pushed her hand forward and the rock went flying towards the tree. A moment before its impact the earth shot upward, forming a wall of dirt that stopped the rock in its path with a resounding *thud*.

"I came as fast as I could," an elegant voice boomed from above them. "You do not have to take it out on the trees." The arbrosprite, Do'hara, climbed down gracefully from atop a tree branch and smiled at Liviah. "You have made new friends since our last meeting, Liviah Cain. I am pleased to see that. This is your sister?" Liviah looked to the others, who seemed every bit as dumbfounded by Do'hara as she had been—all except Andromeda.

"Yes, this is Juliana."

Do'hara bowed before them and spread his arms out wide. "Welcome, Juliana Cain. I am very glad to be able to meet you."

"Um, thank you," Juliana said. "It's nice to meet you, too."

"Where are my manners? I am Do'hara, keeper of this wood. Welcome, fellow guardians of nature." Will, Gus, and Theo gave awkward waves, and Andromeda smiled weakly.

"Do'hara, we need someplace to stay for a while. I was hoping you could help us," Liviah said.

"I see your friend Oliver Hawthorne is not well. I can keep you safe while he recovers."

"Thank you."

Do'hara nodded. "Right this way."

He guided them deeper into the forest, winding through trees and other forest vegetation. The thorn bushes seemed to shift out of Do'hara's path as he walked, and Liviah couldn't tell if it was real or if she was imagining it.

"Hey, how much farther are we going?" Will asked from the back of the line.

"Getting tired back there?" Liviah taunted.

"Well, I am carrying another person."

"Maybe you shouldn't have picked him up by yourself, then," she retorted.

"It is not far," Do'hara said. Soon, they crested a hill, and Liviah could see the mouth of a cave in the valley down below. "You will be safe here," Do'hara said. "The entire valley is enchanted so that only those I lead may find it."

Liviah felt herself grow warmer as they descended into the valley. It had been winter in the forest, but here in the valley, it was pleasant summer. Will carried Oliver into the cave, and the others followed, leaving Liviah outside with Do'hara.

"Thank you," she said. The arbrosprite bowed his head in return.

"I must warn you; I cannot keep you hidden forever. An enchantment like this one is difficult to maintain, and even more so when concealing magical beings such as yourselves."

"I understand. We won't stay long."

"Will Oliver Hawthorne be alright?"

Liviah turned to look at Oliver. Will had set him down and propped him up against the cave wall, and Andromeda was taking care to make sure he was resting comfortably with support for his head.

"Juliana thinks so…I hope so," Liviah answered.

"I hope so, too. He is a very peculiar boy."

"How do you mean?"

Do'hara sat on the ground. "When I came to meet you, I thought for a moment that you were both Eclipse. I quickly realized that the power I sensed was coming only from you, but he was entirely not without a trace of it."

"So, you're saying...what? That Oliver may be an Eclipse?"

"No, no, nothing like that. It was only an inkling of magic I sensed on him. It is likely that it was due simply to his exposure to your magic, but still...forgive me. My curiosity and imagination often get the better of me, and with no one but trees to talk to...well, you'd be surprised what nonsensical stories they like to fill your head with."

Liviah smiled. "Thank you again, Do'hara, for everything."

"You're most welcome, Liviah Cain." He looked as though he were going to say more, but then closed his mouth.

"What is it?"

"I wonder...How well do you know your traveling companions?"

"Not well. Why?"

"The girl Andromeda, she is not an Eclipse."

"What?"

"She is a hylasprite, a guardian of nature's waters. I recognized her the moment I laid my eyes on her."

"But if she's not an Eclipse, why did Ramsey kidnap her?"

"The very question I have been asking myself since you arrived," Do'hara mused.

"I'll let you know what I find out."

"There is one more thing that you should know. For a sprite to leave their dominion in nature is considered an unforgivable offense. It brings shame upon oneself and disgrace upon one's family. She will have lost a great deal, being taken from her home."

"Sprites have families?"

"Of course," Do'hara said plainly. "Did you believe I was born of a tree?"

Liviah laughed, but Do'hara didn't seem to see what was funny. "Where is yours?" she asked.

"Long gone and long forgotten, I am afraid. But that is a story for another time, Liviah Cain. For now, you should attend to your friend."

Liviah turned around to look at Oliver. "Thank you again," she began, but by the time she looked back, Do'hara was gone.

CHAPTER TWENTY-THREE
OLIVER

Oliver's sleep was the kind that you didn't know you were in— the kind where you didn't even realize you had closed your eyes until you opened them again. He sat up, rubbing the back of his head where it had been resting on the hard ground. He looked around and drank in his surroundings. He was in some sort of cave, and just by the mouth, he saw Liviah and all of the other Eclipse talking around a fire. Oliver climbed to his feet. "Where are we?" he called. The others all turned and stared at him as though he were a ghost.

"Oliver," Liviah said. It was almost a whisper. She looked awestruck, but he couldn't figure why.

"What?"

"Oh, he's awake!" Andromeda yelled. She got up and ran over to him, embracing him in a tight hug. He didn't even have time to pull his arms up from his side before she grabbed him, so all he could do was stand there awkwardly until she let go. The others came over as well, and Will clapped him on the back.

"Nice to see you up again!" he said.

"What's going on?" Oliver asked. "And how did we get in this cave?"

"You've been asleep for about two days," Liviah said.

"What?"

"I was beginning to wonder if one of us was going to have to kiss you to get you to wake up," Will said.

Liviah punched him on the arm. "Knock it off, Will."

"Ow! I was just kidding."

"You're joking, right?" Oliver asked. "I mean, I feel like I've been asleep for maybe a few hours."

"We're not joking," Liviah said. "After I blew up the Bastion, you sort of passed out. We all did, actually. You just took a lot longer to wake up than the rest of us."

"Why?"

"Well, Juliana tried to heal you, but—"

"It is because you are human," Do'hara said suddenly, causing Gus to jump. None of them had seen the arbrosprite arrive in the cave.

"Do'hara! What are you doing here?" Oliver asked.

"We're in his forest," Liviah answered. "We came here to hide from Ramsey while we waited for you to wake up."

"It is good to see that you are well, Oliver Hawthorne," Do'hara said.

"Thanks," Oliver replied. "What was that you were just saying, though? About me being human?"

"That is why your body took longer to heal than your friends'."

"I don't understand. Aren't we all human?"

"In a sense, but unlike you, your friends are magical beings. Therefore, their bodies have a certain natural resilience to magical damage that yours does not."

"So, my body is weaker than theirs?"

"Not weaker, only different."

"But I couldn't even heal him," Juliana chimed in.

"It is quite possible there was nothing wrong with him," Do'hara said. "But after as much close exposure to magic as you have had, it is likely that your body required a long rest to recover."

"That's just great," Oliver said. "So, being around you all is going to make me pass out for days at a time." He pushed past the others and walked out of the cave.

"Was it something I said?" Do'hara asked.

* * *

It was a bit colder outside than in the cave, but Oliver liked it. He had spent most of the day out by the little pond in the valley, tossing stones into it and watching the water ripple. As evening drew closer, he heard footsteps behind him.

"I really don't need you to tell me to toughen up right now, alright?" he said.

"I wasn't going to tell you that at all," an unfamiliar voice said. Oliver turned around.

"Oh, Andromeda! Sorry, I thought you were Liviah."

"That's okay." She sat down beside him. "You can call me Andi, if you want. That's what I normally go by."

"Okay, Andi."

"Are you alright?" she asked, leaning her head towards him.

Oliver sighed. "I just hate being the weakest link, you know? I don't want you all to have to take care of me and protect me all the time."

Andromeda laughed softly. "You know you're the only reason that any of us are here, right? We would have been stuck in that tower forever if you hadn't come along. You risked your life against a fortress full of legionnaires to save us. I thought it was very brave of you, Ollie."

A lump the size of an apple grew in Oliver's throat. He hadn't heard anyone call him Ollie since the morning he and Liviah left Nan in the alley.

"Th-anks," he said, the word getting caught in his throat. Andi put her arm around him and squeezed him again.

"*Ahem*," Liviah coughed. Andi pulled away and stepped uncomfortably to the side. "Could I talk to you for a minute, Oliver? Alone." She glared at Andi as she said the last word. Andi took the hint and went back inside the cave.

"You could be a little nicer you know," Oliver said. "She was just trying to help."

"I don't trust that girl."

"What reason could you possibly have to not trust her?"

"How about the fact that she's not actually an Eclipse, but she's been pretending to be one this whole time?"

"What? Why would you think that?"

"Because Do'hara told me. She's a sprite, like him."

"Then how come she's not all green and...planty, like he is?"

"I don't know! She's a hylasprite. Maybe they just look differently than arbrosprites do."

Oliver looked hesitant. It wasn't that he thought Liviah was lying, it just didn't make sense. "She wouldn't have any reason to pretend though."

"You don't believe me?" Liviah asked. "Fine, let's ask her then."

"No, Liviah, come on. Don't do this."

"Andromeda!" she yelled towards the cave. "Actually, everyone should be here for this. Let's go get them." Liviah and Oliver went back to the mouth of the cave where the others were eating some sort of fish Will had cooked over a fire. Andi wasn't eating the fish. Instead, she was enjoying a handful of berries and nuts. Oliver could see the apprehension in her face as they approached, but he knew there was no stopping Liviah once she had her mind set on something. "Isn't it true that you're not an Eclipse, Andromeda?" she asked. Andi's mouth fell open. "Well?"

"Y-yes," Andi answered.

"What?" Will said. "Andi, why didn't you tell us that?"

"I-I couldn't."

"Why not?"

"I just couldn't talk about it! It was just too horrible!"

"Oh, please," Liviah said. "Now she's pretending to be all upset."

"What was too horrible?" Will asked.

"She was taken from her home," Do'hara said, suddenly appearing again and causing everyone to jump.

"You have *got* to stop doing that!" Will said.

"My apologies, William Calderwood."

"What did you say, Do'hara?" Juliana asked.

"She has been forced to abandon her dominion of protection. She will not be allowed to return to it."

Andi sat and cried with her face in her hands. Oliver felt awful for her. He knew what that was like—to be forced to leave his home unprotected, to likely never be able to return. Even as a grudder, he felt a certain connection to the shack at the end of Hawthorne Alley.

"Somebody fill me in," Will said. "Why can't she go home?"

"Andromeda is a hylasprite, daughter of Ala and An'qar," Do'hara said. "She was charged with the protection of one of nature's many waters, which she has now left. This is a great dishonor among sprites. The other hylasprites will not allow her to return."

"I didn't want to leave!" Andromeda said. "I tried to defend the lake! I tried to fight the legionnaires off!"

"I still don't understand why you didn't tell us you weren't an Eclipse," Will said angrily.

"I didn't know what the Legion was going to do with us! I just knew that they wanted Eclipse! I was worried that if they found out I wasn't one, they would have realized they didn't need me and killed me!"

"It's alright," Juliana told her. "It's alright, we understand."

"You do realize this means she could have left the tower whenever she wanted, right?" Liviah said. "If she's not an Eclipse, she wasn't stuck in that tower like the rest of us. She could have gone and gotten help long before Oliver and I got there, but she didn't! For all we know, she could be a spy!"

"Livvy, come on! She's not a spy."

"She could put us all in danger, Juliana! I won't let that happen to you again." Liviah stormed out into the valley, leaving the rest of them behind.

"Perhaps I should go," Do'hara said. "I seem to be causing repeated disturbances."

"Do you think we should say something to her?" Will asked, looking at Liviah

"I'll talk to her," Juliana grumbled, marching after her sister.

"Right, it probably should be you," Will said quickly.

Gus and Theo retreated back into the cave together, both looking anxious about the conversation that had just taken place. Will followed closely after them, and then it was only Oliver and Andromeda left together.

Andi wiped tears from her eyes. "I'm sorry," she muttered.

"Don't be sorry!" Oliver exclaimed. "You did what you thought you had to in order to survive. Liviah will get over it. She's just...well, she gets angry easily, but she always seems to come around after she cools off. We're here for you, alright?"

"Thanks, Ollie," she sniffed.

And there it was again—that pang at Oliver's heart. He wondered if Nan was still alive, or if the Withering Black had finally taken her. "I know what it's like to lose your home and your family," he said. "I lost mine too...I lost the only person I've ever had, actually."

Andi reached over and grabbed Oliver's hand. "Until now."

Oliver smiled and nodded as his eyes began to water. "What's your lake like?" he asked to distract himself.

"Oh, it's beautiful! The most beautiful place I've ever been!" She paused. "Well, until recently, it was the only place I'd ever been."

"I know what that's like," Oliver said with a melancholy smile.

"It's perfectly clear blue, and there are all sorts of animals that live in it and drink from it. The best time is always early in the morning when the surface of the water looks like glass and the sunrise reflects off it. It's unlike anything else!"

"I'd love to see that someday."

"Maybe you will. I wish... I could again."

"I still don't understand. Why can't you go back?"

"When I was taken from the lake, I left it unprotected. I failed the one thing I was *born* to do. Once you leave, you give up your connection to nature. The rest of my family will have taken over protection of the lake. They won't let me come back."

"But they're your family! I'm sure if you went to them and asked if—"

"It's different for us, Ollie. You don't understand. I'm not a hylasprite anymore. You give that up the moment you leave...I'm just a girl now."

"It's okay to be just a girl," Oliver said. "I'm just a boy, nothing special."

"Actually, I think you are." Andi said. She squeezed his hand, and Oliver felt himself blush. "I think I'm going to get some rest."

"I'm going to stay out here for a while. I think I've done enough resting recently."

Andromeda smiled and went into the cave. Out in the valley, Oliver could see Juliana and Liviah sitting beside each other. Liviah laughed and put an arm around her sister's shoulder. Oliver grinned. That was the first time he had ever heard her really laugh. Not an awkward chuckle or a half giggle, but a real, happy laugh.

Night fell over the valley, and the moon slowly became visible in the sky. It was comforting to know that it was the very same moon Oliver had looked up at night after night from Hawthorne Alley. So much had changed—so many things that could never go back to the way they were before—but the moon still looked the same as always.

"Hey," Liviah said to Oliver as she and Juliana came back to the cave, "are you coming inside?"

"No, I think I'll stay out here and look at the stars. I told Andi, I think I've had enough sleep to last me a while."

"Probably," Liviah said. "I'm, uh, glad you're okay."

"Thank you," Oliver said. "I'm glad everyone is."

"Goodnight, Oliver," Juliana said. She looked up at her sister. "I'm *so* glad Liviah met you." Oliver couldn't help but let his crooked smile spread across his face.

"Me too, Juliana. Goodnight." Juliana walked inside, but Liviah sat down next to Oliver and looked up at the sky.

"Ramsey isn't going to stop coming after us, is he?" she asked.

"Probably not."

"And we'll never be safe until he's gone."

"I'm so sorry, Liviah. I know you were close to him."

"Yeah...Well, I guess you never really know who you can trust."

"You can trust me."

Liviah laughed. "I know, Oliver. I do trust you."

"It's beautiful, isn't it?" he said, still admiring the moon.

"Oliver?" Liviah said.

"Yeah?"

"I just wanted to say...I never meant to...I mean, I never wanted..."

"It's okay, Liviah," he said with a smile. "I know."

Liviah nodded and stood up. "Well, goodnight."

"Night, Liviah."

She turned and stepped back into the cave, leaving Oliver alone to watch the sky. Then suddenly, she was back, and her arms were thrown around him in a hug. A rush of comfort came over Oliver, and in that moment, he knew everything would be okay. Liviah pulled away from the hug as quickly as it had happened, disappearing into the cave without ever looking him in the eye. A few hours later, Oliver followed, laying himself down next to Will and Gus. He rolled onto his back and looked up at the top of the cave. He figured he might lie awake there for hours; his mind racing with so many different thoughts. What was life going to be like now? How long would they all be together? Before he knew it, however, his eyelids felt heavy, and Oliver Hawthorne drifted off to sleep, thinking—for the first time in his entire life—how very good it felt to have friends.

Acknowledgements

The process of writing this story was long and difficult. From the start, I was constantly encouraged by the people closest to me. The continued interest of my friends and family—even those who had never read a word—gave me the drive to finish this story.

I give special thanks to all of the readers and editors who helped me through the revision and proofing processes. I truly could not have completed this project without your input.

Lastly, I thank everyone who has remained enthusiastic while waiting for me to finish this book. I hope you have found that your patience was worthwhile.

Made in the USA
Monee, IL
10 July 2020